"And what have you found?"

I ask as we stop at the bottom of the stairs to her flat.

She turns toward me, the swish of her skirt against my khaki pants sends another tingle up my legs, and I pull her hand to my chest, bringing her in closer. The move brings that sparkle to her eyes again, and my heart feels too big for my chest as she looks into my eyes. "Well, today, I found *you*," she says.

Her hand trapped against my chest, I lean in, only slightly taller than her with her in heels, and press my lips to hers. It's a light touch, teasing and testing at the same time. She opens quickly, almost a gasp and I turn my head to properly seal the kiss. There is nothing in my life, not even those drugs I've tried, that ever made me as high as that kiss.

If you enjoy this collection, you can sign up for a free membership at ForbiddenFiction and discuss it with other readers and the authors at the *Divine Desire* story page at http://forbiddenfiction.com/anthology/SPC-1.100011.
We do our best to proof all our work, but if you spot a text error we missed, please let us know via our website Contact Form at http://forbiddenfiction.com/contact.

Also recommended...

You may also enjoy these other ForbiddenFiction collections:

Bi Magic - Best Bisexual Fantasy Anthology
Bi Magic collects nine of ForbiddenFiction's most popular tales of magic, mystery, romance, and of course, steaming hot sex. These high fantasy romps prove that whether you're a man, a woman, a shapeshifter, a fairy, or a trickster god from a forgotten pantheon, you really can have it both ways.
http://forbiddenfiction.com/anthology/SPC-1.100005

Taking Flight - An Erotic Anthology with Wings!
Flight has captured the human imagination for centuries, inspiring poets and lovers alike to greater heights. Is the exhilaration of soaring better even than sex? Is the ecstasy of a lover's touch worth more than all the feathers in heaven? Is one moment of passion on the wind worth the risk of a lifetime? Here are seven erotic flights of fantasy, from gritty dystopian futures and surreal urban discoveries to mythic romances and fleeting moments of enchantment.
http://forbiddenfiction.com/anthology/SPC-1.100004

Divine Desire

An Ecstatic Anthology

edited by Lon Sarver

ForbiddenFiction
www.forbiddenfiction.com

an imprint of

Fantastic Fiction Publishing
www.fantasticfictionpub.com

DIVINE DESIRE
A Forbidden Fiction book

Fantastic Fiction Publishing
Hayward, California

© Lon Sarver, 2014

CREDITS
Editors: Lon Sarver, James L. Wolf
Cover Design: Siolnatine
Cover art: Modified from "The Abduction of Psyche 1895" by William-Adolphe Bouguereau
Internal cover art: Stock images by Feedough, Les3photo8, Mimagephotography, Prometeus, Smoxx78 and Yuriyzhuravov from Dreamstime; werner22brigitte from Pixabay; and José Antonio Gil Martínez and Ivan Bilibin from Wikimedia Commons. Additional art modified from works by Frans Kristoph Janneck. Original art by Siolnatine
Production Editor: Erika L Firanc
Proofreading: Erika L Firanc, Todd Michaels, Kailin Morgan, Kira O'Hara, Jae Knight, JhP323

SKU: SPC-100011-02 FFP
ISBN: 978-1-62234-238-9

Published in the United States of America

DISCLAIMER

This book is a work of fiction which contains explicit erotic content; it is intended for mature readers. Do not read this if it's not legal for you.

All the characters, locations and events herein are fictional. While elements of existing locations or historical characters or events may be used fictitiously, any resemblance to actual people, places or events is coincidental.

This book depicts fictional BDSM; it is not intended to be used as an instruction manual. It contains descriptions of erotic acts that may be immoral, illegal, or unsafe. The characters are not models for the Safe, Sane and Consensual forms embraced by most current practitioners of BDSM. The authors take license with the use of BDSM for dramatic effect. Do not take the events in this story as proof of the plausibility or safety of any particular practice.

We dedicate this anthology to the many Powers who
inspired us in its creation:

To Baba Exu, keeper of crossroads,
and Pomba Gira, the sacred harlot,
Axe-O!

To Maman Brigitte, Mistress of the Ghedes,
Mambo of beloved and restless dead,
Ayibobo!

To Angrboda, fierce Jotunja,
Matron of the Iron Wood,
Hail!

To mighty Perun, sky-bound thunderer,
and draconic rival, earthly Veles,
Dobrodošao!

To mysterious Erlik, of Monoglian Tengri,
keeper of the world invisible,
Bayarlalaa!

To the gods and spirits of ancient Hellas:
Hera and Zeus, Artemis, Pan and Psyche,
Glaucus, Scylla and Great Mother Circe,
IO!

Thanks we give to the gracious gods
Long may your lore in stories be told!

Contents

Crossed Rose

D. M. Atkins

D. M. Atkins has a Master's degree in Anthropology, specializing in the body and sexuality in cultural context. Atkins was on the boards of the *Journal of Bisexuality*, *Journal of Homosexuality* and *Journal of Lesbian Studies*; s/he edited multiple collections, special editions and books. Atkins was also managing editor of *LOCUS Magazine*, the trade magazine for the F&SF field. D.M. Atkins and Chris Taylor co-authored *Faewolf*, a male/male paranormal romance. While most of Atkins' time is spent as publisher and editor with Fantastic Fiction Publishing, s/he does continue to work on original fiction as well as non-fiction.

Chapter 1
Rum at the Crossroads

It's not a place I would normally go—sitting way inland from my home in what feels like the middle of fucking nowhere. I pull my truck to the stop sign and sit, engine idling while I stare at the shabby looking bar across the intersection. "Crossroads Bar," a battered looking sign proclaims. *How original*, I think, the sarcasm in my internal voice harsher than normal. I'm sitting there long enough that a car horn blares behind me, driver even clicking headlights at me in case I was deaf as well as slow. I'm tempted to click on the emergency brake lights instead, but out here in the central valley, I'm not so sure I should push it.

I press the gas, heading across and then pulling alongside the road beside the bar rather than committing to the parking lot. I flick off the lights but sit there in the cab with the engine on. I don't know how long it takes me, watching without trying to admit to myself that I can't decide whether I'm more scared it will work, or that it won't.

"Fuck it." I finally put the truck in drive, pushing the gas as I take a probably illegal U-turn into the parking lot and pull up along aside a truck that looks more beat up than my Ford. Probably a working vehicle, out here in the farmlands of California. I shake my head at the insanity that prompts someone like me to leave the relative safety of the South Bay. There's nothing for it now. It's been a long drive, and I might as well get a drink, if nothing else.

The parking lot was nearly full, so I shouldn't have been surprised to find the small place pretty well packed. More men than women, but all of them seeming to ignore me as I stood there, trying to figure out what I'm to do next. I make my way to the small, battered bar. I have to squeeze in between a couple of men who look like they drove straight in from the fields, and who give my probably too shiny black leather jacket a look before resolutely ignoring me again. I'm relieved until I can't seem to catch the bartender's eye, either.

The steady rumble of conversation is punctuated by the clack of colliding balls. The long lamps above the pool tables break the dark into harsh rectangles of light, almost classy except for the names of the beers advertised and years of dust collected on their plastic surfaces. I look around, seeing the flash of cards, noting at least two of the round tables with games in progress, cash in piles on the tables in complete disregard of anti-gambling laws in the state. *Well, unless you're on native land*, I thought. *As if we all aren't on what was native land.*

With a long sigh, I turn back to my attempt to get the barkeep's attention, only to find the man right there, looking like he's been waiting longer than he thought necessary to take my order. I worry that he'll ask for my driver's license. I don't want to have to explain *that*. Certainly not in a place like this.

"Payphone's in back, if you've broke down, an' there's a local garage down the interstate who does tows," the bartender explains.

I'm taken back by his assumption, and I glance around, confirming that while there's a lot of medium dark skin and dark hair in the room, I'm the only one with black skin. I have to resist the urge to just pretend I'm asking directions to—somewhere. "Yeah, well, how about a Budweiser," I suggest. His eyebrows raise and he looks closer, clearly having read me as "city," but shrugs and puts a glass under the tap, pulling until I think it's gonna overflow. He sets it down on the bar and I pay with cash.

I look back again, trying to spot an open chair at the bar or an empty table anywhere. That's when I see it—one very small table in the very back corner. It's got two chairs and neither is occupied. Taking a breath for courage I'm not sure I have, I pick up the glass and try to make my way through the room. While, before, I seemed to have been pointedly ignored, this time, I feel like every pair of eyes in the room is watching, and every laugh follows me, so that the hair on the back of my neck prickles.

I make it to the table with no mishaps, and am glad my hands aren't shaking too badly as I manage to put my glass down and slide into the corner seat without any accidents. Once again I'm struck by how ridiculous the entire idea is, and find myself vowing to leave just as soon as I finish my beer.

I'm watching the door with probably too much attention when a pretty woman wearing blue jeans and a flannel shirt sets a shot of amber liquid on the table. With a look at her apron, harried expression, and an impatient stance, I realize she's a waitress. She's in her mid twenties and I'm surprised to realize that I don't care if she's attractive or not. She's not what I'm looking for here.

She declares, "Five bucks."

"What's that?" I ask.

"Rum."

"But I didn't order any—"

"You'll need it," she declares, seeming sure despite my confusion. Not knowing what else to do, I pull out a five and then, seeing her look, change my mind and put down a ten and tell her, "Keep the change."

Heaving a sigh, I lean back and close my eyes, rubbing the bridge of my nose to stave off the possible headache from the noise and smoke. *Smoke?* It's not allowed in bars in this state anymore. I open my eyes to find a man standing over me—smoking a cigar. He's a sight to see all right, skin almost as dark as my own, but it's his clothing that makes him stand out. He's dressed in black slacks and vest, with a dark red shirt. His bearded face is almost hidden under the black fedora with a red band and large dark red rose. The smell of rose is powerful, mixing with the cigar smoke in a way that makes me feel almost dizzy.

As I stare up at him, bewildered. He smiles. "You been waiting to see me." It's a statement, not a question, but then with his look at the rum, I realize he's waiting for me to offer.

I do a kind of half stand and gesture to the other chair. "Take a seat?" When he sits back, sizing me up, I add, "I think the drink's for you."

"What's your name, *boy*?" he asks in a way that makes me tense, sitting up in the chair. I wonder if it's that he sees me as younger than I am, or sees more than most would. I'm in my most relaxed pair of blue jeans, good black boots, and black dress shirt. I'm packing, but not in a way that many would understand.

"Davey," I answer.

"It'll do," he says, "An' you can call me Papa, when you call me."

"Papa?" I ask, not sure I'd feel comfortable calling anyone that.

"Just right, Davey; now tell me what you're wanting so we can get this exchange on the table."

It's harder to say than I think it will be. "A woman."

He grins. "Just any woman, or do she have a name, or something we can call her too?"

Maybe he's making fun of me, but I don't care. I wanted this bad enough to drive all the way out here, and I'm not going to back down now. I shore up my courage, aided by another pull of my beer and admit, "I don't know her name, but I know the woman. She's beautiful and I've only seen her the one time. I don't even know how to find her, let alone to ask..."

He blows smoke rings in to the air above us and my nose twitches with the smell of it. "Yeah, they'll get you every time. She's gotta be something to send you out like this."

"Yeah, she is."

I'd first seen her three months before. I had my leathers on—black boots (real leather, spit-shined), leather chaps over my jeans, white t-shirt and a leather vest with no few patches, and a black leather cap. A small black toy bag (duffle to outsiders) slung over one shoulder, I appraised the room. The bdsm club was big, a converted warehouse rented for parties like these. The floor was unforgiving concrete, but they'd found old rugs and gym mats to place around under some of the equipment, and others with pillows for aftercare. There were at least a dozen play spaces, more if you were either very friendly or very careful. I arrived at what might be considered fashionably late, but that had more to do with my own nerves than fashion.

The first thing I heard, of course, were the loud slaps and cracks as leather meets flesh, followed by the cries of pleasure and pain—the two almost indistinguishable. Mixed in with moans and shouts was laughter. No two people made the same sound when struck, many laughing in either delight or nervousness. More noticeable were the peaks when someone really hit their zone and the cries of orgasm drew the attention of other players as well as watchers. It's contagious, making things tighten — hard and wet.

I knew a lot of folks in the scene. I'd played with or even dated quite a few. Now, I did a slow walk around the perimeter of the room, respectful distance; far enough to not "break a scene" but close enough to nod when noticed by friends or strangers alike. One of my exes was, predictably enough, bent over a spanking bench, spread and being systematically tied into place by a top I know as well. The sub's ass was already red from squeezes or slaps. I moved on, already knowing this one well enough to be uninterested.

There was a trio of guys, playing at what to outsiders would look like a big wooden jungle gym. It had ladders on all four sides holding up a platform high in the middle, strong enough for suspension work under it. The sub was wearing suspension cuffs and was trussed up with all four limbs upward, head hanging at one end and his ass on display, already red as the other two took turns at him with large wooden paddles. I smiled in appreciation and watched until the bottom was moaning and begging for what his partners wanted just as much to give him. I moved on when the gloves and lube came out.

It's then that I found them — found her — three players at the rack. The rack was two upright wooden rails with a beam across the top, studded with eyelets. Suspended in that space, spread eagle, and being flogged by a man behind her, was the most beautiful woman I'd ever seen, naked and already covered in a fine sheen of sweat. She had dark hair that was probably all curl, and had been roughly put up into clips atop her head, though tendrils escaped to tickle her shoulders. Her body was a work of art, obscene and beautiful in the way of the classics, with large breasts that bounced and heaved as she writhed. Her hips were luscious hourglass curves over strong legs that looked like they could hold her up for hours of pleasure. I don't know how long the flogging had been going but her backside was already welting up and blushing against her dusky skin. And what a backside! Every time the man behind her paused, she arched back, every muscle begging for more. I had to push my hands into my pockets to cover the urge to reach out and handle that gorgeous ass.

The man taking her apart was tall, white and bald. He was dressed in simple black jeans and t-shirt, already visibly damp with sweat, and jeans that looked too tight for the erection they contained. As he put a carefully aimed strike across her ass, she jerked forward — onto the gloved hand of the woman kneeling in front of her. Stepping carefully to the side, I found a petite red-haired woman with her right hand between the spread beauty's legs, four fingers working in and out of her cunt, while her thumb pressed into the writhing woman's clit.

My beauty's face was rapturous, clearly working herself to orgasm as she managed to ride the kneeling woman's hand and the blows at the same time. The seam of my own jeans was suddenly so tight I felt the urge to shift to one side, reaching down to adjust my package. My lips were dry, and my mouth watered at the same time. I couldn't decide who I wanted to be more: the top taking his leather to her or the one whose hand she rode. I imagined the muscles of her cunt squeezing my hand as I worked it deeper and almost gasped at the sound of the leather strike.

When I drew my attention up again, I found her top had thrown the flogger to the floor and had already ripped open his button-up jeans, cock in hand. As he pressed himself to the bound woman's back, one hand on her hip and the other rubbing his cock against her ass, his lips were at her ears whispering. I could almost hear her begging over the sound of the room. He pulled back, reaching around to take a condom from the redhead, who had withdrawn her gloved hand. The man sheathed his cock in the condom and pushed up into the beauty's cunt from behind. His knees bent to make the angle work, but even so, when he thrust up, she strained up onto her toes. Both hands on her hips, her top fucked her. In front of her, the redhead buried her face in the dark-hair and wet of the beauty's pussy. Cock in her cunt and mouth on her clit, the beauty captured the attention of the room as she moaned loadly and begged — ordered — ☐ ¡mais rápido!" I had to step back to the wall, using it for support as I swear I came with her.

I stood back, never feeling more alone than when I watched her two partners lower her to the padded matt below the rack and hold her, the man comforting her as the redhead helped clean them up. They moved from the space to one with pillows but I didn't dare follow. I felt awkward, even though voyeurism was part of the allure of the scene Many of those who play so openly also get off on the exhibitionism. Suddenly, I felt terribly alone in that large room of people. There was only one person I wanted to touch. I felt an insane rush of jealousy over the two who held her, laughing and chatting as they snuggled. I fled the club and into the cool night.

I flush just remembering her, and even more at the memories of masturbating to the image of her, to imagining myself with her every night since. It's insane to get this worked up over a woman I don't even know. I'd tried, later, to ask friends if they knew the woman, but didn't get anywhere. It was a mixed crowd that night, so she was unlikely to be part of my own social circles.

The look "Papa" gives me seems both amused and sympathetic. "And you want her for yourself," he says.

Looking down at my nearly empty beer, I take a deep breath and sigh. "I want to know her, to make her smile, to bring her not just pleasure, but joy. I want to be wanted by her too. Even if I can find her, what is the chance of that, me being... what I am?"

"Davey boy, you sound like you know how to please a woman, but you need to be *the* someone she can believe in if you want to keep her. Are you that kind? Can you follow through with what you offer?"

I raise my face, stung by the almost accusation in his words, I look him in the eyes. "I swear, I'll be good to her. I keep my promises."

Papa seems to study me for what feels like too long for me. Finally, he nods, picks up the shot and downs it. "Good. I have three things you got to do. First, you take this and carry it with you wherever you go. I mean it; don't open it and don't leave it in the truck or nothing." He holds out a little red bag, drawstrings pulled and tied tight. "And every day, you put a little of that cologne you wear on the bag."

The look I give him must be puzzled because he's grinning again as I take the bag, staring at it. In my palm I can feel something small and metal, in with softer bits. I want to ask what's in it, but I don't. Instead I nod and curl my fingers around it.

"After you find her, you got to bring her a rose every day. But important thing is, you pull off all the thorns. If you hurt her in any way she has not agreed to, you will need to make it up to her."

"Is that all?" I ask suspiciously, because it sounds more crazy than difficult.

Before he can answer, the waitress sets an ashtray in front of him and Papa knocks off the long tip of ashes from his cigar while she refills his shot glass. Both the waitress and Papa look to me for payment so I pull out a fifty and she leaves the bottle on the table as she takes away the cash and my empty beer bottle.

"Good boy; you learn quick," Papa says as he downs the second glass. "If she's the right one for you and you for her, then you find the nearest crossroads to where you live, find the poorest man you can there and hand him all the cash you can afford. Be honest or it won't work."

"All my money?" I ask, wondering if this is a scam. "I thought you'd want my soul or something." I try to laugh at my fear, but he isn't laughing.

"All you can afford. You'll know." Then Papa pours another shot and seems to be waiting for an answer.

I try to pull myself together. "Yes, I'll do it. I swear it."

Papa drinks his third shot, refills the glass and holds it out to me. I don't usually drink rum and I've got to drive all the way back to the Bay Area, but I somehow get this isn't negotiable, so I down it and try not to cough. I only partially succeed, closing my eyes and swallowing hard. When I look back up, he's gone. So is the bottle of rum. The only proof he was there besides the burn in my throat and heat in my guts, is the dirty ashtray and the little bag in my fist.

Chapter 2

Passion and Promises

It's a long drive back to the South Bay and I crash in bed as soon as I get back to my apartment. The next day, it feels almost like a dream, or some really weird movie I saw after drinking too much, but the little red bag that falls out when I dig my keys out of my jeans is a good reminder. I feel foolish when I dab the cologne on the bag each morning and stuff it in my pocket. I tried sniffing it to see what the crunchy bits are, in there with what feels like a coin, but my cologne was all I could smell.

It starts to feel ridiculous after the first week. I wonder if I've really lost my mind, or if living in the San Francisco Bay Area has really warped my perception of reality. Each day I go to my job, sit behind a computer and try to remember that the crazy people who think the internet is actually in their own computers are just the way I pay my bills. This is the home of Silicon Valley, after all, and there are more than an average number of kinky folks in tech jobs.

It's after work one night as I'm driving to a local leather meet-up that something strange happens. I've left my phone at work and don't want to miss the meet-up going back for it, so I'm circling the block trying to find the place, hoping I have the right block, when I see a flash of red. Like a bull, my eyes find it — and her.

She's laughing on the arm of another woman. She's in a red dress that has a full and ruffled skirt, narrowed waist and dropping cleavage. I brake in the middle of the block and flick on my turn signal when the driver behind me honks his horn. *Let him think I'm waiting for a car to pull out.* Her hair is down and the curls fall down her back, but are pinned up on the sides. She's made up like she's going out for the night and the clack of her high heels makes my heart speed up. I want to jump out of my truck right there but have no idea what I'd say.

As she and her friend enter a door, I glance up only to find the name of the very restaurant I was looking for. *It has to be*, I tell myself, feeling for the red bag in my pocket. Just as I squeeze it, the car parked in front of me pulls out, and I have a parking space that quickly. I almost run to get in the door after, but stop to make sure I'm looking good as I stroll in. I see a few folks I know already amidst a group of people who have pulled half a dozen small tables together into one. She's not seated yet, but is leaning over and hugging a man. Folks are teasing them both about the way her cleavage is all he can look at when she does.

"Hey, Davey," a friend yells and I wave back as I make my way to the crowded tables.

Beauty stands up and smiles, big beautiful dark eyes, clearly checking me out. "Maria," she introduces herself, holding out a hand.

"Davey," I answer. "What, no hug for me?" I protest in mock hurt.

To my surprise, and delight, she laughs and hugs me. Too quick for me to really hug back, but then we're being directed to pull up another table and chairs. Somehow in the chaos of shuffling seats, I end up sitting beside her.

It's too easy, I keep thinking as we talk, the pressure of her thigh against my own and the view down her cleavage making me sweat, wondering how it can suddenly be so hot in the room. As the evening wears on, and people leave, even Brooke, the friend she walked to the restaurant with, until it's only Maria and I—and an annoyed-looking waiter.

I offer her a lift home, only to find out she lives but a couple blocks away and walked to the restaurant, running into her friend along the way.

"Then let me walk you home," I offer, nearly begging.

Maria reaches up to ruffle my short hair, allowing her long fingers to somehow trail behind my ear. She certainly knows how to flirt, and my body is a-tingle, things stirring low in my body just from the drag of her nails.

"That's so sweet," she replies and my heart starts to sink. *That's what they always say just before they turn you down.* "Are you a gentleman?"

I probably blush, but I try to look cocky. "I can be gentle, when it's needed. And hard when it's wanted," I promise her.

That gets a laugh, but it's delight not derision. "Oh, I'm gonna have to watch out for you, aren't I."

I capture her hand with my own. "If you'll let me, I'll watch out for you," I promise her.

This time she seems to see something more in me. Her hand squeezes mine. "I'd be honored to have you take me home, Davey."

I leave my truck where it is, hardly even giving a thought to whether or not it will get towed. We walk hand-in-hand like young sweethearts as she tells me what brought her to the neighborhood. She shares a flat with housemates who are friends of friends. She'd moved up a year before from southern California, leaving behind a close-knit Brazilian-American family in hopes that she could find more of what she wanted in life out from under their constant watch.

"And what have you found?" I ask as we stop at the bottom of the stairs to her flat.

She turns toward me, the swish of her skirt against my khaki pants sends another tingle up my legs, and I pull her hand to my chest, bringing her in closer. The move brings that sparkle to her eyes again, and my heart feels too big for my chest as she looks into my eyes. "Well, today, I found *you*," she says.

Her hand trapped against my chest, I lean in, only slightly taller than her with her in heels, and press my lips to hers. It's a light touch, teasing and testing at the same time. She opens quickly, almost a gasp and I turn my head to properly seal the kiss. There is nothing in my life, not even those drugs I've tried, that ever made me as high as that kiss.

I slide my free hand around her back, pulling her in close. I don't want to let go. There's a whistle from someone driving by, and I realize we're standing on a dark street, with only the streetlight a few doors down and light from windows to see by.

I break the kiss slowly, pulling back reluctantly. I whisper, "Let me see you to your door."

She blinks, looking beautifully dazed, and my heart speeds up, delighted that I could put that look on her face. Then she seems to realize that I'm not asking to come up to her room and she's surprised and a bit confused by it. She nods, and I turn us, putting her hand on my arm like a gentleman in one of those silly romances my mother always read.

I lead her up the steps and stop by the door, the porch light almost too bright after the dark. I'm about to say goodnight, but I know I still need her phone and email. I reach for my cell just as I remember I've left my phone at work. She must be in sync with me, because she has hers out already. "I left my phone at work," I tell her. "May I?" I ask, hand out.

It's a test of sorts, but it's also a way to show her I mean it. She hands me the phone and I enter my name, phone number and email into her contacts list. Then I text my own phone from hers, telling myself to remember to call tomorrow when I read this. When I hand it back and she reads it, she laughs again, putting her phone away and pulling out her keys.

"So this means I'll hear from you tomorrow, then?" she asks.

"I promise," I swear. I want to kiss her again but am afraid I won't have the strength to leave if I do, so I end up playing the rest of the role. I take the keys from her, open the door for her, then take her hand and kiss it good night. I practically skip and jump all the way back to my truck.

I text her the next day, before I've even logged into work. Throughout the day, we exchange little bits of conversation. During my lunch break I text, asking: "When can I see you?"

Her reply is, "When CAN you?"

"Tonight?"

She gets off work at a local pub, where she's a waitress, at eight, but I finish my shift by six. I have two hours to work myself up. I know she wants me to take her to bed. I can feel it. And I do not know how to tell her what I really am. It was hinted at in a text. She asked why my gmail came up as "y.davis" and I explained the nickname Davey came about because years before, a work had assigned me the email "dav.y" and the name had become mine. She didn't ask about the name behind the "y," and I wasn't ready to explain.

Too excited to wait, I meet her at the Bahia Bar. I've parked my car and am wading through the evening foot traffic, when I spot the guy at the corner selling flowers. "Roses," I remember from the man at the Crossroads. I buy her a single rose and spend the next couple minutes standing on the sidewalk breaking off a few thorns. One pierces my finger tip and I'm sucking blood as I step into the dark of the bar, my other hand behind my back with the rose.

I see her before she sees me. She's in red again—a red top with thin black straps and a black knee length skirt with a slit up the side. She's bent slightly over the table as she sets down drinks, and I can see every man in the room's watching, her pose hikes up the skirt enough to see the top of her stockings and the clip of a red garter strap. I'm hard and shaking before she rises and turns toward the bar. When she sees me her face lights up. She sets the tray on the bar, and comes right to me.

"Davey, you're early," she laughs in delight as she takes the rose I offer, bringing it right to her face. I think she's going to sniff it, but instead draws it over her cheek and then down her neck, eyes half closed in the sensuous delight of it. My mouth is dry and my gaze following only the trail of the rose over her skin. When it stops just above the swell of her breasts, she laughs. "Come on Davey, take a seat until I can leave?"

I let her take my hand and lead me to a bar stool. I try not to stare too much as I watch her flirt and tease customers. I'm not even sure she knows what effect she's having sometimes, but at other moments I catch the glint in her eye that is the pleasure of being seen. I'm taken back to my first sight of her, on the rack, submissive then but still eager in her grasp on pleasure and the joy of being watched and wanted. This time I'm not jealous, the other men may look all they want, I'm who she's leaving with. Now I feel strong and powerful, and seeing it, she seems to blossom even more, flirting with customers as her eye catches mine.

I'm so aroused I could take her down on one the tables, bend her over and push that skirt up over that gorgeous ass. I could pull the straps on her garters, letting them snap against her skin and listen to her gasps as her red nails scratch against the wood. I can imagine her writhing, pushing up on her toes to get me to do something, anything. Knowing every man in the room wants to be me, I would rub my fingers between her thighs and up against the soft fabric of her panties until I feel the wet soaking them. Slowly, I'd slide them down until they rest at the top of her stockings, trapped there by the garters. Then I'd spread her as open as the panties allow, stretching the fabric so I can gaze at her wet labia. I'd blow over the wet, feeling her shiver before sliding a finger up through the parting lips and finding her bud. There I'd gently graze a few times before flicking it, striking the bud like lighting match. Her moan would quickly be followed by an arch, begging for more. Again and again I'd strike her clit while her fluids drip. When I finally press my fingers into her cunt and rub the clit, she'd explode, feet coming up off the floor so that only my hands were keeping her from falling from the table.

"Davey?"

I blink and laugh at myself. I've been so busy fantasizing I missed that she was standing there ready to go away with me. She is grinning so wide I wonder if some of what I was thinking shows on my face. Holding her rose and her purse in one hand, she easily takes my hand with the other as I lead her out, glancing back at the faces of the men watching her with me.

I take her to dinner, at a place a bit nicer than the one where the meet up happened. We talk more about the scene this time. I've yet to tell her about the first time I saw her, but I do ask her who she knows in the leather group. She explains that she's been having a great time, mostly playing with friends, Ginny and her husband, Roland. From their descriptions I figure they must have been the two at the play party. I'm relieved that she doesn't have a Master, or even a steady boyfriend.

I tell her about a few exes in the scene, including both female and male names to see how she reacts. She nods with approval and I breathe a little easier on that score but we really haven't come close to my story when we're done with dinner.

"Let's take a drive before... dessert," I suggest and she smiles. I insist on paying, and she seems happy with that as well.

"Is your apartment far from here?" she asks after a long kiss in the car, before we've even clicked in the seat belts.

"No too far," I answer, her chin still in my palm from the kiss as I try to read her face. I know what my proffered dessert would be. "I'd love to take you there, but you'd be the sweetest thing there."

That gets me a grin again. "Oh, I think you underestimate your own taste," she insists.

I kiss her again before driving us directly to mine.

We're barely in the door before she tugs at my jacket and I push her up against the wall, taking both her hands and pushing them above head. She arches into me, her hands where I put them as mine trail down both her arms to her body. She squirms and gasps. I slide my hands down her body, enjoying the curves and then down over her hips, squeezing her flesh before finally reaching the hem of her skirt. With the same speed, my hands travel back up, pushing the skirt until it rides up above the black satin panties. I push one leg between her thighs and angle up until she is riding my knee. Then, one hand braced against the door, I kiss her again while the other hand cups one breast, finding her hard nipple under the cloth of top and bra, so I can squeeze it between finger and thumb. It has the desired effect, as she rocks on my knee, grinding against it as I kiss her, working her breast. Her first orgasm with me is there, staining the knee of my slacks with the wetness of her.

The second is when I have her on her back on my bed, hands gripping the metal rungs of the headboard after I suckle her breasts then, fingers working in an out of both her cunt and ass, as I nibble and nip at her clit. My face is wet and my hand sticky when I finally sit back up. She's panting and lying happily in a post orgasmic haze. I excuse myself to go to the bathroom, clean up and bring back a glass of water. She's sitting up when I return. She downs the water and hands the glass back to me. I set it aside as she reaches for me again. I'm still dressed, having only shed my jacket and shoes. She's quiet as she plays with my hair.

"You don't have to, but you should know something," she whispers into my ear, after nipping the lobe first.

I'm leaning against the headboard, holding her. I turn my head to see her face as she rests her cheek against my shoulder. I arch an eyebrow in question.

"You're my guy, my gentleman, no matter what is beneath this clothing. I see you and will feel *you*," she promises.

My heart speeds up and I'm sure she can feel it where she's pressed against my side. I look into her eyes for a long stretch of moments, seeing her understanding in a way that rocks me to my bones. "Can I... fuck you?" I whisper.

"Any way you want," she answers with a kind of breathless excitement.

Chapter 3
Trust, Betrayal, and Thorns

I reach over to the drawer beside the bed and pull out three lengths of red silk. I have imagined them on her before and am now eager to see and feel it for real. It's her turn to arch an eyebrow and I tell her to get on her hands and knees. She happily arches her neck to allow me to tie first the blindfold and then the ties around her wrists to the headboard. Leather cuffs, which I have, would be easier, but I love the look of the red silk against her light brown skin.

I stand then and take off my button-down, leaving on the white undershirt and what it covers, and then letting my trousers drop. She sighs, listening to me as I strip. I exchange the special briefs with their built-in pouch for a harness and a cock that's slightly over average. I roll a condom down my length, making sure she hears me tear the foil package open. She spreads her knees a bit more and I am smiling as I kneel between her legs. I make sure to make the lube cap snap and I groan as I lube myself up. Then my wet fingers find her already wet cunt, playing for a few minutes, my other hand pressing the small of her back as I finger her. She's begging for "*mais rápido*" by the time I position the head of my cock and push slowly into her. I'm greeted with a "yes!"

I'm inside her now and I swear I feel every twitch and squeeze of her cunt as my hands explore that beautiful ass. Too much to encompass in my hands but a great handful at a time, I squeeze and dig my fingers into her with each thrust. It's different from any other time I've tried it. I feel my cock in her heat, feel each thrust taking me close to the edge, wetness covering both my thighs now. I pull out and she cries in dismay. I soothe her as I coax her onto her back, ankles up on my shoulders as I sink into her again. I hold myself up with one hand while the other finds her clit, rubbing with my thumb as I grind with my hips, thrusting deep until she's crying out through another orgasm and taking me with her. I'm on my knees between her legs, sliding out and my face into her belly crying silently and hoping she thinks the wetness is just lube as I clutch her, kissing her belly and delighting in the softness of it. Her feet are hooked around me to rest on my back.

"Davey," she whispers.

"Maria, my love," I whispered to her belly.

We rest like that for a few minutes, with her tied and me held between her legs, my cock resting in the crease between her body and thigh.

Finally I kiss her belly and breasts reverently before pushing myself back. I'm not sure what to do at this point. I know you don't leave someone tied up but I'm not sure I can handle her seeing me yet. I kneel beside her on the bed. "I'm untying you, but leave the blindfold on. Promise."

"If you wish, Davey," she practically purrs.

The moment her hands are free, she reaches for me, pulling me down into a kiss again and I can't resist it, trying to hold myself up while she pulls me to her, hands roaming lower, down my back. I stiffen with the knowledge of the tight bindings she'll feel beneath my undershirt. She doesn't tense or ask, just caressing me as if this was normal. "I'll be right back," I tell her, and go to the bathroom to strip off the condom, take off the harness and put on some loose pants. I wash my face and bring her another glass of water.

She's sitting up cross-legged in the bed when I return — still wearing the blindfold.

"Can I see you now?" she asks and I answer by setting the water down and untying the cloth. Her eyes on mine when she blinks, smiling as she cups my face in both hands. "I really do see you, Davey."

"I'm blinded by you," I admit. "You're so beautiful."

It's wild, and more than anything I've ever experienced before. I feel like Romeo; while I thought I had been in love before, it paled compared to this. Maria is fire. Being with her is as good—no, even better than my wildest fantasies. Wilder even.

Every day I meet her, and bring her a rose. The flower seller near the bar actually starts having one ready for me, with the thorns already clipped off. Our nights are everything, from intense bondage and pain play to quiet evenings watching the latest scifi show on television while I feed her her favorite treats. Even these quiet nights often ended with me indulging in my favorite treats. Ice cream looks amazing on her skin and tastes even better.

Weeks turn into months, and I guess I grow complacent, engorged on the delight of her, and proud of her at my side. I grow to trust in it, in her. But I forget my promises. I don't find that poor homeless man at the crossroads, and give him his due.

I even start to forget my promises to Maria. Our first fight is the night we're supposed to go to one of the local play parties. It's a private invitation-only party where the doors open only for an hour before the fun really begins. If you are late, you are literally locked out for that night.

I was supposed to pick her up at seven, with the party opening at eight. I had my outfit picked out days in advance, my toy bag was resting by the door, and I had bought the rose that morning and kept it in the fridge for later. I was playing a video game while I waited to go pick her up. I got caught up in it, really pushing to top my previous score. I missed her first text and didn't even notice the time until I heard my cell phone buzzing because a call was coming through. I stopped to save the game and reached for the phone just as it stopped buzzing. I was staring at the time and cursing that I was late, even more pissed when I saw the texts and missed call were from her. I panicked. I had no idea what to say. Cowardly as it was, I texted back: "On my way, got caught in traffic. Be there soon."

I ran for the door, made it out to my truck before I remembered the rose and the toy bag, so I had to run back for it. It was ten minutes until nine when I pulled up in front of her house. There was no way to make the party before lock down.

I knocked on the door with a rose in the other hand.

When she answered, the cloud of hurt and anger made me take a step back as if facing a vengeful goddess.

"We'd better hurry," I said, as if we could still make it.

She scowled and without a word, stormed back into her apartment, the door left open. It felt like hours before she finally forgave me. She'd been shopping for new heels and a dress, had probably spent at least an hour on hair and make-up. She'd been really excited to attend the party.

Exhausted, we ended up ordering take-out. I swore to do better next time.

But I don't, not really. I get caught up with work and find I am running late. She's waiting for me at her place, or at work. Her face is set in anger when I finally get there. I lie to try and cover up my mistakes, telling myself it's to protect her feelings, and after a while, I can tell she knows. I suppose something had to break eventually but I really didn't think it was that bad.

It is Saturday, so I don't have to work, but she does. We're going to a concert with friends and I am running late, again. I don't want to face her wrath, but the regular flower seller isn't on his corner. I have to backtrack to the local bodega and buy one of their not-very-fresh roses before rushing to her. Her face is full of hurt, masked in anger, and I feel like shit. I try to soothe by smiling and telling her how beautiful she looks, offering my flower. She sighs in surrender, unwrapping the flower, then pulls it over her face and down her throat. The red wells on the skin before I understand what I am seeing. A thorn cuts her. She pulls the rose away in shock and another thorn, pierces her finger. With a shriek of pain, anger and humiliation, she throws it at me and runs back into the bar. I stare at the flower on the ground for a moment before it catches up with me and I follow. The patrons of the Bahia all scowl at me. The barkeep, Pedro, has his arms, thick with muscle, crossed over his chest. I don't see Maria. Don't know where she has gone.

One of the other waitresses, Rosa, her face full of rebuke but her voice sad, tells me I'll find Maria in the women's room. I go searching, following the signs to the locked door. I knock. No answer. I knock again and put my ear to the door. I hear sobbing, so I knock again.

"Maria, it's me. I know you're in there. Please come out. I'm sorry. Let me explain."

"Go away!" she shouts.

I've been through this before, with other women, and with Maria a few times. Usually she'll get angry and then I'll plead until she comes out. Then I'll make it up to her and it will be wonderful again. Although, previously, it hadn't been in public—and at her work, no less.

"Maria, please open the door. I'm sorry. I didn't know the thorns were there. I didn't mean to hurt you."

The door opens so fast I nearly fall where I've been leaning on it. Stumbling back, I look at her. Mascara runs down her face, her makeup is badly smeared and her eyes are puffy from crying. She holds on to the edge of the door like it's the only thing keeping her on her feet.

"That's the problem, Davey. You don't even know what it is you've done. Leave and don't come back," she sneers at me.

"I'll do better, Maria. I promise."

"You're always worried about being seen as a *real* man. Well, congratulations, Davey. You really are just like all the other men. Leave. Now." She slams the door shut again. I start to knock, only to find Pedro standing beside me.

"It's time to go, buddy," he says in a tone that means arguing could result in a few bruises, at the least. I start to reach for the door again and he blocks me. "Now," he growls, pointing toward the front.

The walk out is the worst humiliation of my life. All those men know that not only did I screw up, but that it's over. She isn't mine any more.

I don't give up that easy. I text, of course. She doesn't reply. I try calling and it goes to voice mail. Nothing I say is the right answer. Not only does she not reply, but she has my number blocked. When I try her work again, I am told I am banned from the Bahia Bar and Pedro says he will call the police if they see me again.

At her flat, her roommate, looking equal parts disappointed and sympathetic, tells me, "What are you doing? The lady doesn't want to see you again. You're pathetic. Go away and leave her alone."

After a week of no sleep, I remember the crossroads. I go to

António, the friend who told me the crossroads story in the first place. I tell him what has happened and that I have to get her back. Does he have a spell? Will the crossroads work twice?

António shakes his head in disgust and, with a more than a little pissed off sounding sigh, tells me I've "fucked up badly" and was lucky that's all that happened. Then he refuses to talk to me about it anymore.

More than a little desperate, I gas up my car, get cash from my ATM and set out for the Central Valley. I arrive later this time, and on a weeknight so the bar is less crowded, but the clientele feels even less hospitable, glaring at me as if they know what I have done. I stand waiting at the bar, watching while the barkeep serves others and wipes down the bar before finally turning to me with a look of utter annoyance. "You shouldn't be here," he says bluntly.

Angry, I square my shoulders. I lay out five twenties on the bar. "I'd like a bottle of rum and two shot glasses."

"I don't want to have to throw you out," he says, but takes the bills and sets the bottle and glasses in their place.

"You won't have to," I tell him, take the bottle and glasses and make my way to the empty table in the back. I don't know what else to do, but I tell myself I'll wait until the bar closes, if needed. Patrons leave and the waitresses keep looking at me. "Papa, I need to talk to you. Please," I whisper under my breath.

I am looking out the window into the dark when I hear the scrape of a chair. I turn quickly to find him sitting there. His vest is red tonight and his shirt black. The hat is the same, but the flower a simple rose bud, not yet opened. "You called."

"I found her," I tell him. Then I spill out my tale, explaining that I know I've messed up with her and will do anything to get her back.

He regards me for a moment and then gestures at the bottle. "Pour."

Hands shaking, I manage to break the seal and fill both glasses, only spilling a little.

He downs it immediately and tells me, "Drink. Then pour."

I do, the burn still making me shudder and my hands shake worse when I pour the second round.

"How much money did you give the homeless man?"

I blink. I'd forgotten. "I... I hadn't yet. Then things just got bad and I didn't think about it."

He shakes his head in a look I was beginning to think everyone in the world shared now. "Let me get this straight. You found her and she was everything you wanted?"

My mouth is dry and my eyes sting. "Even more than I could have imagined."

"You gave her a rose every day?" I nod. "But then you hurt her. Hurt her until she couldn't take it anymore. Then blamed it on a rose?"

I am like stone. I can't move, I can barely breathe. I see everything now, as if I was her. The man suddenly shows up in her life, promising to protect her and be good to her. He gives her what she has been craving herself. He's both sweet and takes charge so that she can feel safe. Then, just when she thinks she has found real love, love that can be trusted, he turns. He forgets, he lies, always expecting her to forgive him. The thorn is the least of many bloodlettings, the others all of her heart.

By the time the vision clears, the room is bleary from my own tears. I try wiping them away but only more follow.

"Take another drink, Davey boy." His tone now is one of sadness, not anger. I take the drink with him, the process of refilling the third round helps me focus enough that the tears seem to slow.

"What now?" I ask. I'm wondering if now is when I offer up my soul to make it better. I'm willing, because going on without her seems like it will be worse.

"Now? Now you go home. I don't want your soul. Your soul is everything you do with it, not a bargaining chip in a poker game. Which you lost, by the way."

"So how do I get her back?"

"You don't."

I'm shocked. I've come all this way for nothing. "So what can I do then?"

"Do? Really? You can start by living up to your promises. You want real trust? Make yourself someone who can be trusted. Give the woman a chance to heal. If you're real lucky, she might give you another chance. If not, maybe somebody else will."

24

He takes the third shot and I choke down mine. When I look up, I'm sitting slumped in the cab of my truck, sun coming up over the farmland in the Central Valley. I'm hung over as I drive back to San Jose.

That week I pay all my bills, set aside just enough from my paycheck to cover basics like gas for my truck and food for me. Then I drive randomly until I find a homeless man near a crossroad. I get out and give him a handful of cash. He is shocked speechless, staring at me as I walk back to my truck and drive home to eat alone.

I become what I said I would. I'm on time for work and friends alike. If I run into a snag, like the interminable Bay Area traffic snarls, I text or call whomever it is I am meeting telling them just what had happened. I don't lie. When I mess up I confess it right away. I don't make excuses. I even find an online transgender support group and find a local therapist I see at least twice a month. I am thinking of legally changing both the name and sex on my driver's license.

I attend meet ups and even a couple play parties, but I don't see Maria. I make sure not to drive by her apartment or work. Occasionally mutual friends would drop little bits in mercy, letting me know she is doing okay.

Days turn to weeks, which turn into months. Every morning I dab the little packet with cologne, even when I don't wear any that day. Once a month, I set aside some money to give to the poor. I know it sounds unrealistic. After a few times with direct cash, I run across a homeless shelter and food bank called, of all things, The Crossroads. I sign up to have the donation taken from my check every month. When the local leather club is looking for a group to do a fundraiser for, I put The Crossroads on the list and am happy to help organize the next event that raises money for them.

So, I've come full circle. A year since the night I first saw Maria, and it's the play party that's a fundraiser for my favorite charity, so I'm here. I don't expect to play, but I'm happy to hang out with friends and enjoy their fun, at a distance. I'm standing to the side watching when I feel a swish of skirts against the leather of my chaps. I look down first, see the red lacey fabric swirl around my calf. As my eyes travel up, I know who I'm seeing, would know any part of her, anywhere. I worry about what I'll see when I reach her face. She looks just as nervous as me when I finally do.

"Hi, Davey," she says so softly I wouldn't have caught it if all my attention wasn't on her. She's even more beautiful than I remember. It feels like a romantic cliché, my heart speeds up and my whole body aches to reach for her.

I smile, it's real even if it feels awkward. I know this doesn't mean anything more than she's not angry enough to avoid me anymore. "Hello, Maria. I... I'm happy to see you."

"Always the gentleman," she says, as if I hadn't broken her heart.

I shrug, eyes dropping for a minute. "I'm trying," I confess.

"So I've heard," she admits as well. Her hand comes up to rest softly on my forearm. I look down in surprise but take a deep breath to steady myself, eyes on hers again as she takes my hand.

That was three years ago. This year, I'm in the running for local Leather Man of the Year. When I was nominated, I took the time to sit down with the committee and explain to them my status as a trans man. They had questions, of course, but they still supported my nomination. Winning would be fun and a great honor, but I have to admit, my status as Master and protector of the most beautiful woman in the world is more important to me. I work every day to deserve her respect.

She does look amazing in red. She's spread on the rack again, red leather cuffs protecting delicate wrists and ankles. A black and red collar around her neck always makes me hard when I see it. We've worked through a few tools and we're really enjoying canes. We both love the brilliant red of the welts and the control that allows me to set a pattern, decorating that smooth skin in her favorite color. She's straining up again, her breasts bouncing as I give them a few gentle taps, enough to sting and make her growl. I don't usually mark them, but it's fun to tease. The taps to her labia are a little harder, but she only begs for more. I vary them so only every other one hits where she really wants it and I can tell she's close to coming, again. This is my cue to take my reward as her top. I sink to my knees, hand already gloved as I point my fingers, thumb tucked inside them. I work them into her cunt as I spread her labia with the other hand and flick my tongue at her swollen bud. Each clench and release of muscles around my hand has my cock throbbing. When my wrists are soaking wet, her juice dripping down to my elbow I feel myself enclosed inside her heat. I suck and thrust in rhythm until she's shrieking her pleasure and pulling me with her.

Now it's my responsibility and pleasure to gently uncuff and lower her to the mat, clean her up and have her drink down a bottle of water before I guide her over to the pillows. Lying back with her in my arms, I am drifting in bliss as I see the sign for the charity above us, "The Crossroads: for those who need help finding their way."

If you enjoyed this story, you can sign up for a free membership at ForbiddenFiction.com and discuss it with other readers and the author at the *Crossed Rose* story page at http://forbiddenfiction.com/story/DMA-1.000243.

SCYLLA'S POOL
ELLY GREEN

Scylla's Pool

Elly Green

Elly Green spins tales of lust and love that re-imagine the ancient myths of the Greeks and Romans, weaving back into those old legends all the arousing and tragic eroticism that was originally present. When not writing, she loves to read about treasure hunting adventurers and watch every sort of dinosaur documentary available.

Chapter 1
Seeking Magic

Inside lives Scylla, yelping hideously; her voice is no deeper than
a young puppy's but she herself is a fearsome monster; no one could see her
and still be happy, not even a god if he went that way.

–Homer, *The Odyssey*

Glaucus grinned at the rare glimpse of a domestic Circe, hunched over her worktable, a sharp-bladed knife clutched in her hand. Her long, black hair was tied back with a scarf, her chiton unbelted and clasped loosely on her shoulders. She looked relaxed, comfortable, ordinary. With a quick glance out the window to her exotic and free-roaming menagerie, spread out in the garden beside her cottage, Glaucus reminded himself this was so very far from the truth.

He had been lucky when he washed up here, many years ago, that she hadn't turned him instantly. After all, he had already been half a monster. Since the moment he'd found refuge with her, the tales of her predilection towards changing men into animals had taken on a startling reality. He'd witnessed her anger many times while serving her that first year. No man except him had been safe.

His gaze caressed the home he had once shared with her. Not much had changed. The walls were still crowded with hanging herbs, in various stages of drying. The dirt floor still meticulously swept, hard-packed where she walked and worked the most. All manner of forged metal pots and pans, glass jars, and clay urns cluttered every flat surface. A variety of smells, both strange and familiar, assaulted his nostrils.

Stepping through the open door, a cool wind off the shore followed him. He could hear the creaking of his boat as it rocked in the rising tide. His splashing charge through the waves should have alerted her to his presence. She was obviously deep in her work, whatever it happened to be. With her, it was better not to guess.

She trembled as another gust of brine-scented wind washed across the threshold. She flicked her wrist, absently, toward the hearth at the back wall of the cottage and a fire roared suddenly to life, casting its glow and warmth everywhere.

Glaucus jumped at the burst of flames. "I see you haven't lost your touch, sorceress."

Circe froze at the sound of his voice, and his grin widened. Not many men could sneak up on her the way he could. With the knife still in her grip, a droplet of fresh blood falling from its edge, she turned around slowly to face him. He caught a glimpse of raw, crimson-edged meat behind her as she moved. Unusually human looking meat. Glaucus swallowed the sudden lump lodged in his throat.

Surely she hadn't progressed to eating the men...

He quickly looked into Circe's twinkling eyes. Her open mouth closed.

"That? Fire is simple magic. You could do the same with a bag of herbs." She was grinning. Her dimples—the ones he found so disconcerting in a woman like her—popped into life. In a moment, she appeared younger. Beautifully attractive.

Glaucus smiled wide in response. Stretching out his arms, he held his palms up in greeting. "You look divine!"

A moment passed between them, full of tension. Glaucus felt it in his soul and in his bones. Circe scared him. He took a deep breath and held his position, keeping the knife in his peripheral. One could never be sure of her emotions. She was a fickle woman. Finally, the knife clattered to the floor and Circe rushed to wrap her arms around his waist.

"It's been far too long! Welcome h—" she began, then clacked her teeth together. He arched an eyebrow at her started syllable, but then forgot as she clasped him tighter, locking her wrists behind his broad back.

He rocked them both side to side, hugging her back just as hard. He had missed her, despite his misgivings in coming to her now. Missed this house. It, and her, had been his saving grace, once upon a time, and the island still held a special, if terrifying, place in his heart. When he'd arrived the first time, he had been near death. He really shouldn't have eaten that magical herb. Sure, it had brought back the dead fish, but why he thought it would be safe for him to ingest, still boggled his mind.

Pushing her back a bit, he took her hands and examined her from head to toe.

"How do you do it, Circe? I swear you haven't changed a bit." His sparkling topaz eyes, stunning in his dark, sea-beaten face, met her gray ones. She batted her lashes in response and summoned a blush to her olive cheeks. Wrapping her fingers in his, he lifted one hand to kiss, then the other. Her hand trembled at the gentle press of his lips on her soft flesh and he searched her eyes for why. She appeared happy—no, thrilled. Leaning forward, she presented a cheek and he kissed her there, too. Her blush deepened. She smelled like amber and rose petals. The scent washed over him and his smile grew, exposing his teeth.

"You tease," she murmured. "Would you like something to drink? Eat?" Glaucus glanced at the meat still on her table, his previous thought returning, then back to her.

"Pork?" He prayed to the gods the guess what right. And that it was real pork and not once a man.

He watched as confusion scrunched her features as she answered, "Of course." Relaxing, he noticed Circe's eyes dart from him to the meat on the table and back. It took her a moment before she realized his reason for asking. "I'm not a monster."

She leaned back and her eyes gazed over his face and down his body. Not unlike his examination of her.

"Are you keeping up with the medicine I gave you?" Circe asked playfully, slapping his upper arm in the same manner.

He hesitated. "Why? Do you see any scales?" Their warm welcome forgotten, he took a stride away, spread his arms and legs, and spun in the middle of the floor. Beseeching her with a worried look, he encouraged her to examine him everywhere. "Please, do not say it is losing its effectiveness." His voice quivered with real fear.

The side effects of that herb had manifested slowly. At first, his skin itched. Then, it had begun flaking off. Underneath, hard, toothlike scales had appeared. He hadn't worried. Sometimes the sun did strange things to a fisherman's skin. He had seen far worse in his years. Though, the blue-gray color was disconcerting. It was the webbing which had begun forming between his fingers and then over his fingers after the first week that had him panicking. That, and the slits behind his ears. When, two weeks after eating the herb, he'd suddenly toppled off the deck of his vessel and discovered his feet had fused together and the toes flattened out vertically, the fear had truly set in.

"No. It works. I promise." She grasped his wrists and pulled his arms down, wrapping her own around his back again.

Thrashing in the sea, he thought the end was near. He had no idea how to swim. Most fishermen didn't. There were monsters in the deep of the sea, and no one in his right mind chose to swim with monsters. Those terrifying creatures would grab a man and pull him under, never to be seen again.

He didn't drown. Instead, he swam, sort of, under the water. The waves carried him. Days later, he washed up on Circe's shore. He was almost completely transformed by that point. Only his head remained human, though his teeth were razor sharp. His body ached, his brain mush. He wanted to die, had crawled up higher on the shore in order to do just that. Fish could not live outside the water. Yet he survived.

"Thank the gods. I am enjoying my new-found immortality, but the fins and tail were a bit too much." He laughed, a little shakily, about it now.

"I remember. You washed up on my beach a wreck." Circe grinned, amused at the memory. He was less so.

It was Circe who identified the herb he'd eaten. She had pushed him back into the water and then sat down in the surf to cradle his head while she explained to him what had happened. She told him he was immortal, but cursed. He would never be fully shark or fully man. A hybrid, she'd called him.

Another word for monster, he had thought. *I am now what men fear. I am the monster who lives in the deep, ready to pounce and kill whoever falls beneath the surface.* The realization had been shocking. He was his own worst nightmare.

A god of the sea, she had amended, after studying his crestfallen face.

All he could see had been the horror of the ocean's depths. Blackness closing in on him, surrounding him, the press of the water from all sides. The screams of dying men and the roar of sinking ships echoing in the overwhelming silence. He didn't want to be like this. Even if it meant giving up immortality. His fear was too great, too ingrained.

"You helped me." His voice was wistful, as his mind returned to the past. She had given Glaucus an herbal concoction that had changed him back into a man, in exchange for some hard labor on her cottage. She had made him promise to stay for a year in payment. He did the best he could regarding the repairs, considering he was a fisherman by trade. She was pleased nevertheless. In fact, toward the end of the contract, he had begun to realize she hadn't cared a bit what he did, as long as he was near her.

He shook his head to clear the memories, his final understanding hanging in the air between them. Standing opposite each other, silence filled the house. *Was that the source of the tension he always felt between them? Did she love him?* It was difficult to believe. He was, after all, a monster. And if she did — despite his monstrosity — there was now a greater obstacle.

"I need some more help. Again."

Her pupils widened briefly in shock and he recoiled, uncertain in his request. *Would she help him? Would she deny him? Should he have come back? What if she got angry? Could she reverse the magical herbs?*

"What kind of help?" Her voice came roughly, as though she choked on the words. Her hands fell to her hips and rested there, balled into fists. She cleared her throat and tried again. "What can I do for you this time? You didn't eat any more questionable herbs, did you?" He cocked his head at her curiously. Her words were lighthearted and silly, but he could still hear anger in her tone.

She waited for him to answer, a small smile softening as silence greeted her. Circe took a few deep breaths. Her body, which had stiffened at his question, relaxed. Her hands flexed and nervously smoothed the front of her chiton.

"What did you eat this time?" Laughter edged her words, now. She tossed her black hair back and fluttered her eyelashes.

His grin returned — she was a making a joke after all — making his whole face brighten. "I'm in love —"

Circe's scream sounded far more like the roar of a lioness than the shriek of a scorned woman. Not that Glaucus would remember. His body crumpled to the floor in a heap, unconscious. The arc of energy she had released sizzled in the air above him, the odor of sulfur filling the room.

Glaucus opened his eyes, well rested and rejuvenated, with a surprising energy that seemed to enliven his every action and thought. He hadn't realized he'd been so tired before. The rising sun was just peeking over the horizon, setting the sea awash in bright pinks and royal purples. *Morning? Had he slept here overnight?* He reconsidered how he felt. *More than one night?*

Sitting up, his gaze roamed over the interior of Circe's main room. Everything seemed as it always had. Embers crackled in the hearth and steaming water boiled in a cauldron hanging over the ashy logs. A caged bird chirped from the far corner. Circe was nowhere to be seen. Tilting his head to the side, he listened for sounds of her from the garden or from her menagerie behind the garden. Nothing.

He hauled himself to his feet and began to search the rest of the house for her. Perhaps she was asleep, though he had never known her to stay in bed past the sunrise. Checking a small bedroom and a then her well organized pantry—it was the only space left for her to be hiding—he returned to the hearth. She was gone.

Her absence made him wary. The island where she lived was vast for one person, with any number of dangers lurking about. Dangers not even a witch could magic her way free from.

Absently, he juggled two items he had found on a side table. A linen bag of scented herbs tied off with a leather band and an attached note, and a jar of creamy unguent, also with an attached note. Both notes bore his name.

He looked down as he toyed with the items. She must have made them while he slept, although he didn't think he'd told her what he had wanted before he'd gone to sleep. *Had she guessed?*

Glaucus read the notes. Apparently, she had. These were just what he had wanted. Special herbs and a potion to make Scylla fall in love with him. The nereid-queen was an obstinate beauty, demanding gifts, passionate words and his never-ending worship, but always holding back. She refused to return his love. Not any more, not with these. He lifted the gifts and inhaled the aroma. Circe had outdone herself; there was no way Scylla would refuse him this time!

Shaking his head, he still wavered. Should he stay or go? Glaucus looked down at the things in his hands again. Go. He should go. Scylla was waiting for him. No doubt, Circe was fine. She was probably off picking more herbs in the island's verdant jungle. Who knew when she'd be back? He knew from experience she could spend an entire day lost in her mind as she collected the herbs.

Having made up his mind, he shut the door behind him as he marched back down to his boat. It rocked gently in the waves.

Circe watched his departure from a behind a thick, moss covered tree. Swiping at the tears she couldn't control, she waited until the speck of his boat disappeared in the shimmering reflection of the sea, then slid to sit against the tangled roots. Dropping her head into her hands, the jungle's fauna quieted as her anguished sobs filled the air.

He had left. Again. And he was in love. With another woman. Her grief turned to self-pity, then anger. Hours passed, the sun high in the sky before she was too exhausted to continue on.

He would return, she knew it in her soul. Especially after those gifts she had left for him.

She lifted her hands and took a deep breath, smelling the strong odor of the herbs picked earlier. She really had outdone herself this time. Smiling inwardly she imagined the havoc the gifts would create. Glaucus would run from his love, whomever she was, and return here. Whether in joy, finally realizing at last Circe's power and her love for him, or in anger at this trick, she didn't know and honestly didn't care. She just wanted him.

Chapter 2
Scylla's Cave

Watching the ruffle and slap of the canvas sails, Glaucus' smile grew. The winds were in his favor this day. The splash of the waves rocked his boat as it sliced quickly through the water. He would be there soon. Back with his love. His heart raced with excitement. He couldn't wait to see her again.

Standing on the beach, looking up the sheer cliff face, he glanced back to make sure the boat was secured. Placing his hands on two rocks, he pulled himself hand-over-hand up to the cave. Hauling himself, at last, over the ledge, he lay there a moment collecting his breath.

"Lover, is that you?" Her dulcet tones struck his heart and plucked it like a harp. Closing his eyes, he savored the harmony of the sea mistress's words. A whiff of the scent of her sun-warmed skin flitted across his nostrils and he groaned. He had missed her so much.

"Yes, I've returned," he said softly, standing. "With gifts." He stepped inside the cave and Scylla's giddy grin greeted him as she rushed forward. Her honey-colored curls swung around her shoulders. Naked and unashamed, the nereid was the most beautiful woman he had ever laid sight on. "Oh, Scylla, you take my breath away." He sighed as his hungry gaze took her in. His heart skipped a beat.

Love. It had to be love.

"Where? Where do you have them hidden?" Scylla used her fingers to search within his limited clothes for her promised gifts. Reaching the border of his tunic, she dipped her fingertips under the hem. His breath caught in his throat and his vision narrowed, completely focused on the beauty kneeled before him. Pulling her bottom lip between her teeth, she flashed her long lashes.

One hand slid up and teased the very top of his thigh, stroking along the angle of his pelvic bone. Glaucus' eyes rolled back into his skull at the sensation of her warm palm so close to his cock. He was already hard. Uncomfortably hard.

She repeated her question. "Where?"

Slipping her hand back down, Scylla tugged at his tunic. He fumbled at his belt, suddenly in a hurry. Working the jar free from his pouch, he handed it to her.

Scylla settled back on her toes and looked at the gift. Tilting her head sideways, she flicked her gaze back to Glaucus'.

"Read the note."

She flipped the tag over and did as he suggested. "To awaken the senses?"

"I'll show you." He took the jar from Scylla and, though he hated himself for doing it, helped her to her feet and pointed her in the direction of the bed. "Lie down."

Before moving to the bed, Scylla turned in Glaucus' embrace and kissed him roughly, rubbing her lips across his with delicious friction. Lowering a hand to wrap her fist around his length, she stroked once through his tunic.

"I'm very happy you came back." Her purr followed her to the bed.

Stunned, Glaucus stood dumbly watching her arrange herself on the finely woven cloth covered straw bedding. Spreading her arms open wide, she kept her legs demurely closed. Squirming on the bed, she raised a knee.

He rolled the jar of unguent back and forth in his palms, warming the herbal paste. Taking long strides closer and closer to the bed, his face hardened and his attention fixated on the source of his growing arousal. Coming to stand at the end of the bed, he popped the cork from the mouth of the jar. The scent of spring blossoms, summer honey, and autumnal herbs filled the cavern. Both lovers moaned at the overwhelming odor. The muscles in his shoulders and back relaxed, his breathing slowed, and his mind succumbed to tender feelings.

"It smells divine." Scylla's full lips parted on the whisper. Glaucus rolled his head back across his shoulders. He felt both drowsy, and more awake than ever. It was a strange sensation.

Scylla shifted on the bed again, this time letting her legs fall open. Her skin glowed with life, glowed with passion and he hadn't even touched her yet. Moisture seeped from between her legs. Glaucus yearned to settle between them and lap at her juice. Grasping her ankles roughly, he pulled her to the edge of the bed. He bent her knees back so she was spread open and available. Dipping three fingers into the cream, he started on her feet, and worked north.

He massaged her flesh, making sure no part of her body was left untouched. Pointedly ignoring the moist center at the crux of her thighs and her pert nipples, he swirled his fingertips through the cream and then across her skin in silky strokes. She began keening and wailing. Her breasts bounced and her hips rose and fell in not so subtle waves, urging him on and threatening to disturb his attention. He stopped, enjoying the view of her so close to the edge. Her eyes sprang open and she glared at him. Her mouth, so soft and pliable before, froze in an ugly line.

"Don't you stop, Glaucus. I will toss you from this cave into the treacherous waters below..." Her voice, pleasant so recently, was now harsh with denied ecstasy.

"I wouldn't dare. Turn over."

Immediately, her entire demeanor changed. Light as a feather, Scylla quickly flipped over. Her girlish giggle returned. She tucked her arms beneath her head.

"Go ahead. Do your worst."

Glaucus huffed at the order. He grinned. This was the woman he loved. Like the sea — the approach of a storm on calm waters was counted in breaths. Easy-going one moment, harsh and commanding the next.

There was only a little remaining unguent. Taking the last of the cream, he smoothed the soothing herbal tincture over her warm ass. She moaned and ground her clit into the sheets under his caresses.

He grabbed her hips in a rough hold and hauled her to him. She squealed in anticipation. Wrapping one arm around her waist, he knelt on the edge of the bed, and spread her thighs apart. The side of her arm caressed his, as she reached under her body and ran her fingers up and down her slit, preparing for his entrance. He watched, mesmerized by the scene. Her folds parted under the ministrations and he almost fainted at the heady odor of her heat.

Moving swiftly, he undressed. His cock was fully erect, purple, and aching. He joined Scylla's fingers with his own, coating his digits with her nectar. Nudging hers aside, he sought out her most sensitive clit and began to circle the flesh. He flicked her nub with his thumb, pressed upon it, then clasped it between his fingers and tugged. She arched at the feeling and whimpered in need, thrusting her hips back at him.

That was the cue he was waiting for. With the scent of her arousal strong, her noise making him crazy, her body laid out like a sumptuous banquet for the taking, and his need for her greater than his self-control, he let go.

Glaucus drove forward with a powerful thrust, entering her sheath halfway before retreating and plunging in again. Taking her without finesse, he slammed his cock into her tight passage over and over. She shook in his embrace. Her fists tangled in the sheet. Her head thrashed side to side, her sweat-soaked spirals tightening delicately. He reached up to run a hand over her scalp and down her curls. He tangled his fingers in her hair, pulled her head back and sunk even deeper into her core. Her inner walls squeezed his cock. The pulse of their heartbeats throbbed in unison. Their flesh seemed to melt together in the rising heat of their lovemaking.

"Faster, dear gods, faster. Move, bastard!"

Glaucus groaned. He didn't want to move. The feel of her impossible tightness was enlightening.

Scylla rotated her hips and bowed her back. The change in position sent him reeling. He was so damned close!

With his hand still caught in her locks, he shoved her forward, knocking her chest down to her elbows, forcing her to the sheets. She fought him but he didn't care. He stretched out on top of her, embedding himself between her folds. Cradling her to his chest, he rolled them over and let go of her hair. She lay atop him, breasts toward the craggy ceiling. Taking her breasts in hand, he kneaded the soft, ample flesh. Glaucus twisted and pulled on her nipples. She whimpered and moaned. Sitting up, she pushed down on his cock.

"Do it, then. Take me!" Scylla yelled.

Glaucus didn't hesitate. He lifted his hips, bent his knees and plunged his cock as deep as possible. She slammed her body onto his cock, meeting each of his thrusts. Racing him to the finish line, she set the punishing pace, pushing him further and further towards his completion.

"Now!" she screamed, the final vowel stretching into a shrill shriek of ecstasy. Glaucus closed his eyes, welcomed the blinding light of his orgasm, and let go. Scylla continued to move on top of his lap, but her motions were easy and languid. Opening his eyes, he could see her skin flush crimson—a full body blush.

"Oh, gods...that was amazing," she sighed. He couldn't agree more. Turning his head on the bed, he glanced at the floor and saw the empty jar. He would have to remember to ask Circe for more.

Side by side, the lovers struggled for breath and tried to calm their racing hearts. Their skin steamed in the cool air of the cavern.

"Do you feel like a bath?" Scylla asked, after a while. She rolled onto her side and propped her head with the palm of her hand. With her other hand, she traced the lines of his physique, wrapped a few strands of dark chest hair around her finger and pulled teasingly. The smile she wore was bliss, pure bliss. Half-lidded eyes, satisfaction gleaming in their depths, had trouble focusing on anything, darting here and there. Glaucus loved her like this. Sated. She was so beautiful.

"I would love one. With you."

She moved slowly, stretching her limbs like a cat as she stood from the bed and sashayed toward the back of the cave. A spring-filled basin was tucked into the corner behind a large stalactite.

Rolling off the side of the bed, he tripped over his tunic. Kicking it aside, he saw his belt and remembered the satchel of herbs. Circe's other gift to him. His other gift for Scylla. Glaucus retrieved the bag and, swinging it on one finger, sauntered back to join Scylla.

"Did you like the cream, my dear?"

Bent over at the waist, humming happily as she fiddled with the collection of combs and sponges she kept beside the bath, the first sight of her swaying ass froze him to the spot and awakened his cock anew.

"Why, do you have more?" She straightened and spun around,

her gaze immediately locking on his quickly growing erection.

Glaucus shook his head, remembered the satchel, then answered, "No, but I do have another gift."

Her features lit. "Please?" Scylla held out her hand and Glaucus dropped the bag into her open palm. She brought it to her nose and inhaled. The scent of plum, peach, orchid, wisteria, and amber all combined to have her on her knees. Weaving side to side, her lips serene, eyes closed, she moved as if in a trance. She drifted on a second sea of passion. All from one whiff.

He laughed at her reaction. "Let me have it back and I'll read the note for you." She handed the linen bag back absently, letting the waves of the aroma wash over her. "To awaken the animal within." Purring where she swooned, he reached down to tuck a stray strand of hair behind her ear. "Which seems to being working already." He grasped her beneath her arms and pulled her back to her feet.

She thanked him with a hug, her purr deepening to the yowl of a cat in heat. Letting her rest on his chest, he chuckled at her current state, already imagining the fun they would have in the bath.

Glaucus untied the bag of herbs behind her back, fiddling with the tiny knot Circe had secured. At last, the leather band undid and drifted to the ground. Dumping the herbal mixture into the bath water, he allowed himself a moment to pull the wonderful scent deep into his lungs. Unlike Scylla, he felt no more than a slight tingle in his cock and between his balls. Shrugging, he didn't think to panic. Perhaps he was stronger, more immune to Circe's magic, than Scylla.

Since they were still naked, he slowly maneuvered her into the bath—nothing more than a deep basin carved naturally from eons of underground water in the rocky cavern's back wall—and then slid down into the warm seawater across from her. Her head fell back and she slipped further into the bath, the water rising just below her heavy breasts. She closed her eyes and sighed, slow and deep. Glaucus eyes settled on her nipples. He hadn't gotten the chance to taste her there yet, and suddenly, he wanted nothing more.

Floating off the slight bench that formed midway in the basin, he slunk across the space between them. He kept low in the water, letting the herb-infused surface lap right above his pecs. Touching her nowhere except her breasts, he used his mouth to lick all around the voluptuous, perky globes. As he licked, he nipped gently on her sensitive skin, loving the savory saltiness of her sweaty flesh. Glaucus' eyes locked on her peak. He craved her dusky, pink tit.

He took it between his lips, rolling the peak back and forth, feeling the areole pebble. Sucking the nipple, peak and areole both, inside his warm mouth, he began to draw roughly, like a starving infant. His hair brushed across her collarbone. Lifting one hand from its purchase on the underwater bench she reclined on, he palmed her opposite breast. He seized her tit between the nails of his thumb and forefinger and pinched hard. Very hard.

Scylla's head whipped up and her hands found purchase in his hair, holding him tight to her bosom. "Gods!" Without consent, her hips gyrated, lifted and wiggled, begging Glaucus for his cock again. So soon after her first orgasm.

Though his scalp burned with the pain of her nails digging into his skin, he didn't let go. Dropping his other hand to her abdomen, he started at her navel and stroked purposefully down to sift through her nether curls. Finding her clit, he punished it as he did her nipple.

She wailed, shrieking unintelligible words.

"Let go," he growled, ripping his mouth from her breast. Delirious, she only pulled him closer. His fingers squeezed her clit and pulled. Scylla yelped and, tilting her head forward, glared at Glaucus.

"Ouch!" She growled.

"Let go," he repeated. They stared each other down, fighting the need for pain and the want for more pleasure. Both desiring, in that moment, domination.

She was the first to relent. Releasing her grip on his locks, she spread her knees and beckoned him with a curved finger. Instead of crawling in with his bobbing staff, ready and poised to enter her, he eased his hands under her ass and lifted her off the bench, holding her poised at the surface of the pool, and pressed his nose to her moist folds. He swooned at the scent. The sweet smelling aroma of the herbs only added to the sweetness of her feminine nectar. His nostrils flared at the overwhelming experience and he hurried to taste her fully. Kissing her with his lips open, he fed on her, slipping his tongue past her slit and, imitating the final act, thrust his tongue as far as he was able into her. He suckled her as though he could not live another day without her on him, in him, everywhere. Her purring resumed with interspersing yips as he happened upon a particular spot over and over again. The spot varied, but her body nonetheless responded. He tried to memorize his actions, but soon lost count and interest. He was too pleased by her burgeoning arousal to care.

Sliding her hands from his head, she caressed the shell of his ears, down to the lobe. Then, taking it between her fingers, she pinched hard with her nails. His head popped up. His shoulders followed, extending her thighs even wider. He dropped his hold on her and let her sink back to the bench.

Now it was his turn to complain. "Ouch!"

Wrapping her arms around his neck, she trailed them lower to his chest. He stared at her, confusion clear. Fingertips gliding along his wet skin, she tickled his ribs and dropped her hands to rest on his hipbones. She forced him to scoot closer so the head of his cock bumped against her slit. She moaned. He groaned.

"I want it slow." Scylla winked. Her eyebrow lifted and one corner of her lips tweaked in a smirk.

"Yes, mistress." He lowered his eyes in an act of modesty. Then, taking her hands in his, he pulled her up so they stood chest to chest. Reaching under the water, he caressed her thigh and lifted her knee, placing her foot on the bench. Crouching slightly, he took his cock in his fist, and lined himself up. His cock teased her folds. His breathing quickened as he watched the joining of their flesh for the second time, this time amplified by the water.

Slowly, bit by bit, ever so slowly, he sheathed his sword in her.

He filled her completely, her core muscles relaxing to ease his conquest. Once in place, his length deep inside her, the lovers released the breaths they held. With one of her legs draped around his back, the other supporting her weightless body, he held her in the perfect position for the long, slow, strong strokes of his staff.

Glaucus reveled in the feel of her tight on his width. He savored each plunge.

"You are divine, my love!"

"So are you..."

The two lovers moved together, lost in the moment. Around them time both seemed to stop and stretch out into eternity. Their climaxes approached quickly, but far too leisurely. He hung on the metaphorical edge, suspended, waiting intermittently for the fall.

"Your nails, dear," Glaucus grumbled, feeling a sharp pain bite at his inner thigh. He thrust forward forcefully, loving the sound of their bodies slapping together in rhythm. Loving the swells that rippled across the water from their union. "Oh, gods, Scylla, stop scratching me!" A white light sparked behind his eye as another stinging graze ripped the thin skin of his abdomen. The climax that seemed so close, was abandoned. Pleasure was gone, but the pain remained. "Oh, Hades..." he screeched as numerous pinpoints of pain erupted at once along his balls and cock. His nerves screamed in agony. He tried to pull free of her, but her legs remained around his waist.

"What? Don't stop." Her lashes fluttered at his sudden absence.

The splash of limbs — not any of theirs — tossed droplets in the air from behind Scylla's body. A drop of the water landed on Glaucus' hand. He eyed it curiously. What in Tartarus was going on? His gaze lowered and he sucked in a sharp breath. Creatures were thrashing beneath the surface of the bath water. Dark, writhing animals, alive, frenzied.

"Scylla?" His voice rose, shrill, as fear and adrenaline coursed in his veins. He lifted his eyes to hers and stared, terrified.

"Glaucus?" His finger pointed down. She looked.

Pulling her leg from behind him, she placed her feet on the bottom of the bath and stood tall. Suddenly nervous, Glaucus watched with her. *What were those things?* Creatures flailed, sending water everywhere. They shifted with Scylla, their snouts and white snarling teeth rising from the water as her midsection cleared the surface. The eyes of rabid dogs glowed in the cloudiness of the churned water. Too many to count. Foam gathered along fleshy lips raised in growls as their snouts broke free of the surface. Scylla scrambled to get away, but with every move, the strange dog heads followed — as though attached.

As she took a step toward him with arms outstretched, panic at the scene before him caused bile to rise in his throat. He could see the fear in her eyes. She was scared. Very scared. Her body vibrated with terror. She opened her mouth to scream. Closed it, then grabbed his arm. Her eyes watered and her lip quivered. She opened her mouth again, this time to beseech him for help. No words came. She was im-mobilized by fright.

He retreated, backing away slowly, all his attention focused on her transformed midsection. His body shuddered as more and more of the monster she'd become rose clear of the water. Every nightmare from childhood on came drastically to life.

Ears pinned back against their skulls, the doglike heads surround-ing her waist began to sway to and fro, nostrils flaring. Like a pack of starving wolves, they were searching for prey. Searching for him. Newly born from her loins, they were very hungry. Locking on to his warmth, their heads swiveled on serpentine necks and lunged for Glaucus. The sharp snap of teeth made him jump and spurned him to swifter action.

He had to get away. She was going to grab him, pull him beneath the water and rip him to shreds. He'd drown in his own blood. He eyed the snarling dogs. Those creatures were hers to command.

Glaucus' calves bumped into the bench and, without glancing back, he climbed quickly over the edge. Crashing to the floor of the cave, he kept his eyes on her as he crawled away.

She found her voice. "Come back, love. Help me."

Tears streaked down her cheeks. Her bottom lip quivered as her pleading eyes dropped from his to stare at the abominations arising from her waist. He followed her gaze and felt his own lips curl in disgust and fear. The creatures' heads thrashed ever searching and their forelegs kicked and struggled. She looked up at him. Her brows were drawn, her forehead creased. Fear and worry marred her once beautiful features.

He looked away toward the basin. Herbs still floated, spinning lazily, on the surface. His gift. Circe's gift to him. It had changed her into this monster.

"Love?" he taunted. "Oh gods, no. You're a—" His voice wa-vered, but grew stronger with each backward step he took toward safety. "A monster." He shook his head and pointed his finger at her. The finger trembled slightly. "Look at you! A nightmare!" He spun on his heels, not even bothering to gather his clothes or belongings, and fled, leaping from the cave's entrance in his haste. Without a glance behind, he rushed to his boat and huddled, curled into a ball, beneath the wheelhouse.

A melancholy howl rang out from the cave, echoed by a dozen more. The eerie noise sent shivers racing down his spine. Clutching his knees to his chest, he blubbered in fear.

Circe stared at the swirling cauldron of water. Scylla was no longer the sea goddess Glaucus had thought he loved.

She stood and stretched, a smile splitting her face. Her eyes roamed her tiny cottage, trying to decide how best to pass the time before he arrived. He would undoubtedly allow his body to revert to his transformed state to reach her fastest. Fear and anger were both powerful motivators.

With that decided, she burst into motion. A new batch of medicine for him was the first order of business. Humming, she pulled a cloak over her shoulders and hurried out into the jungle.

If you enjoyed this story, you can sign up for a free membership at ForbiddenFiction.com and discuss it with other readers and the author at the *Scylla's Pool* story page at http://forbiddenfiction.com/story/EG1-1.000239.

Tomb Brides
Konrad Hartmann

Tomb Brides

Konrad Hartmann

Konrad Hartmann writes action-oriented erotica and a bit of horror, seeking to offer exciting, cross-genre stories. Drawing on mythology, dreams, and the oddities of human experience, he explores the fringes of the imaginative world. Hartmann believes that we all have stories, and that the world will be better for the telling of them. Find his work in Forbidden Fiction's catalog, and scattered across the Web.

Chapter 1
Unnr

Folkvardr retched as the wolf barked its corpse-breath into his face. His hand still gripped a spear, but the beast's paws pinned his arms to the stone beneath. He kicked, but the wolf's body felt like wood against his feet.

The fetid vapor in his lungs, Folkvardr remembered falling into an open tomb, and worse, falling into the rotting corpse within. The smell now blasting from between the wolf's fangs recalled that night.

Was this then the revenge for plundering? Was the curse that he should smell his own decay while his heart still beat? The creature's breath fell in a pattern, making strange sounds. Folkvardr realized these sounds were words; not words in any language, but recognizable only by the way they plucked and gnawed at his mind.

"What would you here?" the wolf asked. The muzzle shot down to his shoulder, nipping his skin. Folkvardr felt the cut and the rasping of a tongue. "You be not jotun nor Aesir nor Vanir. You be not light alf. You be not dark alf. You. Must. Be. Man," the wolf leered as it grated out the words. "And man comes not to Ironwood."

Folkvardr opened his mouth to speak, but the vapor of the breath rolled across his tongue and down his throat like an oily cloud. He gagged and closed his mouth.

"You give me many thoughts," the wolf said. "And many choices. I could devour you now, gulping down your meat and blood while it yet steams in the night air. I could gut you alive, let you die slowly, and later, when decay softens your body and sweetens it with rot, I could savor you then.

"Or," the wolf continued, a rasping chortle in his throat, "I could have you as bitch. Would you like that?"

Folkvardr braced himself. If he could not speak then he would at least scream once in defiance. But when he opened his mouth, the wolf drooled slime in a sticky rope between his lips, and Folkvardr convulsed, coughing and retching as the ooze burned his tongue.

"I can do exactly as I wish with you," the wolf said. "Because you are in Ironwood. You would like a quick fight, wouldn't you? You would fain die on your feet, like a—like a man. Ask for mercy. I will let you stand and fight with your spear. I will tear you apart before you take two steps. But you have to beg for this. No? You won't beg. You don't know where you are. I offer you the easiest fate in all of Ironwood. But still, I wonder what brings you here. Why don't you speak? What is your name?" the wolf asked.

And Folkvardr now felt the dank night air as a fresh breeze, the corpse stench no longer filling his nose.

"My name is Bane-of-Trolls and Lament-of-Curs!" Folkvardr shouted at him.

The wolf's teeth grew large.

"Tell me, oh, Bane-of-Trolls," the wolf said, leering, "what business brings you to Ironwood?"

"To see how high one may stack dead ettins," Folkvardr gasped.

"But you've already failed, oh, Lament-of-Curs. You cannot even start with one."

"Let me stand and I'll start the pile now," Folkvardr said.

"Beg me," the wolf said. "Beg me like a bitch. Beg to be let up. I vow this is the kindest doom in all of Ironwood. You cannot leave now. You cannot go back to Midgard. You are in Angrboda's woods. My name is Skrati."

Folkvardr felt a burning wetness on his stomach. The wolf leaped off from him and was gone. Folkvardr rolled to his feet, his spear in hand, trying to ignore the filth that ran down the front of his tunic.

His heart pounding, he ran in circles through the woods, blood raging, his only thought to find Skrati. He ran aimlessly until the moon set, when he crawled beneath an overhanging boulder and collapsed.

Folkvardr felt the darkness and gasped, feeling a ringing in his ears. He stumbled over something and fell down backwards. Lurching to his feet, he felt a wall of stone and dirt with his hands. He turned at the sound of clicking, and when he saw sparks, realized someone was lighting a torch. The flame lit the room, and Folkvardr saw he was again in the grave mound, the barrow of Alrekr, son of Osvaldr.

The torch spluttered in Unnr's hand. Despite the illumination, her black dress made her blend into the shadows at the end of the chamber. For a moment, Folkvardr saw only her blonde head, and her hands, and the torch floating in the air.

Huld, Unnr's slave, stood with her arms crossed and shoulders slouched, turned half away from her mistress. She stared at the wall or the floor, but rarely at Folkvardr, and never at the body of Alrekr.

An oblong stone, of a mineral different from the others in the local soil, bore runes carved into its face. Folkvardr pointed at them.

"We should leave," he said. "This is a fool's game. What? We bring Alrekr back in vague hopes he will tell us where his gold lies hidden? We face uncertain loot, but certain curses."

Huld glanced at him, at the runes, and stared hard at the ground.

"And why say you that, Folkvardr?" Unnr asked, her head cocked to one side.

"Did you not read the runes?" he asked.

"No. Why don't you read them for me?"

"You can read them at least well as I," Folkvardr said. "And your slave can read them better than you."

At this, Unnr scowled and Huld stared harder at the floor. Unnr walked over to the stone, glanced at it, and then stared at Folkvardr.

"If you won't read them, I will. They say," Unnr said, her stare never leaving Folkvardr's eyes. Her voice grew loud. Hard. Hollow. "I call against the spirit of the dead, against the stalking dead, against they who ride, against those perched, against they who plummet, against the wandering dead, and against those in flight." She stepped close to Folvardr, staring up at him.

"All shall decay and die away," Huld said, finishing the inscription. Her voice crept quietly from where she stood in the shadows.

"Are we dead?" Unnr said. "No. Not at all. What concern is it to us?" She turned and walked towards Huld, grabbing the slave by her thick, black braids. Unnr pulled her towards the center of the room, forcing the young woman to bend over as they walked. Folkvardr noticed the swell of Huld's thighs and breasts beneath the dress as she staggered. He felt his apprehension now mixed with excitement, lust now blending with fear until each offered equal measures.

"Those who fear, should fear," Unnr said, smiling at Folkvardr. She forced Huld to her knees.

"I feel no shame in fearing the rune-master Gyril, only wisdom. I say now before all witnesses here that I take no willing part in this, and what happens, happens not of my will," Huld panted her words out, writhing as Unnr twisted and pulled at her hair.

"I trust you are more willing, Folkvardr?" Unnr asked.

He nodded, a glazed look in his eyes as he stared at Huld. Huld looked up at him, her large dark eyes moist with a silent appeal. She looked at him, he realized, with a desperate hope that immediately hardened his cock.

"Ah, so much for your rescue, my girl," Unnr said. "Your hero's intentions just became visible."

Folkvardr reached for a sack on the floor, and pulled out a length of rope from it. Huld's eyes darted from the rope, to the corpse lying not far away on its bed, and back to the rope. Her body convulsed as she made a sudden struggle to escape.

Unnr pounced on her, strong despite her lithe form, and soon the slave laid on the floor with Unnr's knee in her back. Still, she tried to crawl for the opening, even with her mistress straddling her.

Folkvardr slipped a noose around the girl's neck, and Unnr fastened it like a leash, slipping the knot tight against the neck and pulling the rope with the other hand. Huld's face turned red, and then purple, before she went limp and ceased struggling.

"Give her air, Unnr! If she dies, your efforts come to naught," Folkvardr said.

Unnr stared at Folkvardr, smirking and taking her time in loosening the knot. Huld gasped, sucking in air and coughing, the dust on the floor swirling in an eddy. She grabbed her by the braids again, pulling hard to lift the girl's head from the floor. Huld reflexively reached up to hold Unnr's wrists for support.

Folkvardr clutched Huld's wrists then and wrenched her arms

behind her back, making her squeal. Huld knelt now, and as the man held her arms behind her back, crossing her wrists, she went limp, sagging forward in Folkvardr's grip.

Unnr worked quickly, the rope sliding through her hands like hempen snakes coiling around and around the slave's wrists. Unnr's long fingers wove patterns faster than Folkvardr's eyes could follow, knots weaving upon knots.

Folkvardr eased Huld forward to lay on the stone. Huld wept silently, her tears mixing with the dust.

"Ah, so gentle," Unnr said as she tied the girl's ankles. "She must look forward to kind treatment from you."

Folkvardr ignored Unnr and reached forward to stroke the girl's hair. As he held up the braids, he watched how they shone in the torchlight, almost blue-black in their luster. He stroked Huld's cheek, wiping away the wet dirt. A tug at his belt turned his gaze back to Unnr, who now held his seax in her hand, pulled free from his belt sheath. Huld's ankles were now securely bound. Unnr grinned and Folkvardr wondered if he could actually hear her grinding her teeth. She swept her arm forward in a fast arc, the blade descending towards Huld's bottom.

Folkvardr grabbed Unnr's wrist, stopping the swing only with effort, surprised at the blonde woman's sinews.

"Why would you kill her?" he hissed.

"I. Am not. Killing her," Unnr whispered leaning close to him. Steel shone in the corner of his vision. Too fast to be stopped, Unnr tossed the knife through the air, catching it with her free hand. She slashed towards Huld.

Folkvardr's hand clutched Unnr's throat, only to feel sharp steel against his own. He relaxed his grip, but Unnr did not drop the blade from his neck. She smiled.

"You misunderstand my intentions, dear Folkvardr," Unnr said, her eyes motioning towards Huld. Unnr looked down at Huld. Her dress was now slit to right below her bound wrists, the cut in the linen revealing the swell of one olive-skinned buttock. "However, do remember she is my slave, and I will do with her as I will," Unnr said, again leaning close to Folkvardr.

He stepped away from her and she crouched down, cutting away

Huld's dress in a spiral, rolling the girls across the floor as she pulled away the fabric in one piece. When Unnr finished, Huld lay face down and naked on the floor.

Folkvardr stared at the voluptuous symmetry of Huld's form, at the curve of her full thighs and bottom, the gentle dip of the small of her back, and her narrow waist. He crouched and helped her to her knees. Huld stared up at him, her legs folded beneath her. Tears trickled down and pattered in drops on her full breasts, heaving as she panted, the nipples large and dark.

Folkvardr looked over at Unnr, who was fastening a rope to the support beam overhead. Unnr tied the end of the rope to Huld's wrist bindings.

Folkvardr lifted Huld to her feet. When Unnr finished tying off the rope, Huld stood with her bound ankles together, the rope leading from her wrists to the ceiling mercifully slack.

"You enjoy this, don't you, Folkvardr," Unnr said, circling her slave, running her fingers over the smooth skin. Standing behind her, she cupped Huld's heavy breasts and lifted them, stroking the nipples gently at first. They hardened quickly and Huld stared at the wall, frowning. She winced as Unnr pinched them tighter and tighter. One hand slid to down to the lush black curls of Huld's pubic hair, the fingers plunging in to grip the hair and pull as Huld gritted her teeth.

Unnr released her and walked behind Folkvardr, circling him with her arms. She pushed him forward to stand closer to Huld. He stared at the girl as he felt Unnr's fingers untying the waist of his breeches, reaching in to pull out his stiffened cock as she tugged down the garment.

Huld's face reddened and she looked away.

"Would you like this, slave?" Unnr said, pumping the penis in her hand and rolling back the foreskin. "No, don't look away!" Unnr's free hand darted out and hit Huld's face with an echoing slap. Huld stared now at Folkvardr's cock.

Unnr grabbed Huld by the hair and forced her to bend over, so she leaned forward, her arms stretched behind her by the rope. Folkvardr felt fire course through his brain, and now he grasped the girl by the hair, filling his hand with the silky coils as he pressed his prick towards her mouth.

"Please, no!" Huld gasped, "Not here! Not in the barrow!"

"Your defiance shortens your days, my cunting slave," Unnr said, going to a bag lying nearby.

Folkvardr felt a hot shame as he ran his hands over Huld's body but his penis throbbed painfully. He felt her breasts, unrestrained now as he squeezed and fondled them.

Unnr lifted her dress and slipped it over her head. She was slender and willowy, contrasting to Huld's voluptuous form. Folkvardr stared at her small, upturned breasts and blonde-haired pubic mound as he groped Huld. Unnr smirked and held up a stone phallus, smooth but massive in its dimensions. She wiped grease over its surface.

Huld tried to turn to see what Folkvardr stared at, but the man held her head so she could not see. Smiling coldly, Unnr rested the polished cock against Huld's bottom. The slave squirmed but could not avoid the dildo as Unnr pressed it against her anus. Unnr held it like it was her own penis, and Huld shrieked as Folkvardr watched it sink between her parted ass cheeks.

"Suck, slave!" Unnr barked. "Suck or I will tear you in twain!"

Huld stared up at Folkvardr with wide, tear-soaked eyes and opened her mouth, sticking out her flattened tongue. He shoved his penis into the girl's mouth and moaned as Huld sucked, obedient and fearful. Folkvardr felt control slipping away as he held the girl's face in his hands, feeling the warm scrub of her tongue. He started fucking her mouth hard now, watching as Unnr violated the slave's other end, the stone cock penetrating the hole with a barely audible slick sound. Unnr's eyes were half-hooded, and Folkvardr vaguely realized she quietly muttered strange words as the torches burned dim.

He felt Huld spluttering and gagging around his cock, but the fever in his nerves drove him onwards as he plunged deep and came, ramming his penis into her throat and holding her hair. She coughed and gagged on bile, blowing fluid from her nose as he forced the last drops of his sperm into her gorge.

As he slid his penis out and Huld retched, he listened to Unnr. Her face was tight with effort and she spoke her strange words quickly, her hair hanging in her face as she rhythmically penetrated Huld's rectum.

Folkvardr walked over to the bag lying on the floor, searching it until he found the small pouch within. He held it in his hand for a moment, weighing it. When he looked up, Unnr has staring hard at him. She nodded quickly, never breaking her stream of words.

Folkvardr walked over to the corpse of Alrekr. He stared down, and it felt as though he stood on the edge of a very deep pit, that the floor could shift at any moment, causing him to plunge down to where the dark blue cadaver lay. He forced himself to steady his feet, feeling the stone beneath him. Behind him, he heard the monotonous drone of Unnr's voice, but now there was a swishing sound, a cracking sound, and the squeal of Huld.

He ignored the sounds and forced his fingers to untie the knot cinching the pouch closed. His hands shaking, he untied the cord and opened the pouch. He reeled for a moment, the pungency of the powder making his mouth water sickly. He spat, and tried to avoid smelling it again. Holding the pouch away at arm's length, he slowly began to sprinkle it over the corpse, taking care not to let it fall onto him.

The grains fell like powdered rot; green, the color of a wound turned foul. He winced, and when finished, tossed the pouch away.

He turned to look at the women. Unnr held a lash in her hands, whipping mercilessly at her slave. Huld wailed, twisting and writhing at the end of her rope to avoid the beating. Red streaks, many of them trickling blood into sweat, covered her buttocks and thighs. Sometimes she fell to hang painfully by her wrists, and when this happened, Unnr drove her to her feet by lashing her breasts. When this no longer forced the girl to stand, she dropped the lash and picked up the seax.

Unnr's arm swung in a perfect arc, and the blade slashed the suspension rope. Huld fell uncontrolled to the floor. Rolling the slave onto her back, Unnr straddled her face, the knife poised over Huld's stomach. Grunting and grinding her hips, she force Huld to lick her. Unnr leaned forward over the girl's body. She held the seax by its blade, and Folkvardr heard Huld's muffled whimpering as Unnr began to cut runes into the thighs of the slave.

Chapter 2
Alrekr

Three rows she cut into each thigh, afterwards using the dull edge of the knife to scrape up blood onto the flat of the blade. Unnr rose, careful not to spill the blood. Over to the corpse of Alrekr she walked. She looked Folkvardr in the eye for a moment before she turned the blade, allowing it to spill the blood onto the chest of the corpse. Unnr flicked her wrist shaking as much blood as possible onto Alrekr before turning and walking back to Huld.

Unnr stepped over the slave's inert form, straddling her, with one foot on either side of Huld's hips. Crouching slightly, she held the blade of the seax beneath her crotch. Folkvardr saw Unnr's body grow tense, and then a thick stream of urine fell, steaming in the cool air as it washed the blood from the blade. Huld writhed as the acrid fluid washed the blood from the runes carved in her skin, wincing at the burn.

After the last drop fell, Unnr began to sing her galdr-song. She stared at the body of Alrekr as she sang. Folkvardr felt his skin crawl as the words clattered against the stone walls of the tomb, clanging like steel, jarring in their crispness. Beneath her, only Huld's shoulders shook as she sobbed without sound.

Huld looked up at Folkvardr.

"It cannot be undone. Not now." Folkvardr heard the words, but he saw Huld's lips did not move.

"Awake. He is awake now," he heard her say.

Folkvardr saw movement from the corner of his eyes and recoiled from the grave slab. He felt himself backing into a corner as the figure of Alrekr twitched where he lay. The corpse moved in a way that reminded him of a head-wounded fighter, one mortally wounded, but not dead yet, dancing like a puppet before life seeps out completely.

Breath hissed out in a rattle from between the dead warrior's swollen blue lips. The figure sat up, struggling, stiff muscles and joints crackling as he rose. Alrekr's head swiveled in quick jerks, turning to face Folkvardr. Folkvardr tensed himself. His spear rested against the wall, out of reach, and he cursed himself for leaving it so far away.

A laugh like the rustling of leaves escaped Alrekr's mouth as he opened his eyes and stared with milky, half-deflated orbs at Folkvardr. But now a nearly continuous wail filled the barrow, and Folkvardr saw the mound-dweller turn to stare at Unnr and Huld. Unnr's face was set into a hard grimace, and Folkvardr saw her white form grow paler. She stood with one foot on Huld, holding the slave in place only with effort. Huld's eyes rolled and the girl slobbered and convulsed in her fear, writhing and straining at her bonds. Folkvardr wondered if she would have broken her own back, had Unnr not held her down.

Alrekr stood, his body swelling, growing larger. Folkvardr fought the urge to run, to discard any pride and flee screaming into the night. Only the fact that Alrekr turned away from him kept him in place, for he would have to run past him to reach the opening.

Folkvardr stared at Alrekr's back as the walking corpse turned towards the women. The fabric of the garments stretched tight, pulled taut by the expanding flesh, the blue skin puffing out around the cuffs and neck of the tunic.

As Alrekr stepped forward, the garments began to tear at the seams, each step signaled by a ripping sound, audible only in the gaps between Huld's hoarse shrieking.

Folkvardr could see the sweat glistening on both women — on Huld in her struggle to free herself, on Unnr in her struggle to hold down her slave. While total panic convulsed the slave's face, Unnr's face was set into a mask of stone. Folkvardr could see her limbs shaking with more than the effort to restrain the other woman. He thought of a sailor holding the steering of a ship in a brutal storm, holding onto the only means of survival.

The corpse man stood before the women now, his clothing in shreds on his mottled, dark skin, his body misshapen in un-death.

Unnr stood her ground and Folkvardr admired her, for he knew he would have run. She stood with her feet apart for support, the sinewy muscles of her lean legs and arms flexed, as though restraining not only Huld, but also herself. As he watched the interplay of Huld's shapely form writhing in chaos, and in Unnr's slender figure standing almost motionless above her, he realized he was watching a strange formula working itself out. This was the magic Unnr knew and craved, and Huld knew and feared.

Folkvardr felt helpless, as though he wasn't even in the chamber, but his heart pounded and a thrill pumped through his veins as he watched the women, watched their breasts heave with exertion, watched Huld's legs open and close in her struggle, bound at the ankles but moving like wings.

Alrekr, the size of the man while he laid in his tomb, now stood so large his head almost reached the eight-foot ceiling of the barrow. Folkvardr realized he gripped his spear in his hands. When had he reached it? Parts of the tomb now seemed closer than they should be, and was that a voice now whispering in his ear? As he looked up, he saw Alrekr was looking back at him, a parody of a grin revealing his yellow teeth. They were the teeth of a beast, he thought, stained with the blood and fats of his prey. What would a spear do against this being? Instead of a weapon, Folkvardr used it as a staff, preventing himself from collapsing. Words poured into his ears now, trollspeak, words of a strange language, giving him cravings that made no sense.

Folkvardr watched as Alrekr ripped away the rest of his ruined grave clothing. The cadaver's penis jutted out towards the women, a coal-black monstrosity glistening in the torchlight. Huld closed her eyes now and pressed her face to the floor, no longer screaming but babbling incoherently into the dust. Alrekr stepped forward and Unnr stepped backwards, releasing her grip on the girl, staring blankly at the creature before her.

Alrekr reached down and gripped the rope binding Huld's ankles. Pinching the strong rope between his fingers, he pulled and the rope snapped with a loud cracking sound. Free now, Huld's legs thrashed, her feet seeking purchase against the floor as she tried to scramble to her knees. And then her legs churned uselessly as Alrekr lifted her in the air by her waist. Folkvardr could see the whites of her eyes half-concealed by the black tresses clinging with sweat to her face. Her large breasts swung freely as she struggled in mid-air.

Alrekr gripped her around the waist and lifted her above his swollen penis. As he watched, Folkvardr felt the space between the creature and himself grow somehow thinner. He tried to back up, but felt hands pressing him from behind, and he dared not turn, dared not look at the owners of those hands. Still, the space between himself and Alrekr shrank, until he felt himself very close. He felt something breaking inside of himself, and felt he must somehow be pulled into Alrekr.

His vision grew dark and the pushing of the hands against his back grew stronger. He felt himself pushed against a wet and very cold wall. The hands pushed him into it, pressed him inside of it, and the cold made him scream, the fear gone now, replaced with pain. The cold burned and shrieked in his ears, until he felt himself pushed into warmth. He sobbed, joyful in his relief, and was answered by dry laughter.

He was inside something, now. He was inside something, but he could see everything in the room. He saw Unnr, and she stared back at him, shaking, surrounded by a frosty blue corona. Things moved in the corners of the room, but when he saw a sheep-sized spider with a woman's head, he stopped looking. Something pressed against his groin, he felt warmth against his belly, and as he looked down, he saw he was gripping Huld with his enormous blue hands.

He was inside Alrekr, and yet he could feel the woman pressed against the belly of the giant corpse. He could feel what the dead man felt, but when he tried to move the body, he could do nothing. He shared perception with the thing, but not control.

"So you want to feel death?" a rasping voice croaked. Though Folkvardr could hear with Alrekr's ears, this voice was inside his mind, his mind captive within Alrekr.

Folkvardr hungered for the warmth pouring from Huld. The shared flesh of Alrekr ached and Folkvardr felt something crawling within the muscles. He felt anger for the heat Huld had and he did not. He craved her and felt a hunger to consume her.

"Do not kill her!" he heard a voice shouting at him, but realized he was screaming at himself as Alrekr laughed and mocked him. The craving for Huld deepened.

He felt Alrekr's hands moving over the girl, groping her, squeezing her heavy breasts as she kicked and struggled, her hands yet bound behind her back. His heavy cock slipped between the girl's lush thighs as she flailed, and the pressure of her thighs against his shaft maddened him. Folkvardr felt his hand holding his cock, lifting the girl by the waist with the other arm.

He felt the foreskin rolling back, the crown of the penis pressing against the girl's slit now. Folkvardr wanted to be in her and he howled now within his prison. The organ was impossibly large to fit into her, but Folkvardr would have driven it into her, uncaring in his desire.

Instead he felt a shudder, and he realized the cock was changing shape, growing flexible enough to writhe its way into the girl's cunt. He heard someone sobbing uncontrollably. And then he was fucking her, feeling her flesh wrapped tight around his shaft, absorbing her delicious warmth into himself. He held her under the top of her thighs as he pounded into her, suspending her above the floor.

Folkvardr felt Alrekr's hands and arms growing longer. He felt one finger enter Huld's rectum, pressing in through the tight ring, now wet. A finger of the other hand went towards her clitoris, stoking her with the delicacy of rose petals. Though still mewling in terror, Huld was coming against her will, the muscles of her cunt convulsing around the black shaft that spread her lips wide.

When Alrekr set the girl down on the floor again, Folkvardr begged him not to stop fucking her, but the undead thing only laughed and turned towards Unnr, who was now running for the opening. And now Alrekr held Unnr in his iron grip, her nails digging furrows in his skin. Folkvardr heard the sound of Unnr's nails scraping on stone. It was Unnr that Folkvardr now craved, and a deep relief shook him as Alrekr carried her to the grave bed.

Dropping her so only her head and upper back rested on the stone, he held her by the legs, spreading her open wide to expose the flushed pink of her vagina.

Unnr tried to cover herself, putting her hands over her slit. Folkvardr laughed to see and feel the black organ of Alrekr, now slick with Huld's moisture, become like a serpent as it writhed and pushed between her hands. He felt his penis push deep into her cunt, her tight hole almost pushing it back out. Unnr's eyes rolled back and she gasped.

Folkvardr felt panic rise for a moment as he felt the flesh changing again, this time forming tiny tongues above, around, and beneath his cock. He could even taste Unnr as the tongues scoured the edges of Unnr's stretched labia, her clit, her asshole, each tongue giving a different flavor.

He was going to come now, and he almost feared what would happen, as if he were slipping off a cliff. A smell like the air before a lightning strike filled his nose, and soon he felt himself spinning, a euphoric glee stabbing him in the brain as he felt come surge through his cock and into Unnr's pussy. The woman was convulsing and smiling, but all sanity was gone from her eyes.

Folkvardr woke to coldness, and as he opened his eyes, he saw the milky predawn light in the sky. His heart raced for a moment and he quickly looked at his hands, relaxing when he saw that they were his own. He rose and checked his weapon, noting a fine speckling of rust on the spearhead. He sharpened the blades and ate a meager meal, but did not linger long in his shelter, for the rocky outcropping overhead reminded him too much of the barrow. He craved an end to that memory. It could only end with Alrekr's destruction, or, perhaps, his own. The women were surely dead. How many more would die because of the creature? And Folkvardr would bear the shame, for he and Unnr awakened him.

The sun rose as he walked, casting a diseased light through the branches of Ironwood's dead trees. Dry leaves crunched under his feet and he watched carefully, his spear ready.

"Ah, well, one of us is lost," a voice spoke and Folkvardr whirled in his steps, spear aimed at the source of the words. An old woman walked behind him, bent almost in two as she walked with a cane. She looked up and smiled at the weapon that almost pierced her. Folkvardr saw her lips bore odd scars.

"Then it be not I," Folkvardr said, feeling sweat chill on his brow.

The old woman walked forward, ignoring the spear as it slid across her, tangling in her garments before Folkvardr recoiled and pulled the weapon free.

"Come. Let us walk," she said, never pausing in her step.

Folkvardr paced her, never taking his eyes off of her and maintaining a safe distance.

"Do white-haired ladies claim many warriors where you come from?" she asked, laughing softly.

"No. But ettins do," Folkvardr said.

"Really?" she asked. "Be they so common in your land?"

"We make certain they never become common," he said.

"Ah. So you must be the ettin-slayer, so famous in these parts. I smelled Skrati on you."

Folkvardr stopped. The woman did not.

"Come on," she said, and Folkvardr felt a quick pressure against his knees so he fell heavily in the leaves. He lurched to his feet.

"Come on!" the woman called out, neither turning nor stopping.

Folkvardr walked, and the woman reduced her pace until he caught up with her.

"You doubt me, but trust at least these words: do not tarry in this spot. Those who wish to meet you here are less desirable traveling companions than myself," she said, chuckling.

"Who?" he asked.

"I will do you the favor of not answering that."

"And what do you want?" he asked.

"I want to see how far you will get," she answered.

"I will go as far I need to."

"You cannot go far enough to destroy Alrekr. He has gone to a place you cannot go. Truthfully," she said, turning and smiling, showing teeth that should not belong to an old woman.

"What do you know of him?" Folkvardr said, grabbing her shawl as they walked.

"Knowest thou, how to put to sleep?" she said, cackling. "No. That you did not know. Only how to bid. Ha ha! You knew only how to wake him up. Did you like walking with Alrekr? Did you like being one who walks after death, tasting the blood of your people on your lips and doing all the things that crawl about in your black heart? Ha ha!"

Folkvardr was trying to shake her, but she was unmovable, only walking on.

"But now, if you see Alrekr again it will be by his choice and to your disadvantage. There is nothing to be gained of it for you," she said. "But you might be interested to meet friends of yours in Ironwood."

"I have no friends living," Folkvardr said, his teeth clenched.

"Ah! Would you speak so cruelly of those with whom you have shared so much? Would you truly say that of Huld and Unnr? The slave and her mistress, though I know not which is which?" she asked.

"They live?"he gasped. He found himself more relieved for the sake of Huld than of Unnr, and the thought surprised him.

"Oh! Naturally, they live! Here in Ironwood even! They are guests of a most prominent lady here, none other than the very lady of Ironwood!" she said, mocking astonishment.

"Angrboda!" Folkvardr cried out, choking on the name. Angrboda, bearer of Loki's seed, mother of the wolf Fenrir, mother of the Midgard Serpent, mother of Hel, mother of countless wolves by hordes of giants. Ever did her womb bear foul fruit.

"Though, I must say that Alrekr brought them here in a shameful fashion. No matter."

"You are she!" Folkvardr shouted.

"No," the old woman chuckled, standing up straighter now, growing taller, and younger. A beard sprouted from her face, and soon a powerful young man, fair of face and bearing stood in her place, still walking. He still bore the scars around his mouth.

"No. I am not she," the man said, laughing. He slapped Folkvardr hard on the back, sending him sprawling in the mud. "But find Angrboda and you will find your ladies!"

Folkvardr wiped mud from his eyes and when he blinked, the man was gone. But a fat lazy fly circled the air thrice above him and flew in a straight line towards a small mountain that poked its head up above the tree-line in the distance.

Chapter 3
Angrboda

Folkvardr walked until hunger overtook him. He stopped long enough to eat a bit of his cheese and bread. The food seemed to spoil quickly in the fetid air of the forest, but he did not like the looks of the game he saw in Ironwood.

He remembered the mountain and kept his course until nightfall. Though he hated the way the trees seemed to suck all of the light and warmth from the sunlight, he hated it worse when Sunna abandoned her hopeless effort to light the forest, and left on her path beyond the mountains. Then the stench of decay seeped up from the soil, befouled by the poison fungi that sprouted like disease from the flesh of the earth, and in the dimming light drained energy from him.

What do I seek? he asked himself. *I came here to destroy Alrekr. But I believed the women to be dead. What if I can save them, yet, even if it cost me a chance to slay that undead thing? Should I even save Unnr, whose will made all of this manifest? But then I am just as guilty.*

When he found an area with a small cave-like shelter, he wondered for a moment if he'd only walked in a circle and arrived at the previous night's camp. But it was dark now and he did not favor walking far by night in these woods.

Huld wanted no part in this, Folkvardr thought. *I must at least bring her out of this place, and out of whatever torments she now suffers. I will bring her and Unnr out, and then worry about Alrekr.*

As fog rolled in and damp sunk into his bones, he decided to make a small fire, though the light might bring unwelcomed visitors. Did the trolls not know he was here already, anyway? What did it matter? If he was a fey man, then so be it, he reasoned. Better to perish by a warm fire than to die shivering in the dark.

By the light of the fire, Folkvardr saw he lay not in last night's shelter, for the stone in this one was marked by an unknown hand. Lifting a firebrand and holding it closer to the boulder, he saw it was covered with runes, if runes he could call them, for their shape and order were completely alien to him. He puzzled over them until sleep overtook him.

He heard babbling and wailing, and realized he was lying on the floor of the grave. He sat up in time to see the massive bulk of Alrekr walking towards the opening, the flailing form of Huld under one arm, and the cackling form of Unnr under the other. Folkvardr rose to his feet, but his legs failed and he crumpled to the floor, watching as Alrekr carried them off. He called out to them, but heard only the sound of heavy hooves beating the ground outside.

He stared at a torch lying on the floor until the light burned out. Then he screamed at the darkness and plunged headlong towards the opening.

Folkvardr woke to find himself standing in the forest, the miasma reminding him that he was in Ironwood. Mani, the moon, stood high in the sky and Folkvardr silently thanked him for the little light he gave now. He looked about for his campfire. He had built it incautiously high before falling asleep, and it should still have been visible if he had not wandered far from the camp.

He crouched as he heard hoof beats and reached for his spear before realizing he'd left it at camp, or lost it somewhere in the darkened woods. He knelt behind a fallen tree as he tried to place the direction of the sound, his knee sinking into the black mud.

Was it many horses? The noise came from one direction, and then the other, but it never sounded like more than one horse at a time, until the horse appeared mere yards in front of him, thundering down upon him.

Folkvardr ducked, and the mare leaped over him and the fallen tree, the animal's bulk blocking Mani's light as the beast flew through the air. It landed behind him, spraying him with mud as it ran away, churning the muck with her hooves. The pounding on the earth shook him, making him want to hide.

He stared at the horse as it ran into the forest, his heart thumping with fear that grew hot and melted into rage.

Folkvardr rose to his feet, grinding his teeth and wiping mud from his soiled clothing. But when he turned he saw a maiden standing between the trees, staring at the moon, her white shift gleaming in the silvery light. She tucked her dark hair behind her ears.

"One day," he heard her say as she stroked her belly. The words skittering along the leaves and into his ears. She was fair of form, her limbs perfectly shaped, her full bosom heaving as she sighed deeply before turning to look at him.

Folkvardr leaned against the tree when her eyes met his. He saw her clearly, in a way that defied the night's shadows. Her eyes were black, and no white showed surrounding her irises. Yet they glittered and shone with a light that was not light.

"You found me," she said. "Fárbauti's son said that you would." She held out her hand.

Folkvardr walked towards her. He heard something inhuman scream far away to his left, and something far away to his right answered it. He took her hand. His skin tingled under her fingers. He realized it was actually moving ever so slightly, every inch of skin delicately twitching. The thought of tiny animals came to mind, but he pushed that thought away. Her eyes stared into him. A musky smell made him feel dizzy, made him want to be with her.

She held his hand and led him as they walked, and the forest no longer seemed so dark. Where Mani's light failed, the fungi illuminated the way. When they walked through streams, the water felt cool and refreshing on his feet and legs.

And wherever they walked, shapes slipped in and out of the darkness, pacing them. The realization they were very large wolves startled Folkvardr for a moment, and the laughing howl of one of them made the beauty of the forest shimmer for a moment, and almost collapse. But the woman stroked his cheek and smiled with her white, pointed teeth. He watched a frog, shining and silver in the light, as it ate a smaller frog. He laughed and no longer cared about the wolves as they walked.

"You have traveled far," she said to him.

"Indeed, I have," Folkvardr said, happy to speak with her, eager to hear her talk.

"Why?" she asked, pivoting to stand in front of him. She looked at him, he thought, like a farmer looks at a hog before cutting its throat.

Folkvardr searched his memory. Why had he come to Ironwood? It was hard to remember now. He grinned as he found an answer, for he hoped to please her.

"To find you!" he said.

"How do you know that you have found me?" she asked.

"Of course I have. You are next to me and I am holding your hand," he said.

"But how do you know who I am?" she asked, smiling in a way that sent a tremor through Folkvardr's heart, for he feared if the smile should leave her lips.

"Who else could you be?" he asked. "I can feel it."

"Then, you know my name?" she asked.

"Yes. You are Angrboda," he answered.

"Am I?" she asked. "What if she is Angrboda?" The maiden nodded her head in the direction of Folkvardr's other side.

He turned to look. A woman walked on his other flank now. Her hair was like red flame, her eyes like icy-blue sapphires. She was naked save for a string-skirt. Folkvardr felt himself shaking. As he watched, something dark rippled over the woman's body, and he realized it was fur growing and covering her entire body. She hunched low, on all fours now, and ran away, her shape changing completely into that of an enormous wolf.

Folkvardr turned back to the dark-haired girl, and she flickered in the corner of his vision before he saw her completely. But now she smiled again, pulling him along by the hand as they walked.

"Come," she said, laughing in silver. "If you would like me to be Angrboda, then I am she. And why would you seek me then?"

"To slay Angrboda and rescue his women!" Folkvardr heard, the voice of a giggling girl pealing next to his ear, but when he turned to look, no one was there; only the wolves, still walking along in the woods around them.

"Yes. That is so," Folkvardr said, his stomach sinking as he remembered. "I did. I did come to kill you. But," He tried to remember how he felt. It seemed he'd come to kill her, to destroy Alrekr, or at least put him to sleep again. "But that was so long ago," he trailed off.

"And what of Huld? What of Unnr?" the woman asked.

The names startled him.

"Yes! But," he stuttered. He knew they were important to him once, but could not understand why now. The path felt hard beneath Folkvardr's feet, the ground stony. . He looked up and saw huge jagged stones, larger than halls, rose out of the earth around them. Like massive teeth, the stones jutted from the soil. Folkvardr thought some of them must surely fall over, for the angles seemed all wrong. The stones stood where they should have fallen, and hung precariously on the slope of the mountain rising before them.

The wolves no longer followed them here, but other shapes lurked in the shadows of the stones. Folkvardr wondered where they were going, but it was enough simply to follow her and watch how Mani's light danced in her shiny black tresses. He felt things touching him now as he walked, sometimes caressing him, sometimes jabbing him roughly, but he ignored them all and walked on.

"You will see them again," she said.

He frowned, irritated at being reminded of them, and of his original idea of slaying Angrboda.

"But who first told you my name?" Angrboda asked him.

"One who wore many skins told me. She, or he, told me to find you here, in Ironwood. And then I would find Unnr. And Huld," he said, slowly remembering.

"Ah. Perhaps you met an ancestor of mine," Angrboda said, singing the words.

"Perhaps," Folkvardr said.

He felt her pulling him hard by the wrist now, and looked back. The slope pitched down steeply beneath them. The rocky ground rose steeper and steeper, and soon Angrboda was more lifting him by the arm than holding his hand. He staggered and lost his footing often, sending stones rattling down the mountain, but his guide never released her grip. Though she kept him from falling to his death, he struggled to keep on his feet, for when he fell she only dragged him up and over the jagged stones. He felt himself bleeding from a dozen small cuts, but she never stopped the ascent. When he looked where she stepped, he saw the once-dainty feet now bore horny, black talons that scraped and gripped the rock.

He struggled to breathe now as the air thinned, the cold stinging him as he gasped to fill his lungs. Mani rested on the far side of the mountain now, taking the light with him. The stars in the sky felt very close to Folkvardr, and he wondered if they would soon be able to touch them, for the mountain seemed to have no end.

Folkvardr felt himself pulled over a ledge, his arm nearly yanked from its socket, and he waited to fall over a precipice. Instead, he found himself on flat stone. He no longer knew if he would fall or ascend, but collapsed instead, and shut his eyes.

When he opened them again, he found he was burning with cold, the wind cutting and ripping at him. But there was a hole in the rock wall above him, and somewhere within, flames flickered.

He remembered everything now, and cursed himself for his weakness. He'd been close enough to strike Angrboda, yet he did not, could not. He could not descend the mountain without dying, for he had little clothing, no rope, and it was night. Perhaps it was always night here, he thought. He did not know where Huld or Unnr were, and the cold wind would soon kill him.

He rose, his body aching, and gripped the rock face before him. He climbed slowly, using the small openings to inch his way up. He reached the ledge and pulled himself up and into the hole. He curled up and closed his eyes, eager to at least die in warmth. A new wave of pain swept him then, as his numb limbs now coursed with warm blood, burning his nerves.

Folkvardr opened his eyes. He was in a cave, and fire burned in many pots resting in niches in the walls. He rose and followed the passage forward until it forked. Taking one turn and then another, soon he no longer remembered his path.

Emerging into an open chamber, he saw a large fire burned from a pit in the center. He heard stone grinding behind him, and found the passage behind him no longer existed: only a stone wall. Exhausted, he collapsed and sat with his back to the wall. Hunger twisted his stomach, but the fire warmed him and sucked the last vestige of cold from his bones.

Something moved within the flames, and as they parted, Folkvardr felt the fire pulling the breath from his lungs. Angrboda stepped out of the curtain of flames now, and his breath returned, burning like cinders within him. She stood naked before him, larger now, her breasts heavy and full. He felt her black eyes somehow pressing into him.

And now wolves walked into the room from somewhere beyond the pit, skirting the fire and approaching Angrboda, each of them massive. They sat down next to her, licking their yellow teeth, firelight dancing in their eyes as they stared at Folkvardr.

All the wolves sat but two. These last two wolves carried ropes in their teeth, and at the end of one rope crawled Huld, at the end of the other, Unnr. Both women wore heavy iron collars, and the mark of the birch decorated their backs and buttocks with spidery lines of crimson. Huld crawled on hands and knees, and looked at Folkvardr with a mixture of relief and fear. But Unnr walked on hands and feet now, her rear posed high in the air, and feral intensity blazed in her pale eyes.

Folkvardr rose to his knees as Angrboda approached him. Her arms encircled him, and the hunger burned hotter in his stomach as she pressed him to her breast. He opened his mouth and took her large nipple into his mouth, sucking. He felt tears on his cheeks as warm milk spurted into his mouth, honey-like in its sweetness. His hunger felt endless as he drank and drank, feeling his cock swell.

Angrboda pulled him to the floor as she laid down, holding his head fast to her breast as she nursed him. He felt his tattered clothing being pulled from him and looked to see the red-haired woman from the forest undressing him. As he knelt over Angrboda, kneading her breast, he felt a tongue on his anus, licking and penetrating him as a warm, slimy hand pumped his cock.

Folkvardr felt the flesh shifting under his hands, as Angrboda's belly swelled and rippled. Her torso stretched, a row of breasts swelling out from her distended form. He was almost pushed aside as the wolves pressed in against him, each of them seeking their own teat, snapping and biting at each other. All around him whirred flashing fangs and hot wolf's breath, until the winners took their spoils and lapped hungrily at the milk flowing from Angrboda's nipples.

Folkvardr fought desperately to maintain his place, clawing and biting at the snarling forms around him, feeling come pumping out of his penis as the ettin-woman's long tongue fucked his rectum. But he held his own place and when he had drunk his fill, he stood, a buzzing in his head.

He saw Huld on all fours, trying to bear the weight of an enormous wolf now mounting her. The beast's forelegs were clenched tight under her arms, and he growled as his hips pumped furiously. As her shoulders sunk lower, Folkvardr saw she was pushing back with her broad ass, using her hips to bear the wolf's weight. Folkvardr watched as she first winced and bit her lip, but soon her mouth was opened and she was yelping, her face flushed as she cried out. The wolf leered at Folkvardr, and he recognized Skrati now.

Many of the wolves now dozed before the fire, but two others yet stood. Unnr crouched, her head under the belly of one, suckling the creature's red penis as it licked its lips. Behind Unnr, a wolf bitch licked the fluids dripping from the blonde's cunt, her long tongue licking the crease.

Folkvardr felt himself pulled to the floor by strong hands, and then Angrboda was on top of him, pulling his penis into her slit. He felt his body quiver involuntarily, and an orgasm shook through him, the giantess's vagina clenching and milking the sperm from him.

He wanted to run away then, away from the black mirrors of Angrboda's eyes. She smiled at him then, her teeth sharper and whiter now, and held him by his shoulders, pinning him to the floor.

He struggled to push her away, to climb out from beneath her, but she only laughed, clenching his prick inside, forcing him to stay erect.

She leaned forward, and as he felt her teeth biting into his shoulder, he felt his will slipping away. He no longer felt the floor beneath him, only Angrboda as she milked him of sperm again and again. He heard howling and smelled blood as her teeth nipped and nicked his skin.

Darkness fell over the fire like a curtain. Folkvardr felt himself falling, seeing nothing but blackness. Cold air buffeted as he fell and he willed himself to feel nothing.

He remembered the sensation of being on a horse, and when the blackness left him, he found himself lying in cold grass, his limbs locked with a warm body. He stared into Huld's eyes as they embraced.

Laughter devoid of sanity rattled in his ears, and he looked up to see Unnr dancing next to them where they lay outside of the barrow mound. Strange runes, freshly carven, trickled blood down the skin of her stomach.

Huld and Folkvardr rose and stared at the rising sun. An old woman walked by them and looked at Unnr, pausing for a moment to watch the blonde woman's mad dance.

"Ah, well, one of us *is* lost," the old woman said. She cackled and turned away, and Huld and Folkvardr watched as she disappeared into the woods.

If you enjoyed this story, you can sign up for a free membership at
ForbiddenFiction.com and discuss it with other readers
and the author at the *Tomb Brides* story page
at http://forbiddenfiction.com/story/KH1-1.000176.

Hera's Punishment

Natasha Neil

Natasha Neil is a writer of novels, short stories and nonfiction works. She lived in San Francisco, Japan and France before returning to her native Los Angeles where life is surprisingly easy and people are nicer than you would think — unless you're driving. Natasha has always found history in all of its forms fascinating, and is currently obsessed with uncovering untold truths in Persian, Greek and Roman history for use in her work. She finds the process of researching her subject matter nearly as enjoyable as writing about it. She is happily married to a spouse who is nothing like any of her characters.

Chapter 1
Binding the Lightning Striker

Long ago when the world was young, the gods grew tired of the rule of their king, Zeus. His brothers, Poseidon and Hades, resented his dominion of the sky, thinking both their realms inferior to his own. His wife Hera was weary of his many mortal and immortal lovers. So together the gods of Olympus conspired to bind the Lightning-Striker and usurp his power.

White-throated Hera went to golden-haired Aphrodite and begged the Goddess of Love and Beauty for a loan of her magic girdle. With the golden girdle taut around Hera's waist, she sought out her husband in their palace on Olympus.

Zeus was looking down into the woods of Arcadia. He had spied a beautiful dryad with voluptuous breasts and hips made to be gripped firmly. He was imagining how he would disguise himself as a cloud of mist and encircle her so Hera would not see. He could almost taste the dryad's silken skin, feel the moisture he would enrapture her with.

He sensed his wife Hera in the doorway and was suddenly aware of how he must look to her. He had lifted one of his muscular arms and was busy stroking his dark, pointed beard. His white *chiton*, trimmed with gold, shimmered like lightning. The sunlight itself kissed him as the dark hairs sprouting from his bulging arms and thighs caught the light. His golden crown glittered in his dark brown locks that fell in waves to his massive shoulders. He smiled to himself. He knew he was magnificent.

"What are you doing, Lord of the Skies?" Hera asked.

He turned to look upon his wife. She was the most beautiful of all the goddesses and the coldest. Her skin was as white as the moon.

Her light brown eyes always entranced him, even when burning with fury. Lithe and petite, Hera made up for her physical smallness with her tenacious anger.

She was wearing the peacock gown he had given her after one of their many fights. Fifty peacocks had been killed to make her garment, which shimmered with iridescence. The gown caressed her curves, and he felt the same dull ache of unfulfilled lust he always did when he looked upon her. Thoughts of throwing her down on the bed filled his mind, but she usually refused him. Instead he turned his gaze back out the window, to find a creature who would yield to him more easily.

"Just watching the mortals to see how they fare," he said.

But Hera surprised him by coming behind him to stand on tiptoes and kiss the back of his neck. He was distrustful of his wife's affection, but her full lips parted, and she pulled her peacock feathered gown over her head. She wore nothing but Aphrodite's glittering girdle, her own golden necklaces and peacock earrings. Zeus knew Aphrodite's girdle was enchanted and that his wife had come to seduce him, but this knowledge did little to help him. Released from her gown, her special fragrance of apples and amber wafted over the King of the Skies. His shaft grew hard and his eyes heavy-lidded.

"And, how do they fare?" Hera asked, turning away from him. Though she was small, her buttocks were rounded and full. They were irresistible to him. Every time he saw her behind, he yearned to cup the plump flesh in his hands.

Zeus sensed the danger, but like a dog after a piece of meat, he followed her to his golden couch.

"Wife," he said, sitting on his bed and reaching for her pendulous breasts, "what has come over you?"

She caught his hand with her two smaller ones, keeping it from her breasts. She gazed at his hand, which had thrown so many bolts of lightning, caressed countless women, and killed Titans and men alike.

"It has been too long, husband," she said, and pulled his hand between her thighs, trapping it there. She stood above him, stroking his neck and trailing her hands to the golden pin that kept his *chiton* clasped. He laughed at her attempt. No one but he could unclasp his lightning bolt pin. It was one of the many ways he protected himself. He gripped her inner thigh with his captured hand and grasped her buttock with the other, teasing her crevice to distract her from his pin.

He pulled her toward him, onto his lap, ready to take her quickly, but then remembering one of their arguments, slowed his pace. He looked lustily at her pubis, the dark hair there glittering with gold. He began to tease her vulva, exploring her with his strong fingers, trying to draw her out. She was damp, but he wanted her to moisten for him before he took her.

Surprised by his hesitation, she urged him on, pushing him onto his back and straddling him. Her sex rode high on his belly, rubbing against the silken fabric. She put her hands next to his head, offering him her breast. His tongue lashed out at her hardened nipple, pulling it into his mouth. He knew his dark beard tickled her skin, but she paid it no mind as she struggled again to unclasp the pin on his *chiton*.

Seeing her distraction, he ran his hand over her haunches. He was unable to resist squeezing and kneading the flesh. She normally pushed his hands away, but today she allowed it. Feeling the fullness of her rump, he gave her buttocks a slap, savoring the sound and the hard sting he brought her. Since she did not protest, he slapped her again. She gasped but endured his hands and mouth.

Unable to remove his *chiton*, Hera began to pull the shimmering fabric up over his thighs. His hard cock, ravisher of so many goddesses, mortals and nymphs, stood waiting. She never touched him with her hands or mouth, but seemed eager to have him inside her.

The King of the Gods knew something was amiss, but he did not care. Perhaps it was Aphrodite's girdle, or simply how long it had been since she had last come to him. Looking at her erect nipples, her breasts pushed up by the golden girdle taut around her waist, he wanted to make her moan for him the way she had when their marriage had been young.

She moved to ease his cock into her, but he stopped her by slipping his finger into her glistening vulva. He gently stroked her until he caressed her bud with his thick fingers. He had recently learned how to touch her to kindle passion and was rewarded by feeling her moisten with desire.

"Queen of the Skies," he said, trying to sound amorous, but seeing the flame of anger in her eyes, he realized he had chosen his words foolishly. Their last argument had begun with her asking to be called the Queen of the Skies as he was King. She had asked for more power, and he had denied her, telling her to be content with simply being the Goddess of Marriage.

"Take off your *chiton*, husband, I want to feel you beneath me."

He looked up into her cold eyes and unclasped his lightning pin. She pulled his glittering garment over his broad shoulders, over his wild beard and held it wide so it did not tangle in his crown. The King of the Gods lay naked beneath his wife, and she smiled down upon him.

Zeus could see that despite the acrimony between them, his naked form aroused her still, and he could not fault her for it. He had arms stronger than any god, for he alone was able to wield lightning; a chest broad as the oak that was sacred to him. And his cock, well, he laughed to himself, it was heavenly.

And today she seemed to agree. She mounted him, and for the first time in centuries allowed herself to enjoy his oaken shaft impaling her. She did not usually come to his bed or desire to be on top, but today, all was changed. He moaned deep in his throat. He could easily finish with her quickly, but he wanted to take his time with her. Despite his mistakes, the Lord of the Skies wanted to please his wife.

"Wife," he said, "sister, Hera, what has come over you?"

She rode him harder, reaching down to pinch his wine-dark nipples. He shuddered and moaned, letting her ride him like an Amazon to war on a stallion.

"Perhaps," she said, slowing her thrusts and stroking his chest, "it is time for you to give me another child. The others have been so disappointing." She leaned forward, putting her hands next to his massive head, trapping his wild locks, and teasing his mouth with her nipple. "Perhaps it is Aphrodite's girdle." He sucked her nipple fiercely as she fed it to him and slowly pulled it out. She bent to him and bit his neck, hard.

Releasing his hair, she sat up straight upon him, his hands coming to her breasts. She leaned back, putting her hands behind her, between his legs. She felt the tenderness of his inner thighs as she pushed his legs apart and began to ride him hard again. Feeling the tightness of his sac, she slowed her rhythm.

"Keep yourself for me, husband. Do not spill your seed yet. Do you think you can do that for once?"

This was how it had always been, as soon as he felt tenderness for her, she insulted him. Electricity buzzed between his fingers and she pulled her breasts back. He flicked the extra energy away from her and took her by the hips, feeling her rock back and forth, harder and faster until it took all his strength not to come into his pleasure. He felt like begging her for mercy and was torn between longing and resentment, but before he could decide, the goddess came into her pleasure, arching her back and moaning. As the muscles of her inner walls squeezed his shaft tightly, he could resist no longer. He shuddered and spurted his seed deep inside her. They moved together, gripping each other fiercely, pushing into each other, wishing to be one. Their bodies glistening with golden sweat, the King and Queen of the Gods shared a moment of complete accord.

Unable to bear herself upright any longer, Hera collapsed upon her husband. His strong arms enfolded her, and he stroked her tiny waist for a moment, with only the golden mesh of the magic girdle between them.

"Wife," he whispered, "that was…" He thought for a moment to tell her he loved her, to apologize for his infidelities, to acknowledge the many times he had hurt her, but overcome by pleasure, Zeus-Lightning-Striker closed his eyes and fell into a deep sleep.

Hera lay still upon him, completely content for a moment. Slowly, she eased off him. She removed herself from his bed and unfastened Aphrodite's magic girdle. Silently she pulled her peacock feathered gown down over her head.

Hera went to the door and opened it. There stood the other Olympians: Hades, dark and foreboding, pale in the light of the golden sun, but smiling at what was to unfold; Poseidon Earth-Shaker, wild-haired like his brother and almost as strong; Apollo, God of Light and

Truth, but in this case, ready to be a part of deceit. Hephaestus bore a lopsided grin and held the manacles he had made especially for his mother's husband; Ares stood in the shadows wearing his dark helm and holding his spear. Athena and Artemis had not been told, but Aphrodite stood smiling, as did Demeter who had never forgiven Zeus for allowing Hades to take Persephone as his wife. Hermes, the God of Ways, with his winged sandals and helmet, stood in the shadows, unable to resist a good scandal.

The Olympians silently surrounded their king. Hephaestus put the special cup-shaped manacles over Zeus' hands, and then the others all descended at the same time, tying him fast with magical rawhide thongs. He was slow to wake, but realizing his wrists were bound together, his eyes opened in rage and he struggled and kicked. Poseidon and Hades held him fast; each god caught one of his kicking feet with two hands and held them while Hephaestus tied his ankles together with a magical strip of rawhide. When it was done, the gods laughed to see their king bound naked and helpless.

Tied by a hundred knots, Zeus fought still, his muscles straining. Hera smiled to see her husband's eyes widen in shock, unable to believe that the magical thongs prevented him from changing his shape. This kind of betrayal by one god was no surprise, but by all of them! He shouted obscenities and threats, swore to kill them all, but with his hands manacled and his lightning bolts out of reach, he was powerless.

"You would do this to me?" he bellowed. "I am your elder! I am your king!"

Hades approached his captive brother. The richest of all the gods, owning every precious stone beneath the earth, the God of the Underworld was not known for speeches or for his smile. He reached out a strong, pale hand. His nails black around the edges, he stroked his brother's naked thigh. His hands were cold as night and his touch sent a shiver through the King of the Gods. The shock of being at the King of the Underworld's mercy hit Zeus hard. Hades inhaled as if he could smell his brother's fear.

"Cloud Gatherer, you always claim to be the eldest, but you are not. I was the first living born son of our mother, and you tricked me into ruling the darkest realm. I tire of my lands. Shades do not make good subjects. Why should you have all the power and all the fun? I rather thought you should take my place and live in my land. See how you like that. And I will take your place and rule the skies."

Zeus raised his brow at Hera, as if questioning her plan. She cursed him again for seeing that she had not thought this through. She had wanted only to see him bound, to be done with him, but she had not thought about where she would live once he was overthrown. She would still be his wife, and as such he could command her to live with him in Hades, but before she could speak, Poseidon interjected.

"What now? No, no, brother, I am to rule the skies. You can have dominion over the seas. It will be quite an improvement after the Land of the Dead."

"No," Aphrodite said, gently laying one hand on Poseidon and the other on Hades. Her ocean-blue eyes met Hera's and she handed the Goddess of Love and Beauty her magic girdle. Aphrodite tied it fast around her waist. The tight golden girdle pushed her alabaster breasts higher so they almost spilled out of her light-pink gown. Though she stood clothed, the gods could easily imagine her naked: waves of desire lapped at them. "My lords," she said, "I thought I would take back the seas, from whence I came. After all, I am the one who was foam born, should I not rule the oceans? Do you not feel the rise of the waves when you look upon me?"

Neither Hades nor Poseidon could reply. They gazed at the Goddess of Love through heavy-lidded eyes. Hades clenched his hands into fists over his thighs. Hera suspected from the way he held his body taut that he pictured Aphrodite in his dark palace, chained to his bed, begging him to ravish her. Hera shuddered, wishing she did not know her brother Hades so well.

Poseidon's pink tongue darted out of his mouth as he stared at Aphrodite and Hera had no doubt that he did indeed feel the rise of the waves, the pull of the tide and the tumultuous thrashing of the sea as he stared at her breasts, her girdle working its magic.

"No," Demeter said, breaking Aphrodite's spell and pinching the Lord of the Underworld. "Hades should have the skies." She had only supported this coup with the hope of freeing her daughter Persephone from the realm of the dead.

"Whoever rules the skies," Apollo said, "will share it with me, for

I am the Lord of Light!"

"I will take the Underworld," Hephaestus said.

"If you do, I will not live there with you!" Aphrodite said.

"You don't live with me now, wife. But I suppose we could rule the seas together."

"Yes," the Goddess of Love and Beauty said, "so that's settled. We will take the seas."

The gods began to argue and threaten each other in earnest. Zeus began to laugh.

"You need me!" He thundered. "You need me to rule you and to unite you in hatred. Without me, you will do nothing but fight. It will come to war. I command that you free me! If you free me now, I will not punish you." His glowing eyes stared at each god in turn, settling last on his wife.

Hera saw Ares smile at his father's words. She knew war was why he had come. Demeter and Hades appeared uncertain. Apollo grimaced and Hera could see that Zeus' foolish son feared making yet another bad choice. Poseidon glared at Aphrodite. All knew how strongly the pull of the tide beat in his veins. His brow furrowed. Hera doubted he wanted to relinquish the seas.

"No!" Hera cried. "We will decide as you did to begin with—draw lots."

"Yes," Hades said, "only I will hold them."

Zeus laughed at Hades' suggestion. Zeus had held the reeds the last time, and Hades had never forgiven him for getting the skies. No one trusted Hades; it would not do for him to hold the reeds now.

As the gods argued, Hades and Poseidon almost coming to blows, Zeus noticed Hermes slip out. He would greatly reward the God of Ways if he were freed. Zeus tried anew to burst his bonds, but the rawhide thongs held him fast. Bound and naked, the King of the Gods refused to be humiliated as well. He would get out of this, and when he did, he would punish these traitors: his wife, his siblings and his sons. Even in his anger, he knew he would forgive Aphrodite after ravishing her in the violent waves. He would grind her against the wet sand as the waves crashed against them. He would not allow her to wear even her girdle... Tartarus take that girdle! He tried to think of a punishment for her, but every time he looked at her, he could only picture her naked body undulating in the foam.

Zeus focused on the others instead. He would punish Hades by returning him to his realm and forbidding him from seeing the light of day for centuries. The Lord of the Underworld was already miserable. Dashing his dreams of rising and then mocking him would be enough. And Demeter, she would suffer for Hades to go back to his lands. Apollo and Poseidon, he would make into slaves, yes! And to a mortal! Zeus laughed softly to himself, his eyes glowing with fire. Ares he would curse. Zeus had never liked his combative son. No one did. He would make Hephaestus his servant. The Smith God would make him anything he needed. And if Hephaestus disappointed him, Zeus would have him watch as he ravished Aphrodite. Despite his bonds, he smiled. He rather liked that idea. His mind turned to Hera, his traitorous wife, unfaithful sister, conniving queen. He would think of something exquisite for her.

Chapter 2
Zeus, Unbound

Zeus was taken from his reverie by a scream. It was Hera, shrieking. Thetis the Nereid stood before him with hundred-handed Briareus. For a moment the Olympians protested, but once the hundred-handed Titan set to work unknotting the rawhide thongs, they fled.

"Seize my queen!" Zeus commanded. As Hera turned to escape, four of the Titan's hands gripped her. She struggled and squirmed, trying to escape his hands, which manacled her wrists and ankles. Her eyes filled with terror and confusion as she tried to change her shape and found she could not.

"Your gown is charmed, dear wife. I had it sewn by the Fates especially for you. As long as you wear it, you will keep your current form." Zeus smiled to see the rage in Hera's eyes. Her helpless anger grew as the Titan held her fast and completed untying the King of the Heavens, finally removing the manacles Hephaestus had made.

Zeus sprang up, fury in his eyes. He held back from striking his wife, thinking instead of how he would savor her punishment later. He thanked Thetis, and Hermes, who stood behind her quietly smiling. He owed them both a boon.

He grabbed his *chiton*, slipped it on and clasped his lightning pin. Then he snatched up his lightning bolts and began hurling them at the other gods fleeing over the islands. He bellowed his rage over the land and seas. Destroying ships and temples, he roared and threatened his brothers and sons. If they did not return to face their punishment, he would destroy all their sacred lands, their cattle, their temples, their priests.

The gods dared not return to Olympus, but sought shelter in their sacred lands. Hades and Poseidon returned to their realms. Poseidon bore the worst of Zeus' rage, his open seas exposed to the Lightning-Striker's fury. Hades was safe under the earth, but Demeter's fields were easy targets for Zeus' bolts. The King of the Skies burned only a few before the Goddess of Harvest came to him begging forgiveness. Since she was the first, he forgave her easily and returned to punishing the lands of the other gods who had betrayed him.

While he threw bolts and sent out threats, Hera was held fast in Briareus' hands. When Zeus' rage had cooled a little, spent from throwing so many lightning bolts, he went to Hera. He had the Titan lift her so her beautiful feet dangled off the marble floor. He walked around her, savoring her helplessness, her silent rage and fear. Briareus held her away from his own body, as Zeus moved behind her. In her struggles, Hera's hair had become undone and fell wildly around her face. The King of the Gods lifted the silken tresses off her neck, caressing her tenderly.

She began to tremble, as if expecting him to strike her, but his anger had gone past fury and into a realm of calm calculation. He ran his hands over her body, stroking the peacock feathers on her gown. He lifted her breasts, teasing the nipples so they rose. His hands encircled her waist, his fingertips meeting over her belly.

"Why did you do it, wife?" he asked.

Hera kept her face passive, pressing her lips together tightly. It seemed her anger had also gone cold. It was not like her to keep quiet, for she was normally one to rage. But Zeus saw that she would hold her resolve for silence, so he began to pull her gown up to her calves, to her thighs and over her buttocks. Briareus tried to look away. Zeus surmised the Hundred-Handed One had not lain with a Titaness in some time.

"Go on, Briareus," Zeus said. "My queen has such a lovely ass. Why should I be the only one to enjoy it? I'm sure she offered herself to you in exchange for freedom. You might as well see what you've given up in the name of loyalty. Here, hold this." Zeus passed the Titan the hem of Hera's gown, the beautiful peacock feathers crushed and crumbled.

Hera bucked wildly, thrashing about in Briareus' vice-like grip, trying to make him drop her gown to cover her nakedness. Zeus knew the humiliation she felt for the hundred-handed giant to see her this way, her glittering pubis and white buttocks displayed like one of Aphrodite's sacred whores. She tried to kick at Briareus, at Zeus, but he only laughed and caught her foot in his hands. He unlaced her sandal. Laughing at her powerless anger, he dropped the sandal to the ground.

"Even if your foot struck me with all your force, dear wife, it would only feel like a feather." He plucked one from her gown, and slowly ran it along the sole of her foot. Zeus knew his wife was not normally ticklish, but trapped in her mortal form, her skin was sensitive and the bottom of her foot, normally well protected, was especially vulnerable. She squirmed in Briareus' hands as Zeus slowly stroked her insole with the peacock feather. He ran the feather back and forth along her foot until she bit her lip to avoid crying out.

Though Zeus enjoyed watching her struggle, his mind returned to her betrayal. His face turned dark. Storm clouds came into his eyes. He released her foot and dropped the feather, his eyes glowing with fire as he looked at her half naked body.

"Yes," the King of the Gods said, "a fine ass, but, Briareus, do you not think it could do with some color?"

The Hundred-Handed One said nothing as Zeus walked behind Hera and gripped her buttocks. Briareus held her gown with a different hand, to give the king more room and Zeus noticed how the Titan casually put one of his hands over his member. Zeus did not mind that the Hundred-Handed One was aroused by his wife. He could hardly blame him.

Zeus pulled back his hand and struck Hera's rump. She caught her breath, but did not say a word. He struck her again, hard and fast. He would make her beg his forgiveness. By the time he was done, she would swear it would never happen again. He reveled in feeling the supple flesh of her mortal form warm from his slaps. She would know his dominance and never defy him again. Her alabaster haunches changed to pink, and he continued striking her with the flat of his hand until her buttocks were crimson.

"Yes," Zeus said, "that is very satisfying. Briareus, do you not think that is better? Does she not have the loveliest ass on all of Olympus, perhaps even on Earth?"

Hera turned her head, glaring at her husband and the Titan who held her.

"What is it, wife? Do you feel betrayed that I would allow someone else to see you naked? Tell me you did not offer yourself to him."

Hera said nothing and Briareus' face reddened. He switched the hands that held the goddess, giving Zeus his answer. The King of the Gods could see that the Hundred-Handed One longed to stroke that red rump.

"Go on," Zeus said, "you can give her just a little pat. I would not normally allow another to touch my wife, but you deserve a little something."

Hera struggled in the Titan's grip, a low growl coming from her throat. Her eyes, piercing as daggers, stared at the Titan.

"My king," Briareus said cautiously, "I am here to serve you, but I must refuse your offer." He added two more hands to hold Hera steady. "My queen, please. I mean no disrespect. I am only a servant of the Lord of the Skies, nothing more."

Zeus laughed, thunder boomed over the gathering clouds.

"Ah," the King of the Gods said, "Briareus, the Hundred-Handed, I see how you have lived so long. You fear offending my wife, for if you do, she may well track you to the ends of the earth and have your head struck off. Remember this Hera, if I ever set you free, this Titan was wise and did you a kindness, though I will not."

Zeus stepped closer to his wife and stroked her buttocks, making her tremble at his touch. He knew then that a part of her enjoyed the torment as her anger and arousal combined. He pinched the burning flesh of her buttocks, squeezed her and struck her again. He was rewarded by a low moan deep in her throat. He wondered how long she could stay silent, how soon he could make her beg.

He wrapped his arm around her waist, pulling her enflamed buttocks to his hard cock. She pushed back against him, and he cupped her sex, probing her with his finger. She was wet with desire. After centuries together, perhaps he was finally beginning to understand his wife.

He wanted to take her then, fuck her hard while the Titan watched. He would thrust his cock into her anus, as if she were a man. And then when he recovered from the first time, he would take her as a woman, again from behind. But he remembered their argument about how he always pleased himself too quickly and decided this time, he would wait. This time, he would make her wait.

The Lightning-Striker moved his finger against her bud, making her shudder in anticipation. Then he withdrew. Her body stiffened in surprise as he told Briareus to drop her gown. Zeus stood behind her and breathed into her ear, biting the lobe gently. His shaft was hard against her as he whispered, "Wife, you remember Leto and Io? You remember how we fought after the births of Artemis and Apollo? After I gave birth to Athena and you to Hephaestus? Remember how I flogged you and struck you with my bolts? Well, that will be nothing compared to what I will do to you for this." He kissed her neck savagely and gripped her buttocks, but Hera did not say a word.

Zeus ordered the Titan to bind her wrists and lock her in an enchanted room with no windows. He left Briareus outside, to guard the door. He would let her suffer and worry over her fate.

In the throne room, Zeus drank nectar from a golden chalice. He would think of the best torment for his wife and while he did, the other gods would come to beg forgiveness.

Aphrodite came first, wearing her magic girdle and glistening with beauty. She knelt before Zeus' golden throne, her breasts heaving as she wept, claiming to have been coerced into betrayal by Hera and Hephaestus. The Goddess of Love and Beauty confessed to being fickle and foolish and pleaded for forgiveness. But she knew the price of betrayal. Despite his plans for her, he could not resist when she came to him on her knees and wrapped her arms around his calves, kissing his thighs and lifting his *chiton* with her teeth.

The King of the Gods moaned and fell back in his throne, completely spent.

"Will you forgive me, Lord of the Skies?"

"Yes," he said, "but..." He had not even cupped her perfect breasts nor ploughed between her milky thighs. He had said yes too quickly, and her breasts hypnotized him still. She stroked his thigh and pulled down his *chiton*. As she leaned on the throne to rise, he gripped her hand.

"It will not happen again, Foam Born..."

"No, Lightning-Striker. It will not. But if Poseidon ever fails, I would be happy to rule the seas." She smiled and licked her red lips. They shared more than one secret now. The Goddess of Love and Beauty rose and turned around. Glimmering, she walked away. Zeus regretted not taking her from behind.

Poseidon and Apollo came next. The King of the Gods knew they would come; it was only a matter of how many of their temples he would destroy first.

The light behind Apollo's eyes was dark with defeat and shame. "Forgive me," the God of Light said, kneeling at his father's feet. But Poseidon made no such move.

"I am surprised at you, brother," Zeus said, ignoring his son. "I thought you loved your realm. I did not know you wished to take mine."

"It was folly," Poseidon admitted, his voice rough like sand upon skin. But he would not apologize.

"You will both be punished for this," the King of the Gods declared. "I will make you slaves—to a mortal." Seeing the shock on their faces, Zeus laughed aloud. He opened his hand and offered Poseidon a thick golden collar to put around his own neck.

"I will not," the Earth-Shaker said.

"If you do not, I will destroy every temple, every boat in the sea. The mortals will worship you no longer. They will make no sacrifices and you, dear brother, will be forgotten."

The God of the Seas snatched the golden collar from Zeus. With hate sparkling in his blue eyes, he fastened it around his bulging neck and clicked the lock shut. Zeus thought it very becoming on him.

Apollo's face had turned bitter and Zeus suspected his son was holding back golden tears.

"Don't worry, Lightbringer, I know you are more delicate." The collar he had had Hephaestus fashion for Apollo was a lighter gold, and the leash he would wear had a finer chain. Apollo took the collar and snapped it on his neck, wiping his eyes.

"You are to serve King Leomedon. You will build a great city for him. It is to be called Troy. The Fates say it will be known for all time. And just think, perhaps you will impress them so that they will build you temples. I know how you both long to be worshipped."

Neither his brother nor his son said a word as they left Olympus.

Zeus smiled every time he thought of Poseidon wearing the collar. He was beginning to think his ordeal had almost been worth it.

Ares he cursed with ill favor. The God of War would fight, but he would seldom win. He would have no temples and few worshippers. Hephaestus was now his creature. The Smith God had to make Zeus whatever he bid. He had made the collars for Poseidon and Apollo and the golden cuffs that Zeus would now put on his treacherous wife.

Chapter 3

Queen of the Skies

The Queen of the Immortals did not struggle as Briareus brought her out, nor did she speak. She only stared defiantly at her husband. Zeus knew she expected him to take her forcefully, but he had chosen a different punishment, one she would not forget. He took her from Briareus and walked her to the edge of Olympus to the place where the clouds gather and turn pink as the sun rises and sets.

"Wife," he said, "sister, it has been too long since I have given you jewelry." He brought forth the golden cuffs. Her eyes grew wide. The cuffs were thick and strong and would hold her fast. She offered him her slender wrists, a light of defiance in her eyes, refusing to give him the pleasure of seeing her resist. He snapped the cuffs on, seeing the fear she tried to mask. He lifted her up into the clouds. Her feet struggled to find purchase but touched nothing but air.

Zeus attached the cuffs onto an invisible hook, leaving Hera dangling over the earth. He could see how she tried to keep her gaze calm as she stared down at the land below, but for one moment he saw the flash of terror behind her eyes. The skies were clear, all of Hellas stretched out before her, and Zeus smiled to himself, all of Hellas could see her as well.

"Wife, our wedding night lasted three hundred years. How long shall I leave you here? What is the appropriate punishment for trying to steal my throne? For conspiring with the other Olympians against me? How could I forgive this?" Floating next to her, he stroked the back of her neck. He waited for her tears, for her apology, for her promise it would never happen again, but she only glared at him with disdain.

It was as if she were giving him permission. He looked at her, hanging there and laughed. "You said you wanted to be Queen of the Skies, and now you are. I will leave you here until I am satisfied. And until I am, you can watch. I will not have to hide from your prying eyes any longer!"

He looked down to the woodlands of Arcadia where he had spied the beautiful dryad when Hera had first come to him. In a flash he was next to her tree. The dryad gave a cry of terror, but he gripped her wrists and pulled her to him.

"I am the King of the Gods, and you, sweet creature, will be mine."

"Please," she said, "it is an honor, Lord of the Skies, but I fear your wife. She will kill me."

Zeus kissed her throat, pulling off the gown of leaves she wore to cover her naked body. Her breasts were fuller than he had hoped for, her dark brown nipples big and hard. He took one into his mouth while caressing her thighs, slowly moving his hands toward the mossy green hair of her pubis. She trembled beneath his touch but did not resist as he gripped her buttocks, which he was disappointed to discover were slighter than he liked on females.

"You need not to worry about my wife, beauty. Give yourself to me and I will give you divine children."

He had intended to take her from behind, but now that he beheld how little meat she had on her bones, he decided to lie her down on the soft, dewy grass. He pulled her down and climbed atop her. She lay beneath him, her eyes big with fear.

"Mercy," she cried weakly, addressing the heavens.

Zeus' laughter boomed, shaking the ground and making the girl go pale.

"Who do you beg mercy from, sweet creature?"

She looked away from him, her moss green eyes filling with tears. Centuries ago, he would have enjoyed forcing himself on her, but now remembering Hera's complaints against him, and how much more enjoyable it was to truly seduce a woman, he had a different idea.

The dryad would not speak, so he spoke for her.

"Perhaps you have heard that the gods are brutal and rough? Do you beg mercy from some kindly goddess in hopes that she will turn you into a tree before I take you?" He stroked her green hued cheek, wiping away her sticky tears.

Remembering how Hera had chastised him for how he had hurt her the first time, he resolved to try something new.

"It is true that I am the ravisher of the world, but this time I will be gentle. And since my wife is occupied, we have plenty of time. I will take you slowly, little dryad." He kissed her neck, enjoying the woody-earthy smell of her. He stroked her nipples tenderly.

"No goddess will have mercy on you now," he whispered, "better you learn to enjoy it."

The dryad looked up into his eyes as if suddenly understanding. He could see her taking in his muscular form, his far-seeing eyes and the crown perched within the locks of his flowing black hair. Her panic seemed to be replaced with awe. He was the King of the Gods and he wanted her. He was the King of the Gods and he would have her. He bowed his massive head to her breast and tenderly licked her with his tongue, gently stroking her. She lay rigid under his mass and gradually began to relax, her taut limbs loosening as the wild look in her eyes was replaced with a sudden understanding of pleasure.

She seemed to like the way he suckled her breasts, so he worked at one then the other, feeling her gasp at the pleasure of it and shudder when his beard tickled her. He ran his hands over her waist and played with the mossy hair of her pubis. She tried to keep her legs firmly together, but by sucking her nipple while stroking her, he was able to make her yield to him and slowly her thighs parted, so he could delve his finger into her. It had been too long since he had turned an unwilling maiden to a willing one. And he was well rewarded when she began to ooze sap. When she was sticky and wet, he knew she was ready for him.

He inserted the head of his shaft into her opening. She was so tight. It had been too long since he had lain with a virgin. The dryad trembled, but Zeus stayed still.

"I will not take you by force," he said, reveling in the idea. "Go on, you move to me."

The nymph was hesitant at first, but encouraged by his hands, she arched her pelvis toward him. He lifted her thighs so her knees were bent, opening her to him more fully. Her fine brow rose in confusion and then understanding came as she stared into his eyes, offering herself to him.

"Go on," he said, taking her nipple between his fingers. She moved cautiously at first, wincing and then pushing up against him, she began to undulate beneath him, seeking to find pleasure she never knew existed. She moaned, and he thrust himself into her.

Zeus had never been so patient with a maiden. Feeling her taut skin against his shaft, opening for him, made him burrow into her. She gasped in pain as he broke her hymen, but her blood against his cock was too much for him, and he was only able to wait a moment before spurting his seed inside her.

The dryad cried out at the force of his ejaculation. Swooning between pleasure and pain, her body clenched and then lay still. For a moment he thought he had killed her, but she had merely fainted. As he rose, he felt a drop of rain and then another. He looked up into the skies, thinking of Hera watching him, how jealous she must be! To have taken the dryad so slowly was yet another victory against his wife.

He eyed the naked girl on the grass, his golden fluids leaking from her parted thighs. The rain fell harder. He would go find another nymph—no, perhaps a mortal would be better, a princess or queen. He would have to ask Hermes who the most beautiful mortal was these days—it was so hard to keep track. The rain on the grass looked slightly yellow and Zeus held out his hand to catch a drop. Smelling the pungent liquid in his hand, he realized it was not rain but a token of his wife's jealousy.

Rage filled him. Even bound, his wife insulted him still! Perhaps taking another woman was not the only way to stoke Hera's ire. Seeing the supine form of the naked dryad he had an even better idea. They both needed a bath now. Why not take one together in his palace?

Holding the girl in his arms like a child, he rose to Olympus. He stopped first in front of Hera dangling helplessly among the clouds.

"Wife, is there anything you want to say to me now?"

Hera glared at him and the girl. The dryad began to stir. She rubbed her eyes and opened one. Her dark brown hair, tinged with green, was undone and half covered her heavy breasts. The dryad looked at him with confusion as if trying to decipher what he could want from her now. She sniffed, confusion overcoming her lovely face. Then she turned her head and saw the Goddess of Marriage, her arms hooked above her head, her eyes ablaze. The tree nymph stifled a scream and fainted in fear.

Hera laughed and spoke for the first time. "Are you having fun, husband? Has this one won your heart for the moment?"

"Yes, I thought I would try taking her in our bed."

Her eyes narrowed to slits.

"Promise me, sister," he said, "that it won't happen again. Beg my forgiveness, wife."

Hera glowered. She was stubborn like Poseidon, like Hades and Demeter and like Zeus himself. She would rather hang in the sky than beg for anything.

"Go on," she said. "Enjoy your little whore. You both smell like piss anyway."

Zeus flew to his palace. He had his slaves bathe the girl and took a bath himself, trying to calm his anger. It had always been like this with Hera. Sometimes he thought he should never have forced her to marry him. He should have chosen Demeter or Hestia; his other sisters were more even-tempered, more docile and calm. They would never fight him like Hera did, nor would they ever bed him with the same burning passion. Demeter had some of the same anger, but she was too wounded whereas with Hera, her anger was a challenge for him to fight against.

Or perhaps he should have married a Titaness like Leto or Mnemosyne. He had loved Leto, but she had proven to be a coward. Pregnant with the twins, she had run from Hera's wrath. Had their places been reversed, Hera would have stood and fought. He had been angry at his jealous sister at the time, but in a way, he had also been proud. They had not even been married yet, and Hera's jealousy had been magnificent. Mnemosyne was a good mother, having borne all nine of the muses. She never would have incurred his rage the way Hera did. Her jealousy over his many affairs, would not have manifested into screaming fights. Her quiet nagging would have driven him to Tartarus.

His other lovers were a good respite from his angry wife, but none of the others had the same connection as he and Hera did, despite or perhaps because of their animosity. He thought back to how aroused she had been after he had beaten her. He had always suspected that their fights fueled her passion and in truth, he longed to go to her, but he was wounded that she had betrayed him so deeply.

He would leave her there, hanging in the sky until she begged his forgiveness. He took the dryad to bed with him. He hoped it would be thrilling to take a mortal into his own chamber, but her fear and confusion were not as arousing without Hera to watch. He took her quickly and, not knowing what else to do with her, let her sleep next to him. She snored softly like the wind in the trees, and it kept him awake. But then he realized it was not the nymph that would not let him sleep, but a sound that only he could hear, his wife quietly weeping.

He was glad. Let her cry! She deserved it. She should have cried sooner. It should have been her tears of regret raining down on him. She should have asked him for mercy as soon as the Hundred-Handed One freed him. She should have gotten down on her knees like Aphrodite and begged his forgiveness with her mouth! Yet the sound of her tears grated on his ears and despite himself, his heart began to ache thinking of her misery. He had no regrets about the times he had struck her, or made her burn with jealousy. He felt no remorse for the women he bedded whom she then tormented, turned into trees or animals, or killed, but suddenly the thought of her hiding her golden tears from him as she dangled above the earth with only one sandal on made him long to comfort her.

When Hera saw Zeus hovering over the clouds, she wiped her eyes on her upper arm. He stroked her cheek, but she looked away, ashamed he should catch her crying. He wiped her eyes with his first finger and rubbed her lips with his thumb. She parted her lips slightly at his touch.

"Husband," she whispered, "brother." She had not known how long he would leave her. Seeing him with the dryad, slowing stroking her in the grass had infuriated Hera. But it had also renewed her passion. Zeus was hers. Her brother, her husband. He did not belong to anyone but her, and she hated him for not realizing it. But his punishment had worked as he had wished, raising a fear that he would abandon her and force her to watch him seduce nymphs, dryads, mortals and goddesses for as long as he liked.

But now, he had come for her. Feeling his gaze upon her, his thumb on her lips, the fire of her anger began to change to passion, as it always did.

He encircled her waist with his hands, lifting her slightly. He drew his lips to hers and kissed her. She allowed his tongue to delve into her mouth and kissed him back, pressing her body to his.

He gripped her tender buttocks, and she gasped at the pain and desire coursing through her. She did not know if he would release her, and she did not care. At that moment, she was only glad that he had come for her, that she had his complete attention.

"Promise me, wife."

She leaned forward, straining in her bonds to reach his ear. "I promise I will never again conspire to usurp your power, husband. I swear it by the River Styx." She nipped at his ear and added, "Now, if only you could promise to be faithful…"

He kissed her neck, biting her gently. "You do not really want that. Do you, wife? You do not really want all my attention, all the time. My need is too much for only one woman. You would hate me even more if I did not chase others, and I suspect sometimes that you enjoy the opportunity to rage."

She said nothing, for she could not deny it.

"Tell me," he said, "what would you have done if your coup had been successful? Where would you have gone? If Poseidon had the skies, Aphrodite and Hephaestus the seas, where would that leave you? Your place is by my side, as my wife. None of the others cherish you the way I do."

"Cherish me," she spat. "You humiliate me with every new conquest, rutting around like some randy goat, worse than Pan, fathering demi-gods on mere mortals, Olympians on Titanesses," her voice grew raw as she struggled, helpless in the sky, her only power her anger, "while I, I the Goddess of Marriage have born only disappointments." Her voice cracked and she wished to take the confession back, but it was too late, the true source of her anger had been exposed.

The King of the Gods stared at his wife in shock. After centuries together, tempestuous fights, years of animosity and passion, he was finally beginning to understand her.

He had not realized her deep disappointment in their offspring: Eileithyia, Goddess of Childbirth, Hebe, a mere servant, and Ares, the God of War, a bellicose fool, hungering for mortal blood. What were they compared to Leto's children, Artemis and Apollo, or even the muses? She had kept it from him. He had always thought her jealousy to be only for the women.

"I thought I was giving you something to do," he uttered in earnestness. "I thought it was a game between us, sister. Our game. Were you not jealous of the others before we were even wed?" he caressed her cheek, wiping away her tears.

She did not answer him with words but assented by pressing her cheek into his palm.

"Come now," he said. "Let us be honest. Do you not thrive on the challenge of catching me as I enjoy the challenge of escaping your watchful eyes? You have always loved me, Hera, as I have always loved you. Though my desires are too much for only one, my heart is not."

She did not answer his question, but her eyes softened. He knew that a part of her delighted in the acrimony between them, thrived on him tormenting her flesh after rending her heart.

"Sister," he said, "wife, it is you I always return to. It is you I chose to marry. You I desire. Let me give you another child, one to make you proud."

"I do not think it possible, husband," she smiled coyly, "but I'm willing to try. Release me."

"No," he said, "I want to take you here, above the world, as my queen, the Queen of the Skies."

He stroked her neck and placed his hands on the neckline of her dress. Slowly he began to rip the fabric. She moaned at the sound and the anticipation of his hands on her. Ripping her gown wide open, he took one breast in his hand and the other in his mouth, sucking her savagely, the way she liked.

She arched her back and gasped, but soon opened her eyes in discomfort.

"Zeus, I can't. They can all see us."

He caressed her breasts, enjoying her pale flesh in the moonlight, thinking of all he would do to her while she hung in the sky.

"Yes," he said. "The other Olympians can see what happens to anyone who attempts to usurp my throne. I should let them all watch." Her eyes began to harden at his words as her passion began to change again to anger. "But," he added, "since I wish for us to be reunited, not just in flesh, but in spirit," with a wave of his mighty hand, he summoned clouds to gather around them, making a soft chamber of seclusion, white in the moonlight.

"Is that more to your liking, wife?" But he did not wait for her answer, for he had decided to surprise her. Centuries ago, when he first had her, he had been too quick, thinking only of his own pleasure. Now he would appease her. He knelt on his cloud between her feet, and cupping her buttocks, still raw from his ministrations, drew her to him. He enjoyed seeing the shock in her eyes as he brought her mound to his mouth. Despite her disbelief, she parted her legs for him and let him explore her with his tongue.

The King of the Gods had never done such a thing before, and he enjoyed it more than he expected, but he was sure that his wife would be the only one he did this to. Still, he could tell from the small moans that escaped her lips that she appreciated his attempts.

Kneading her buttocks, he brought her closer, lashing her bud with his tongue until she let out a pleading sound. He licked her hard and she shuddered, pulling hard against the golden cuffs and coming into her pleasure.

"Husband," she moaned, "I did not know you could… that was…." Then recovering a bit, he saw the familiar spark of jealousy. "Have you…"

"No, wife," he said standing. "By the River Styx I have done that with no one else, will do that with no one else. But if you do not believe me, I can go, leave you here, alone in the clouds."

"No," she said. "Stay."

"You want me then?" he asked, a slight mocking tone in his voice. He would like nothing better than to make her beg him to take her.

But Hera did not say a word as she swung back, and using her momentum, lifted her legs, wrapping them around his middle. She entwined her ankles together at his back, her one sandal digging into his buttocks.

"You cannot escape me brother, we are bound together for eternity."

"Yes," Zeus said. Unable to wait a moment longer, he lifted his *chiton* with one hand. The moonlight glittered on his shaft, hard and thick as oak. He moved the extra fabric of her gown out of the way and they came together in one motion. He thrust himself into her as she rocked hard over him. She had never felt so good to him, silken and ripe, the perfect sheath for his sword. He gripped her buttocks with both hands, kneading the flesh and pushing himself deeper into her.

"Oh," she gasped, pushing against him, "Husband," she pulled against the golden cuffs, holding him taut between her thighs "brother," she whispered, "Zeus."

He pounded against her, harder than he ever could with a mortal, feeling the heat and desire within her mount until Hera arched her back and cried out, "Lord of the Skies! My king!" she shuddered against him, her sex sucking his shaft so hard he ejaculated like a bolt of lightning.

They held each other longer than usual. He, savoring the moment and she, uncertain of what he would do next.

"I should leave you here," he whispered. "It is what you deserve and then I will always know where you are."

"I promised, husband. Release me, my king."

He untangled himself from her and floated a moment, gazing at her. Dangling in the sky, the golden cuffs so large on her slender wrists, her beautiful peacock gown in tatters, and her body exposed in the moonlight. She was so small and helpless. He felt a strange sensation he could not recognize. It was new, a stirring in his heart, but it was neither desire nor rage. He thought again of her crying alone in the sky and realized the sensation was pity—for her, for being his wife, and for loving him.

He reached up and unhooked the golden cuffs. He held her in his arms and floated to the solid ground of Olympus.

"Thank you, husband," she said rubbing her wrists. She smiled at him, her face flushed from desire. With a complicit look in her eyes, she pulled off what was left of her gown and laughing, vanished.

The King of the Gods stood dazed. Not yet prepared to gather his wits, he stared at the emptiness where his wife had just stood. Then, hearing a scream from his palace, he realized what was to happen.

He materialized in his bedchamber. Hera had kept her mortal form. She had covered herself with a hastily thrown-on red gown that fell awkwardly across her breasts. The dryad cowered naked on the marble floor, prostrating herself at the goddess' feet, her eyes huge in fear. Kneeling on the ground with her buttocks in the air, Zeus saw that she did indeed have the ass of a boy. He watched his wife's keen eyes study her.

"Please," the nymph moaned, her voice shaking. "Protectress, have mercy. I beg you!"

Hera smiled seeing her husband's wild eyes, daring him to intervene.

"Mercy," the Goddess of Marriage said. "Yes, and protection." She lifted her white hand and shot a bolt of magic at the tree nymph. Zeus blinked, unable to see the girl at all. For a moment he thought his wife had killed her, just sent her straight to Tartarus. But he looked on the ground and saw a small creature, soft with a hard shell and strange eyes that roved around the room. The creature inched away from the immortals slowly, leaving a sticky trail behind.

"You took her so slowly, husband. So very slowly, this form seems fitting for her now. Pity, though. I shouldn't have offered mercy. It would be so satisfying to step on that and crush its shell. Oh, but…" she looked down at her feet and up in annoyance at her husband. The goddess snapped her fingers and her other sandal appeared on her foot. "That's better."

Hera stood up straight, power coming back into her eyes. Even though Zeus had just had her, he wanted her again. He half wished he had left her hanging in the sky.

"I will keep my promise to you, husband, but I am weary from your punishment. I think I shall take myself to Canathus for my annual bath to renew my virginity. Perhaps when I am ready to lose it, you can show me all you have learned." She looked down at the slow moving creature that a moment before had been a beautiful dryad.

"So slowly," Hera laughed. Then the Goddess of Marriage stared at her husband. Looking into his face in the way only she could, seeing what others did not.

"You need some nectar and ambrosia to bring the color back into your face, brother."

Zeus realized she was right. He was tired. Hera should be the one to look wan, to need nourishment, but she seemed pert and strong, as if taking his divine seed and transforming the dryad had given her energy enough.

She glanced again at the thing moving across the marble.

"You should have one of your slaves, Briareus perhaps, deliver her back to earth before someone steps on her." Hera began to laugh before adding, "But she could be carrying your divine child, Lightning-Striker, so perhaps you should keep her here where you can watch her."

He looked from the tiny creature on the floor to his wife in confusion. Hera grinned.

"Well, goodbye, husband. I'll see you when the fancy strikes me, but I'll be watching you. You know that." She disappeared.

Zeus stood in silence staring at the slow moving snail, frantically trying to move away from where the goddess had been. He picked the creature up by its hard shell and put it in his hand.

"I cannot change you back," he said, holding the once lovely dryad in his hand. Its cold, slimy body inched across his palm, still trying to escape. He began to laugh then. He would make sure his next conquest was a worthier challenge for his wife.

Notes: This myth was found in *The Greek Myths* by Robert Graves. This story is pretty consistent to Graves' version except for three parts: In Graves' story all the Olympians except Hestia were present at the coup, only Thetis the Nereid brought Briareus to Zeus' rescue, and Zeus attaches an anvil to each of Hera's ankles while she hangs in the sky, which just seemed like too much. The part about the dryad and the origin of the snail was invented by the author.

If you enjoyed this story, you can sign up for a free membership at
ForbiddenFiction.com and discuss it with other readers
and the author at the *Hera's Punishment* story page
at http://forbiddenfiction.com/story/NN1-1.000214.

In the Death of Winter

Annabeth Leong

Annabeth Leong has written erotica of many flavors. She loves shoes, stockings, cooking, and excellent bass lines. Forbidden Fiction publishes many of her dark erotica titles. Find her at annabetherotica.com or on Twitter @AnnabethLeong.

In the Death of Winter

"What if the god does not come?" Sarant asked.

Bolormaa ignored the postulant's words. She pulled the young woman's fur-lined robes over her head and discarded them, revealing a lush body, rosy nipples, and red-brown hair between her legs to match the tresses on her head. Sarant smelled sour under the heavy garment, which did not suit the muggy night. Bolormaa scowled and slapped away a mosquito.

Mud, heat, and rain had no place on this night, and yet they tormented her. The pleasures of the underworld should keep the sun long below the ground. Tonight, frost should crunch under her feet. The winter touch of Erlik should lie heavy on the land.

"Will you send me away if he does not come?" Sarant pressed.

Bolormaa sighed. "Child, he will not come. He is dead."

She uncoiled a rough length of hemp and bound Sarant's wrists with it. The god would have liked this one. The cuts that had covered Sarant's body when Bolormaa found her had nearly healed. Most village men would reject the girl as hopelessly disfigured, but Erlik favored signs of inner strength.

Bolormaa's bones creaked when she hoisted Sarant's hands above her head and fastened them to the branch of a great larch tree. The young woman's nipples had already grown hard. Sarant panted with excitement, and the smell of her arousal stung the old woman's nostrils.

"Why are we doing this if we know he will not come?"

Bolormaa tugged and tightened the ropes, grunting. "Because I am an old fool, and I cannot give up hope that he might."

Bolormaa had seen only twenty winters when her husband stripped her bare and threw her to the mercy of the Longest Night.

"Let Erlik have you!" The slamming door denied her the light of their hearth fire, leaving her under the darkness of a moonless, starless sky.

She shivered against the outside of the heavy door. Bolormaa's feet blushed red, slipping on the thin, knobby layer of ice that had built up across their entryway in the early hours of the night. Chill air whipped past her, chapping her exposed flesh everywhere. She tried to cover herself, wrapping her arms over her breasts. Another blast of wind confused her senses. Her thighs burned with cold, and her back pricked with icy fire. She rubbed her palms against her legs to warm herself, but the next gust hardened her bare nipples to the point of pain.

"Please!" She pounded on the door. "I'll die out here!"

The door quaked dully from the other side. Her husband had dropped the heavy wooden bar in place across it.

Bolormaa slumped in the meager shelter of the doorframe. She hated the man. His reedy looks masked a cruel disposition, and he subjected her to beatings by day and painful rutting by night.

She hated herself more for waiting at the doorstep like a good doggy, praying to be let back in. On impulse, she plunged her hand into a pile of snow beside the narrow walkway to the house, savoring the punishing, clarifying pain.

"Great Lord Erlik," she whispered. "*Will* you have me?"

Gritting her teeth, Bolormaa lifted her naked body upright and spread her arms. She took one step, then another. The soles of her feet stuck slightly to the icy walkway stones.

Bolormaa could not hope for relief from the cold, so she forced herself to run. Tears formed in the corners of her eyes in response to the dry air, then froze to the sides of her face. The effort did slowly heat her body. Her skin blushed angry red all over. Her lungs opened to bigger breaths, each stabbing into her chest like sharp steel.

She ran from her home, out of the village, and into the woods. Her jaw chattered so violently that she bit her tongue. She sucked on the wound, tasting the metal in her blood, and ran on. The snow beneath her feet rubbed them raw and burned hot as desert sand.

Her body could not take such punishment long. Bolormaa's face had gone numb and stiff despite the furnace in her lungs. She could not tell how each step landed — she could not feel her feet at all. Each heartbeat struck her chest with the force of her husband's fists.

Bolormaa had to rest. She dragged to a stop in the snow, coughing and gripping her thighs. Her confused, struggling body convulsed. Falling to her knees, she could not muster the will to rise again.

The snow here caressed her bare skin. It warmed and comforted her. She sank more of her body into it.

A clump of icicles cracked off the branch of a nearby tree, stabbing the piled drifts. Bolormaa forced her head up. Dull illumination gleamed from the ice in the skeletal branches and ghosted off the snow.

A hand thudded onto her shoulder.

Bolormaa lacked the breath to scream. She craned her neck back and up. The hand connected to a winter-pale arm, which led to the chest of a tall man standing behind her. Ropes of muscle and tendon rippled below his wrinkled skin. He stood naked, hairless except for the thick, jet-black eyebrows that belied his apparent advanced age. Horns grew from the top of his head, tangled like tree roots. His fingers dug into Bolormaa's chest just above her ribs, hooking painfully under her collarbone.

Bolormaa resisted the urge to twist away from his grip. The combination of awe and fear he inspired left no doubt of his identity. "My Lord Erlik?"

The god smiled, pressing a finger the color of packed powder to her mouth. She kissed it reverently, and did not resist when he pried her jaw open into a painfully wide "O." Erlik studied her expression, gave a satisfied nod, and tapped her lips with a chipped fingernail. They rang like glass.

Bolormaa managed to produce a small, terrified sound in the back of her throat. His touch had frozen her mouth immobile. Her saliva transformed to a block of ice that trapped her tongue and radiated aching cold into her cheeks. Erlik kissed her on the forehead and stroked her hair.

Though cold, this contact did not freeze her flesh solid. He ran one finger down her throat, her breasts, brushing lightly over each of her hard nipples. A blush rose to Bolormaa's face and neck when her cunt clenched in response.

He released her shoulder and stepped around to her front. Her eyes widened at the enormous, ivory cock that bounced erect before him.

Shame and fear battled the desire within her and won. Bolormaa scrambled up, her mouth still beyond her control. The god's hands darted out to snatch her wrists before she could get away. She whimpered at his painful hold, but cold had weakened her body too much for her to fight.

Erlik jerked her tight to his chest, his cock a thick column of ice against her belly. "You asked me to take you, did you not?" he rasped into her ear. "To save you?"

Bolormaa managed a tiny nod. Her face contorted around her immobilized mouth. Her eyes poured forth tears that froze as soon as they were shed, coating her cheeks with frost.

"I think you know what to do," the god said. Bolormaa squeezed her eyes shut and sank to her knees before him.

He trailed his fingers over her cheeks. The gentle touch lulled her, leaving her unprepared for when he snatched a fistful of her hair and fed the entire length of his cock into her helpless mouth.

Bolormaa's throat spasmed around his cockhead. She pounded her fists against his thighs and scraped her knees against the snow in her efforts to pull her face off the implacable thing. The god held her effortlessly in place, his freezing cock embedded to the hilt in the deepest heat of her throat.

Slowly, he pumped in and out of her face. His cock skated across her lips and tongue with the unearthly smoothness of ice against ice. Finally, Bolormaa stilled her fruitless struggles and looked up at him. He seemed to have been waiting for her to meet his gaze. His ink-black eyes bored into her as surely as his cock.

"You have a choice to make," he said. He drove into her throat until she gagged. He held the back of her head with both hands and listened to her gurgle around his cock. Bolormaa could not breathe. She choked, alarm heating her numbed body. She clawed at him desperately until he thrust her away, just before she lost consciousness.

Bolormaa lay on her back in the snow, panting through her frozen-open mouth. The god knelt straddling her, his still-hard cock resting on her cheek. "I have three gifts for you tonight, if you accept them," Erlik told her. "You've earned the first. I will bring you safely through this night. The second gift will hurt more, and the third will nearly kill you."

He caressed her jaw. "How much do you want of me?" His touch thawed her mouth. Bolormaa stretched her lips, weak with gratitude. He offered his finger, and she willingly sucked. Warmth spread through her mouth and traveled down into her chest.

Erlik withdrew the finger and raised a thick eyebrow.

Bolormaa considered him. She turned her head slightly to peer at the great cock, its velvety skin smooth on her face. Erlik towered above her. Here was real power, not her husband's cruel shadow of it. Bolormaa kissed the tip of the god's cock. "Please give me all," she whispered.

Bolormaa surveyed Sarant's restrained body. She had lifted the young woman's wrists high enough to force her onto her toes. Sarant's muscles strained to hold her balanced, creating lovely lines around her tensed muscles. The position lifted her breasts and emphasized her height. Blindfolded now, Sarant's head twisted sometimes toward a cracking twig or gust of wind.

Bolormaa stroked the postulant's side, then stretched upward and kissed her temple.

Sarant groaned and turned away. Bolormaa gripped her chin. "Pray to him."

"Lord Erlik," Sarant began obediently. "Winter-touched, dark Lord of the night and the hidden sun, pierce me with your icy spear of truth. Lead me across barren fields and strip me bare of clothes and flesh. Reveal the skeleton of my strength with the harsh caress of your winds. And when my heart has frozen solid from the pain, crush it in your hard hands, Lord, and take me, remake me — to die and be born again forever in the ecstasy of your stern embrace."

That solstice night with Erlik, Bolormaa's stomach burned with the pain of the god's seed. The cold mess of it froze and shattered while traveling down her throat. She feared shards of it would pierce her on the inside.

After emptying himself down her throat, the god removed his cock from her mouth and wiped it against her hair. Bolormaa watched her black hair blanch white at his touch. "You are marked as mine forever," Erlik whispered. "You will gain all the power, respect, and trouble that come of this."

Bolormaa clutched her guts and whimpered. The god's hand on her shoulder stilled her. His fingers found her nipples, circling them with his chilly touch. He squeezed them into thin, aching points, so stiff with cold that they would not return to their customary shape. Erlik gripped both nipples firmly and pulled up.

She gasped and squirmed to get her feet in place under her. "Do you still wish to receive my third gift?" Erlik asked. He kissed her, her still-thawing cheeks so cold that even his icy tongue felt hot and harsh.

"Yes," Bolormaa declared. The god guided her onto all fours in the snow.

Erlik placed the head of his cock against Bolormaa's cunt but did not push inside. He leaned forward and gripped her nipples again, pinching until she screamed and fought him. Slowly, the god increased the pressure, pulling until she had no choice but to impale herself.

The stabbing cold of his rigid member reached steadily farther inside her. "Please," Bolormaa gasped. More and more of it entered her, until it seemed far longer than what had been in her mouth. The god's cock bottomed out inside her, but still he pulled her nipples.

Bolormaa stopped moving, unable to take any more. Erlik did not relent. She feared he would tear her nipples off. Bolormaa could not bear the pain in her breasts, nor the pain of his cock. The torment intensified until it transformed to helpless insanity. She flung herself into both anguished sensations, swinging forward and stretching her nipples to the breaking point, and then slamming back until she thought his cock would rip her in half.

The god toyed with her, sprouting cold claws from his fingers and piercing her body with them. For the first time, Erlik grunted his excitement. The chill he radiated intensified. Bolormaa's skin went numb all over. Aside from a dull pounding at the deepest depth of her womb, she could no longer feel his cock inside her. She could not tell what his hands did to her breasts.

The god moaned and cold surged through her. Bolormaa's body froze solid. She could not speak, struggle, or feel. She heard the god's body slamming against hers. She could not see him or mark the passage of time.

Erlik screamed and rammed against her. The seed he pumped into her womb surged within her. Bolormaa felt as if she could not contain it. Erlik touched between her legs, finding her bud. A sharp poke chipped through the ice that covered it, exposing the tender flesh to the wind and the god's harsh fingers. Bolormaa could feel nothing but the god pinching and tugging on her most sensitive place.

She came, the spasms of it bursting through the icy layer that immobilized her. Bolormaa howled at the pain of her splintering skin.

Erlik withdrew his cock from her. He touched her behind the ear. "Now I will be forever inside you."

Bolormaa collapsed forward into the snow. Through her shock and pain, she smiled.

"Mother Bolormaa, are you still here?" Sarant sounded frightened.

The dark flicker that now passed for night had begun. Erlik would not come, but the solstice must still be celebrated in full. Bolormaa kicked some leaves.

"Why didn't you go to the temple of the Summer God after Tengri murdered Erlik?"

The old woman grunted and spat. "I'm a priestess, not a whore. I will not be passed along with the cheap spoils of war."

Bolormaa squinted at Sarant. The girl should suffer more. Bolormaa had lost two fingers and three toes after her night with Erlik, and the blizzard of his seed had stolen her tongue's sense of taste.

She squatted on the ground beside Sarant and pinched her inner thigh. The girl cried out. Bolormaa did it again, harder, leaving the impression of her fingernails in the young woman's skin. The third time, she drew blood.

Sarant screamed and kicked. Bolormaa dodged the blow easily, cackling. She took out another length of rope. "Do you want me to tie your ankles so your feet can't support you?"

The postulant whimpered. Bolormaa smiled and pinched her side, just under her ribcage. The girl flinched, but bit her lip and took the pain.

Bolormaa wound the rope around the girl's chest methodically, length over length until the rope lifted and squeezed the girl's breasts. Her rosy nipples reddened and grew. Bolormaa shaped Sarant's breasts into cones and bound them tightly with the rope while the girl whined and gasped. Finally, she stood back to admire the purpling flesh.

"Please," Sarant begged.

"Please, what?" Bolormaa tweaked a swollen nipple.

"Please. It hurts."

"It's supposed to hurt. If Erlik had come for you, you would be wishing for mercy right now. But in the end, you would give yourself to him more completely than you thought possible."

"Why are you hurting me so much if he's not coming?" Sarant wailed.

Cold rage rose in Bolormaa's belly. Why, indeed? She had always felt the god's presence in the pit of her stomach. That had ended when Erlik died, obliterated as thoroughly as her beloved snow. She squeezed a tortured breast in the palm of one hand.

"Why did you come to me?" she hissed.

Sarant swallowed, her throat working desperately. "Anything seemed better than my home."

Bolormaa's anger softened. "The pain is what sets you free of that," she murmured. "Remember that."

Her fingers traced the young woman's scarred flesh. She traced the curve of her hips, tickled Sarant's inner thighs, and soon delved into the warm, wet place between her legs. "He would have been pleased with the taking of this virginity tonight," Bolormaa murmured.

Her fingers tingled strangely. She wanted to hurt and help, to strip bare and transform, to destroy and make new. She pushed one finger all the way inside of Sarant. The young woman let out a frightened yelp. "Mother, your hands are so cold!"

Bolormaa slapped the bound girl's face with her free hand. "Do you want the gifts of Erlik or not?"

Sarant's protests fell silent. Bolormaa added a second finger. Sarant's moistening slit provided a pleasant warmth that traveled up her arm. She pounded her fingers in and out of the girl, her aching old woman's joints forgotten.

The postulant struggled against the ropes, her breath hitching. Bolormaa sat on the ground, forcing the girl's legs apart. She easily overpowered Sarant's straining thighs. Reaching up, Bolormaa made her hand into a spear point. She aligned it with Sarant's slit and shoved viciously upward, tearing through her barrier. Sarant shrieked, but Bolormaa did not let up, using her other hand to rub vigorously at the bud between the young woman's legs. She continued to force her hand deeper inside.

"Cold, cold, cold!" Sarant cried. She tried to dance away, but only succeeded at spreading her legs wider. Bolormaa's hand disappeared inside her passage, and the old woman stared in wonder as frost spidered over the girl's legs and lower stomach. She kissed and licked Sarant's bud. The postulant gave in with her entire body, her muscles gripping powerfully at Bolormaa's wrist.

The old woman looked down. Ice covered the larch tree's roots. Bolormaa's arm had lightened by several shades. The hair between Sarant's legs glowed white.

Bolormaa eased her hand out of the girl and stumbled to her feet. Sarant panted and shivered. Bolormaa yanked the blindfold off Sarant's head.

"My Lord Erlik?" Sarant gasped.

Putting her hand to her head, Bolormaa discovered a tangle of rough horns. Exploring further, Bolormaa found a freezing, implacable cock between her legs. Slowly, a smile spread across her face. "You have a choice to make," she said.

If you enjoyed this story, you can sign up for a free membership at
ForbiddenFiction.com and discuss it with other readers
and the author at the *In the Death of Winter* story page
at http://forbiddenfiction.com/story/AL1-1.000042.

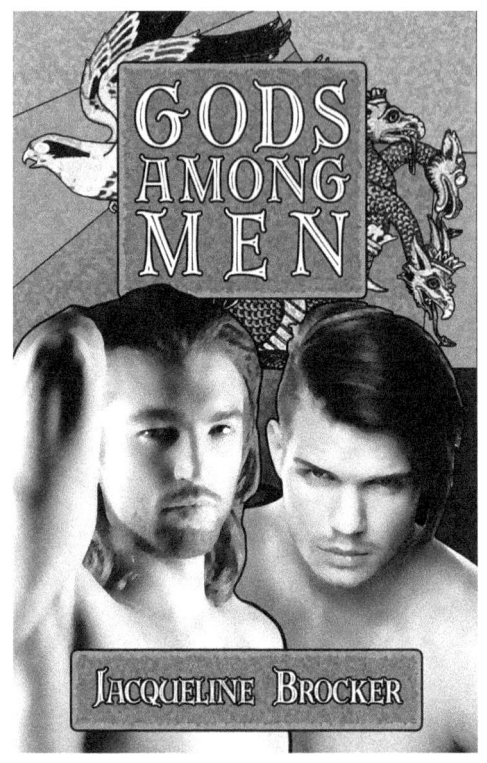

Gods Among Men

Jacqueline Brocker

Jacqueline Brocker lives and writes in Cambridge, England. Her short erotic fiction has appeared in anthologies such as Smut Alfresco (House of Erotica), Under Her Thumb and Best Bondage Erotica 2014 (both from Cleis Press). Originally from Australia, when not writing she is a Scottish Country Dancer, a recent convert to Lindy Hop, and dabbles in foreign language (current dabblings being German and Korean).

Chapter 1
Rain

Croatia - Present Day

Nikolai

Nikolai leaned languidly against the frame of the window of his second-floor study and watched the bay below, and beyond. The water shimmered with the afternoon sun. Yachts and fishing boats bobbed at the docks, and in the distance windsurfers sped along the Adriatic. Vendors sold cold lemonade along the boardwalk while mothers and fathers pushed prams and held dripping ice-cream cones for their capering toddlers. Three old men sat on a bench: one stared vacant out over the harbour while the others contemplated a chessboard. A pair of teenagers kissed and giggled as they sat on the low wall above the water. Other groups played in the water or sunned themselves on the beach. Nikolai smiled; this was summer at its most perfect, for the day was pleasantly hot, and peaceful.

That was, until Ilya charged along the harbour road in his bright red American Mustang. He parked the car, slammed the door and stomped up the boardwalk. Straight towards Nikolai's house.

Nikolai narrowed his eyes, glaring down at Ilya. Although he'd been expecting a visit, he ground his teeth together.

There he was: Ilya Gromovnik. The same nick-name as his father, also the namesake of St Ilya. All of them — saint, father, and son — called Gromovnik; that is to say, Thunderer. Ilya Gromovnik, owner of the furniture factory, the largest employer in town, president of the chamber of commerce. So well-respected by everyone in the town for his capacity to employ many people, to be good to them in return for their complete loyalty; for his generous donations to public works (the painting of the town hall, the play parks for children, the new local museum); for his gorgeous, buxom wife Dobrana and that brood of children. How many did the man have now? Six? Nikolai had lost count.

His striking looks aided him too. Ilya was a tall man, his chest square and broad. As he charged along the boardwalk, the sun caught glints of his close-cropped coppery hair and long, neatly kept beard. His features — handsome and with a hawk-like nose — were creased in anger and he walked as if he owned everything that lay before him.

Nikolai supposed in many ways he did. Not only did he have his factory, but he also had his house on the hill that overlooked the town with pompous pride. It was high enough that anyone in the market square could gaze up over the rooftops and see Ilya's home, watching over them all. Like a beloved god.

Beloved. Nikolai snorted. *Feared is the better word.* For who would dare to cross a man who could make drug cartels scurry away to neighbouring towns with a single phone call, an action the police could not take? Who would fight with a man who, when riff-raff sailors made trouble when they came ashore, would ensure said sailors would be found floating in the harbour the next day? And those who failed to give him proper respect or decided to try and run the town or their business a little differently had felt Ilya's wrath, and found themselves friendless or destitute.

Lord and protector. In a town where councillors were weak-willed and the police ineffectual, who needed a mayor when they had Ilya Gromovnik?

Nikolai sighed. He was well aware of the power of Ilya's rage. Well aware, too, that everyone in town knew that he and Ilya despised each other. Even now in the bay below, the teenage girl turned her head. Likewise, a father pushing a pram saw Ilya's progress; stopped to grasp his wife's shoulders and whisper something into her ear. The man who'd been staring dumbfounded out to sea started as Ilya passed him, and a child's ice-cream tumbled to the ground as the kid froze to gaze at Ilya. As Ilya closed the distance, Nikolai could feel and hear — even through the glass — Ilya's thundering purpose and the hush that fell over the bay. Only the gulls continued to chatter.

They were not business rivals; Nikolai ran a shipping business. He, too, was a member of the chamber of commerce. Longer than Ilya at that—he suspected that Ilya would have blocked his application had Ilya been a member first. However, he kept a number of smaller operations running that the upright and self-righteous Ilya would have loved to have seen abolished. His dance club, for instance, which on paper was perfectly legal, but where Nikolai well knew all kinds of licentious and illicit behaviour took place. His patrons—mostly tourists, male and there for other men—as far as he was concerned, were dancing and embracing the joys of life. Nikolai turned a smirking blind eye to what else besides dancing went on there.

Someone at the chamber told Nikolai he was surprised that Ilya hadn't run him out of town yet. Nikolai had only grinned. Ilya probably would have if not for Nikolai's generosity: people in need of loans found themselves with a discreet envelope slipped through the door. Builders would arrive at a storm-damaged house and do the repair work, refusing payment and shrugging when asked why they had come. No trumpeting, no fanfare, but Nikolai was aware that his name was mentioned. He'd have preferred otherwise, but secrets were a near impossibility to keep.

The only kept secrets he knew were the ones between himself and Ilya.

People left in Ilya's wake, quickly packing their bags and rushing up the beach. On the horizon, dark clouds began to gather, the signs of a sea-born storm, bringing with it a suffocating heat.

Nikolai sighed, rolled his shoulders back, and stood up straight. For all his irritation and hatred of Ilya, this meeting was unavoidable. *Inevitable.* The wheel that had been set in motion since they were children was now rolling towards a climax that neither of them could ignore.

Ilya

Ilya's mind was set with determination, and he was governed by red rage. He let his emotions reign freely on his face. The path cleared before him. People raced to their cars and motorbikes. He heard the whispers of 'Ilya' and 'Gromovnik' and 'Nikolai' in the air.

Good, he thought. *Let them all know that I will no longer tolerate Nikolai's scheming.*

More importantly, he would not give in to what had been drilling through his mind and body this past month.

These past years, you mean, a quieter voice said in his mind. Ilya ignored it.

Soon, Ilya stood before Nikolai's house: it was a fortress of glass and steel, crouching back into a rocky outcrop. So modern and fashionable, possessing none of the traditional values that Ilya held so dear. This home was not suitable for children; Ilya would never have let his near this place. The house may have seemed transparent, but it was another facade for Nikolai's wretched subterfuges. It was no surprise that Nikolai lived here, right at the end of the bay. He'd want to keep his activities well out of sight from the public. A pity that Ilya could see it from his own house on the hill!

Fortress it may have been, but Ilya could have kicked it over with his rage.

Instead, he tested the glass door in front of him, discovered it was locked, and so smashed the glass pane nearest to the handle to let himself in.

That's when he discovered that it wasn't a house; it was a jungle.

Lush green hangings fell from the walls. Potted plants loomed tall, and the furniture was upholstered in a deep, velvety dark green. It was open-plan living, with a mezzanine towards the back—over which a vine grew, thick with broad leaves—and a dining area to one side.

A man built like an ox and wearing a tight t-shirt sat at the dining table. Bodyguard or boyfriend? Maybe both: he carried a side-arm. Ilya didn't know or care, but when the ox saw Ilya he leapt to his feet. He was nearly beside Ilya, hand at his weapon when a smooth voice spoke from from above.

"Risto, that's not necessary. Leave him."

Ilya's eyes shot upwards. Nikolai was standing on the mezzanine, one hand leaning on the balcony. His black hair was slicked back with hair gel, and his pointy features were filled with mocking arrogance. He wore a dark silk shirt, as green as the surroundings and his eyes, with a snakeskin belt holding up his tight black jeans. A gold scarf was draped around his neck. He was dressed as if for a nightclub. Ilya doubted if he'd ever worn proper clothes, like the shirt sleeves and plain slacks Ilya wore then, or if he had any sensible jewellery. Ilya's watch and gold ring were as far as he'd ever go.

Risto's hand hovered a moment, his gaze trailing slowly between Ilya and Nikolai. Ilya watched the gun, ready to duck if Risto should grab it.

Nikolai said, "Leave us, Risto. I can defend myself against Ilya should he prove troublesome."

Risto looked sceptical. *As he should*, Ilya thought. Nikolai had long arms and legs, but was slender, with little muscle, while Ilya could have broken Nikolai into pieces. As he might well do, with or without Risto there.

A wave of Nikolai's hand, though, and Risto obeyed, moving up the staircase, passed Nikolai into the upper level of the house.

When he was gone, Nikolai chuckled. "He is new. How is he to know of our old friendship?"

Ilya scoffed. "That is not what we are."

Nikolai feigned surprise, but soon his mouth curled into a languid smile, teasing, taunting even.

"I suppose I should fetch some champagne. This is an occasion to celebrate; in all these years, you have never been in my home before." A pause as he cocked his head; all pretence. "Nor have I been to yours, have I, Ilya?"

Ilya only glared.

Nikolai smirked, then descended the stairs, steps like a slinking cat. He slid onto the couch, hand out in an inviting gesture.

"Please, Ilya. Take a seat."

Ilya crossed his arms and remained standing. Childish perhaps, but he'd not give in to any of Nikolai's suggestions. Not today of all days.

"Suit yourself."

Nikolai began to toy with that ridiculous gold scarf. It was made of material like a harem veil, opaque and alluring.

"Are you here to simply glower at me? Come on, Ilya, talk."

Words were not Ilya's strength, so he went straight to the point. "You are taking bribes from Mishka to support the application for his club."

Nikolai twirled the scarf, cocked his head to one side, trying to convey the picture of innocence. Ilya held himself steady, keeping his arms over his chest as if that could contain his bubbling anger, and glared at Nikolai.

At last, Nikolai sighed.

"I suppose it is no surprise that you have found out. You have your informants after all. Yes, it is true. Me, and a number of other members of the chamber, as I'm sure you know. But what concern is it of yours?"

It took Ilya great control not to splutter. "It is illegal."

"I think you'll find it is a legally grey area, my dear Ilya."

The words came at last, and they fell out of Ilya's mouth. "Do not call me your dear, and do not pretend that what you are doing is the right thing. The man wants to open a sex club. Do you really think that is appropriate for this town?"

"I think it will add a certain kind of appeal." Nikolai held the scarf below his eyes, peered at Ilya and fluttered his eyelashes. Just like a harlot. "You may even get something out of it yourself."

Ilya flexed his hand opened and closed again. He would not give in and punch Nikolai, or touch him in any way. He would do this the right way. He had to.

He spoke carefully, his voice controlled. "We are in a fortunate position with our chamber of commerce. The planning section of the council which allows us to vet applications for new businesses has served all of us well. If we start to be open to bribery, we will undermine ourselves."

Nikolai dropped the scarf. His voice was still casual when he said, "I am less open to bribery than seeing it as an added bonus. Mishka is a sordid man, and it would serve me well for him to think he has me in his pocket. He made me the offer of money without my asking, and it hardly seemed good business to say no."

You would you dirty little schemer, Ilya thought.

"Nikolai, this is serious." Ilya took a deep breath, and tried to appeal to Nikolai's goodness—assuming he had any. "He wants to open it where families will be coming for holidays, right on the promenade. Our town is for everyone, not the coarse and the sexually depraved!"

Nikolai shrugged.

"I am not the only one taking the money. Why don't you convince someone else? You only need to convince two of them to change the vote to what you want. I am sure they will respond very well to your threats."

Ilya stepped closer to the couch with the intent of looming over Nikolai. "Your refusal will send a better message. I do not want only a minority vote. Mishka needs to understand that no one will accept his money or wants his club."

"Such regard for my power. I am very flattered."

Ilya closed the distance between them, nearly hitting Nikolai's knees. He glowered down at him. "You will do this, Nikolai. You will meet with Mishka and tell him the deal is off. Then you will contact the other chamber members and tell them to do the same."

The leisurely look disappeared, and Nikolai's face went as hard as stone. "Do not order me around, Ilya."

Ilya's fists curled up. "You will do as I say, Nikolai."

Nikolai sprung to his feet, teeth bared. "Make me."

In an instant those two simple words pushed Ilya over the edge. Yes, he would make Nikolai bend to him and his demands, and he would do it the only way he knew how. As his body rushed with enraged arousal, Ilya said, "I will."

Ilya threw himself at Nikolai. He grabbed his chin, forcing Nikolai's face up to his, and snatched Nikolai's lips into a biting kiss. Nikolai tried to lean away from Ilya, but Ilya urged his bulky frame right up against Nikolai's slender body. Nikolai groaned, knotting his fingers into Ilya's beard. Nikolai's erection pressed into Ilya, and Ilya's cock responded. Ilya relished the hardness, but refused to give it attention.

Outside, thick rain began to fall, splashing into the bay and hammering against the glass. A distinct clap of thunder sounded in the distance. Inside, a moist warmth began to form between Ilya and Nikolai's bodies.

Many centuries ago...

The land remembers.

It remembers the centuries aeons before written records began, before Christ, before the one God and his saints swept away the pantheons of old. When humanity gathered in small villages and lived off the land, existing between terror and hope of the fickle ways of the gods that stalked above and amongst them. It remembers days of bronze, of forests yet unconquered by farms and cities.

In such a time, in the sky high above the world where it is airy and clear, standing proud in a golden chariot pulled by a buck goat, Perun rode across the clouds. His eagle perched on one arm and his axe was fastened to his back. Beneath the chariot lay the land: mountains and steep valleys, green forests, rich and abundant fields of wheat. Cattle and sheep grazed, and the farmers looked after their flocks and herds with patience.

It was a perfect day, busy with the activity of life. Perun stroked his long, coppery beard, and was content.

Then Veles came in the form of a dragon from beneath the ground, from the base of a great oak tree. He shot into the air like a giant lance, his body green-scaled and terrible, his fangs long, his eyes golden with greed, and his wings like a giant bat's, veiny and leathery. He, too, surveyed the lands, flapping his great wings just above the treetops. He saw the tender flesh of the waiting cattle. He licked his lips. With a sudden swoop, he snatched a cow up in his jaws and tore it to shreds in the air, devouring it in his flight. The farmer below wailed in horror. Hot blood gushed down Veles's throat. His stomach was sated, and he smiled.

Perun, watching the whole scene from above, angry at the dragon-god's mischief, shouted out to Veles. Veles turned, hovering in the air like an awful cloud. He winked at Perun.

"Greetings, Perun, God of the Sky and the Thunder. Why do you scream at me in such rage?"

"Oh Veles, God of the Underworld. You are meant to protect the cattle! And now you have caused a poor farmer much grief."

Veles laughed, low and rumbling. "I, too, must eat."

"Then you are nothing but a thief."

Veles sneered, lips curling around his fangs. "And you are a stubborn overlord who frightens the people to your will, Perun Gromovnik, with your fury and your lightning that kills with a single strike. You dare to presume you are better than me."

The eagle at Perun's arm shrieked, flapping its wings. Its eyes and Perun's bore down at Veles, ferocious, enraged. Again Veles only laughed. The sound filled Perun with greater anger. He urged his chariot downwards, like a bolt from the blue, towards the mighty dragon Veles. Veles beat his wings and dove towards the earth. His body was filled with the vitality of the meal he had consumed. He would give Perun a merry chase, across the four corners if he had to.

As they had always done and always would.

Croatia – eighteen years ago

Nikolai

At the end of the day, the gymnasium was usually empty. Even the staff would have gone home. So Nikolai would go to the punching bag and practice alone. Boxing was his favourite of the sports at the gym, and despite his slightness, he was among the best. It was a status he could not maintain without practice, however: he did not wish the others to see just how hard he worked at it, or learn his techniques. So this time of the day was the best.

That evening, Nikolai hopped and darted around the punching bag, hitting it with teasing taps and thudding blows. The first hits designed to foster confusion in his opponents, followed by direct hits that would leave them dazzled. He was on form, and—though he sweated and his heart raced—he smiled.

It was the largest gymnasium in town. It was an old building and held a space for weights, a boxing ring and wrestling mats. The changing rooms were a little grubby, but it was a place of activity and community for all the young men. While no sign indicated that women were not welcome, most didn't enter, or if they did they did not linger: such was the scent of maleness in the air. Outside an old elm tree stood, too close to the building in the minds of some; they feared it falling and destroying the gym. But there it remained, for people loved it.

For Nikolai it was more than just a place for exercise and sports: it was the battle ground on which Nikolai and Ilya fought for the minds of men.

Nikolai smirked as he thought on that, and pictured Ilya's face as he landed a triple punch on the bag.

It was an old rivalry, a war that had begun when they were still children. Nikolai remembered being only five years old and looking across the classroom to see the solid boy with the proud face whom everyone wanted to love. His own scrawny body had failed to inspire such devotion, but he traded marbles for sweets, was generous with his friends and so found his own place. But in that instant, in that first look, Nikolai knew Ilya hated him and that he hated Ilya. He could not explain why; he only knew that their hatred was mutual and that was that.

Of course the children flocked to Ilya's side, his father being the richest man in town, and Ilya destined to take over the factory from him. Ilya's father was benevolent, but he was a proud man who was not easily crossed. Everybody knew when he was angry. They called him Gromovnik.

And Ilya became him as he grew, Nikolai thought, taking another punch at the imaginary Ilya.

Nikolai did not mind the attentions Ilya received. He had his friends and he also had his place. As he grew up he swapped marbles and sweets for sexy magazines and videos (the teenagers he traded with knew not to ask questions about their providence). He found himself giving away the money he began to accrue. Though quietly. There was no need to puff out his chest and brag about it.

In the year before he was due to graduate, Nikolai began selling hashish. A risk, but worth it for the proceeds he made. He knew Ilya watched him with piercing eyes, waiting to catch him off-guard. He was careful, but the day came when — on Ilya's evidence — Nikolai was expelled with no diploma to take into the world. His father had been angry, but when he saw Nikolai's self-accumulated wealth, he'd shaken his head in amazement and urged Nikolai to go into business school.

Nikolai knew he wouldn't need that. He started a small business in the docks, keeping smaller and more shadowy businesses on the side.

Ilya, meanwhile, finished school with good marks and joined his father's factory, and began courting the loveliest girl in town, Dobrana. Theirs was a relationship from a Hollywood film, as much for everyone else to enjoy as it was theirs, replete with public displays of chaste affection. Nikolai found it sickeningly amusing. His own interests lay with older men who he sought out in darkened pubs and one ill-lit park on the outskirts of town. He learned that he liked the fierce grip of another man's hand on his cock, and how to best use his tongue on theirs.

Nikolai slowed his punches down, practicing his technique over his speed. He considered where he and Ilya stood now; each kept their distance from the other and that suited them both fine. The gymnasium was another matter. They might be out of school, but the same battles for their favours continued to play out there.

Most still wanted the attention and favour of Ilya. They regarded him with solemn respect, and stood aside for him when he walked. Not grovelling, for it was understood Ilya liked confidence, pride in oneself. But they would never stand in Ilya's way if he had his mind set on some goal.

Nikolai snorted. Only a fool would stand in front of a charging bull. And indeed some tried. They found themselves shunned by others, not always for reasons they could fathom. And because it is a man's duty to survive and to show he could fend for a family when the time came to have one, they turned instead to the shadows, where Nikolai operated. What good operatives he had, too, for Nikolai found the gymnasium the perfect place for his latest scheme: selling steroids to the attendees.

How easy men were to convince that they needed to enhance their strength and virility.

Nikolai swung at the bag one last time, landing his punch with a grunt. It flung back with juddering force and Nikolai smiled, satisfied.

Sweat dripped from him. He picked up his towel and bottle of water, and was drying his face when something caught his eye.

Ilya was leaning against the wall. He'd clearly been watching Nikolai. Watching and waiting.

Nikolai's blood ran hot. He ran his knuckles across his still girlish chin, conscious of how Ilya's short and sharp beard made him appear so much more like a man. But he did not bare his teeth at his old enemy. He stood nonchalant, with his arms folded. Ilya could speak first.

Ilya took his time, but at last he said, "You punch well, but I wonder how you would fare on the wrestling mats."

Nikolai filled his mouth with water, swishing it around before swallowing. "I am told it is not your size that counts, but the way you move."

Ilya raised an eyebrow. "So you've been told? Well... why don't we see if that's the case?"

"Now?"

"Yes."

Nikolai chuckled, and his already hot blood began to boil.

Chapter 2
Lightning

Croatia – eighteen years ago

Ilya

Ilya took his place on the mat. Nikolai went through some absurd routine of wiping himself down, drinking more water. As if it might help him win. Soon enough he would know Ilya's will and wrath.

Ilya thought himself a tolerant person. As much as he hated the devious little man, as much as they had their factions in the gymnasium, Ilya was content to leave Nikolai alone. But something had changed that Ilya could not abide.

Drugs had begun to circulate at the gymnasium. The kind that would allow a user to become stronger, faster, better than the others. At first, no one knew where they came from. It didn't take long for Ilya to suspect their source. Nikolai would spring and bounce across the boxing ring, seeming a waif but with a sneaky punch. He never took the drugs himself (as far as Ilya could tell), or kept them on his person; even after Ilya sent his men to raid Nikolai's locker, they found nothing.

But Ilya knew. And he wanted it to stop.

Nikolai bent forward, kicking his legs up as if about to start a race. His face showed that he thought this was all a game. Ilya's lip curled up in a sneer. Everything was a game to that man —apart from his little business in the docks, everything else he did was all about hedonistic pleasure, about giving to people what sated their basest needs. No sense of civic duty or pride, just fun and games and consequence be damned. Like the hashish, like the steroids.

Like the men he was rumoured to be fucking. A vision of Nikolai in congress with another man flashed before Ilya. He stopped the thought before it could... grow.

Ilya had been with two girls his own age, but was now keeping himself for Dobrana, who wanted a long engagement for the best possible wedding. That was the right thing to do. Nikolai wouldn't know the right thing to do if it reared up and struck him.

So, Ilya reasoned, it was his job to do the striking.

Across the mat, shirtless, only in shorts — Nikolai's tight and fitting, Ilya's hanging loose — the two men circled each other, padding the mat like panthers, eyes hooded like hawks. Nikolai sometimes slapped his thighs, and he wore his damnable grin, the one the seemed as if he was keeping a secret that only he had the pleasure of knowing. Ilya, meanwhile, was still, quiet: he felt no need for sudden sounds. Patience and watchfulness, he knew, were how you won at wrestling, not with darting games. And nothing would distract him from his task.

Nikolai lunged first. It made Ilya smile. That was his first mistake. He caught Nikolai, stumbled backwards, and Nikolai briefly grinned in triumph, only to find himself on his side, Ilya's shoulder pressing his down. He heard Nikolai gasp and saw his panicked eyes. Ilya chuckled, but Nikolai locked his legs around his own and twisted until Ilya too was on the ground, Nikolai half on top of him.

Nikolai bent in, close to Ilya's face. "See, I told you—"

Ilya pushed back at Nikolai's shoulder and once more Nikolai was on his back. Nikolai tried to squirm away, but Ilya held him firm in his grasp.

"Now that you cannot get away, I want to—shit!"

Nikolai had bit Ilya's hand: a sharp and decisive bite. Ilya wrenched back and Nikolai rolled away.

Ilya shot a furious look at Nikolai.

"That's against the rules."

Nikolai shrugged. "But it worked."

Ilya snarled, got on his haunches. *Two can play at that game,* he thought. He launched himself at Nikolai who deftly moved out of the way and caught Ilya's legs, lifting them just enough to throw him back onto the mat. Ilya winced and cursed when Nikolai fell on top of him, trying to press his small weight against Ilya's body. Nikolai managed to twine himself enough around Ilya so Ilya couldn't move.

"So, I am here, you said you wanted to... what?"

Ilya jerked, but he was quite subdued. He could only move one hand and that hand was very close to Nikolai's... crotch.

The cotton stretched over Nikolai's cock and balls, making them appear soft and vulnerable. The scent of salty sweat rose from his body. His skin, Ilya knew, would be sensitive to touch, and his cock and balls even more so.

Ilya began to reach forward, inch by inch. "I want to talk."

"Well then, talk." Nikolai smirked as if he'd won already.

"No. I mean, I talk," Ilya grabbed Nikolai's cock through his shorts, "and you listen."

Nikolai yelped, his arms going limp around Ilya. Ilya, not letting go, threw Nikolai back. Nikolai landed on his side, whimpering. Ilya tightened his grip.

Nikolai beat the mat with his fist. "Not... fair..."

Ilya hooked his fingers through Nikolai's hair, and forced his face onto the gym mat. "Says the man who bit me."

The sight of Nikolai trembling, of his face twisted in pain, sent a shot of arousal to Ilya's own cock. It shocked him. But Nikolai was so close, their bodies locked together, it was almost as if they were one. Ilya stroked the cock he already held. A more tender hold, but still firm, and he realised that Nikolai was growing hard, too.

Nikolai tried to lash back, but Ilya's grip was too much. Ilya had to grin at the feeling of total power over Nikolai, his nerves crackling. With Nikolai's hardening cock in his hand, Ilya knew exactly what he needed to do to teach Nikolai his lesson.

Swiftly, Ilya grabbed Nikolai's shorts and pulled them off his body, leaving Nikolai naked on the mat with Ilya looming over him.

"Ilya!"

Nikolai's voice held a warning, but Ilya's hand rubbed his cock, then splayed to stroke down its length, to catch his balls and rub the whole of his sack and cock at once. Nikolai swore, but he thrust his hips into Ilya's hand.

Of course he would.

Ilya lifted Nikolai's buttocks off the mat, spreading his legs. He rubbed harder. Nikolai gasped, and Ilya delighted in knowing he liked it despite himself.

Ilya leaned down to speak straight into Nikolai's ear. "I thought size didn't matter... little Nikolai."

A snigger. "It still doesn't. What do you have that's better?"

Ilya's hand left Nikolai's cock and pulled his own shorts down, revealing his erection. Nikolai swallowed. Ilya smiled: he knew his cock was huge, red and hard. It wanted attention. He was not betraying Dobrana, for this was not sex; this was necessary education.

So Ilya flipped Nikolai onto his knees, and spread his legs once more. Nikolai reached to pull away, but Ilya's grip on his hips was too strong.

Ilya spat into his hand; for his comfort, not for Nikolai's. He smeared the spit on the blade of his hand, divided the cheeks of Nikolai's arse, pushing momentarily at the puckered hole.

Nikolai beat the mat again.

"Don't you fucking dare!"

Ilya paid no heed. He took his cock in hand, angled it to Nikolai's hole, and shoved it inside with a grunt.

Nikolai shouted like a loud and sudden bell. "Fuck!"

Ilya threw his body over Nikolai's back, grabbed Nikolai's wrists to hold them down, and drove his cock in deeper. "Yes! Until you say yes, I'll fuck you."

Ilya began to rock his hips, his cock sliding in and out of Nikolai. It was as though he could tear Nikolai in half, and Nikolai's grunting sounds gave credence to that thought. Ilya relished the motion of his body, the total power he had over Nikolai in this moment. And oh, how Nikolai was tight, tighter than any woman's cunt—and there was something almost better about this. Pleasure seared through Ilya, though he told himself it was necessary, a duty, to subdue the arrogant little shit.

Ilya paused, half inside Nikolai. "Now you will listen to me!"

"Fuck you!"

Three times Ilya slammed against Nikolai, leaving Nikolai whimpering, barely able to hold himself up. But Ilya knew his spirit was not yet subdued, even if his body was. It would take more than that with Nikolai.

Ilya spoke again, murmuring into Nikolai's ear. "The steroids? You will stop selling them. Do you hear me?"

Nikolai made no response.

Ilya dropped his voice and pressed his lips right to Nikolai's skin. "I said... do you hear me?"

Only a nod.

Ilya continued to pound into Nikolai until Nikolai's voice came up, taunting, "I hear you... but I will not stop."

"You will stop."

"Why should I?"

"Because..."

Ilya drove his cock all the way into Nikolai and held it there while he kept speaking.

"If you do not, I will find you, and once again..."

He drew back, leaving only the head inside Nikolai.

"I will fuck you."

Nikolai hissed, his head twisting around to glare at Ilya with hate. A hatred, Ilya saw, streaked with need for Ilya's cock.

Ilya began thrusting again, harder and faster than before. Nikolai tried to stretch away from Ilya only to be dragged back for more. Ilya watched as Nikolai bit his lip, a moan barely suppressed under it. Ilya pounded again and Nikolai expelled a tortured sound.

A small victory.

Keeping Nikolai to him was like trying to contain a bundle of coiled springs. Ilya had to grapple with him to stop him from scrambling away. He would make Nikolai take this, take all of Ilya's cock. His cock could have burst with the incredible intensity as Nikolai's tight channel contracted around it again and again. Then Nikolai moaned like a whore, flooding Ilya with the desire to come.

Ilya spoke again, his vicious thrusts punctuated with his words. Each of them jabbing Nikolai with pain and rippling pleasure.

"You. Will. Stop. Selling. Steer. Oids. Do. You. Un. Der. Stand!"

Nikolai screamed, "Yes!" His body shuddered as he came.

Despite himself, Ilya was impressed, for neither his hand, nor Nikolai's, had so much as brushed Nikolai's cock since Ilya had penetrated him. Yet Nikolai shot his load all over the mat, his come splashing against Ilya's knees. His whole body shuddered, and he squeezed the orgasm out of Ilya's cock. Ilya coated

Nikolai's insides, and thrust until the last wave of it fell.

Ilya pulled Nikolai's head up by the hair, forcing Nikolai to meet his eyes.

He smiled, showing all his teeth.

"I'm glad we understand each other."

He dropped Nikolai back on the mat. With a sharp tug he withdrew his cock and was filled with a pure satisfaction.

Ilya stood, keeping a close eye on Nikolai who still lay on the mat, exhaling slowly. He looked like a gym towel rung out after being used to wipe away sweat. Ilya smirked. *Serves him right*. Ilya waited until Nikolai caught his breath, crawled away and left the gymnasium.

Ilya found some towels and began to clean up their sweat and cum, invigorated with purpose. He hummed, proud that he had done the right thing and taught Nikolai a lesson. Then a sudden, sharp crack echoed through the gymnasium. Ilya started, gasping. The sound had come from outside. He left the towels and moved slowly through the gymnasium towards the front door.

The elm tree was on fire. Ilya scanned the sky, saw the thick wooly clouds hanging there above the pelting rain. It must have been lightning. Ilya's eye went wide at the sight of the beautiful tree burning. A branch snapped off and fell onto the roof. Ilya cried out, and raced to call the fire brigade.

When the firemen arrived, they immediately set to work with their hoses and water.

"Anyone inside? Anyone with you?" one of them asked Ilya.

Ilya shook his head. "I was alone."

Nikolai

Nikolai's body shook as he pulled his clothes on, gingerly packed his bag and hobbled out of the gymnasium.

As he hauled himself home, rain began pelting down. He wrapped his arms around himself and hunched his shoulders. Nothing could ease the ache inside him. He winced with each step. When he heard the sirens, he turned to watch their progress, and saw above the tops of the houses, the roof of the gymnasium and the elm tree alight. Nikolai began to smile, before his mouth spread into a devilish grin.

Centuries ago...

The chase was on.

Perun pursued Veles through the skies and over the hills, down low valleys and rollicking over houses, urging his buck goat forward. Veles swam through the air, glancing over his shoulder, his laughter mocking. He breathed noisy fire to distract Perun.

Then Perun brought out his stone arrows. He threw them at Veles. The dragon only writhed out of their range.

The arrow struck a great elm tree standing by a field of corn. It split directly in half. A young girl in the field cried out, seeing the arrow as lightning from the heavens. Her lips trembled as she cast her eyes nervously to the sky.

"Great Veles flies, and Great Perun is angry."

She ran from the field to her father's house, declaring that they had to make a sacrifice of a bull soon. The thunder was coming again.

In the sky above, Veles laughed, a hissing bellow.

"You will have to aim better than that, Perun!"

And he dove straight into a dark forest.

Perun screamed in fury. He grabbed another arrow, aiming into the forest. It would surely strike close this time, and indeed, it struck the tallest oak. The oak crashed through the trees, a leafy, fluttery wave of destruction as it fell and smacked against the other trees. Foxes, squirrels, wild boar, deer and a lone wolf all scattered in a terrible panic.

This time when Veles emerged, wings still beating hard, he bore a large scratch on his shoulders. He craned his head over his shoulder, lips curling in a sneer. Perun smiled, feeling his triumph imminent, and aimed another arrow.

Veles shot straight over the cornfield, towards the barn. Perun cursed as the dragon vanished through its doors.

The girl and her family ran from the house and headed toward the town. The other people needed to know that the gods were doing battle; a sacrifice had to be made and they had to find a suitable ox. Perun aimed towards the barn and hurled his arrow once more.

The lightning struck the barn with such force and heat that the wood, the straw and the leftover grain caught fire. Soon the whole barn was ablaze and Veles, screaming at his wretched luck, took to the air once more.

As the farm blazed below Perun stood with his hand on his hip. "Give up your flight, Veles! You cannot outrun my arrows."

Perun's eagle laughed as well, its head flinging back cawing.

Veles felt sorry that the barn was alight; the barn had given him shelter. He twirled away from Perun, dashing to get away as fast as he could, though as he departed, he threw a bag of coins through the window of the farmers' house; a recompense for the damage done.

He glared at the thunder god still pursuing him. How dare he suggest Veles was no more than a thief? Well. This thief was going to make Perun's task the hardest it could possibly be.

And still, the chase was on.

Croatia - ten years ago

Ilya

Summer was approaching an end. At an outdoor cafe on the town promenade by the bay, Ilya and his wife Dobrana sat with their three children. Two children occupied themselves with a quiet game—they were well-behaved—while Dobrana fed the toddler in a highchair, cradling her pregnant belly and smiling as she did.

Ilya, however, seethed. In his line of sight, Nikolai draped himself over a bulky, muscular man and turned sporadically to wink at Ilya.

Eight years ago the fire hadn't spread through the gymnasium. No one ever did learn about what passed between him and Nikolai. But ever after people associated Ilya's quick call to the fire department—

thus saving the gymnasium — with the end of the steroid trade.

Ilya married Dobrana soon after. They named their first child Ilya, keeping with the family tradition. Ilya continued to work at his father's factory, and now that his father was considerably ill, he took over most of the duties of running it.

Nikolai did not marry. Ilya doubted he ever would. His shipping business expanded, as did his shady deals. He'd kept his word: he had stopped the steroids at the gymnasium long ago. But his side business branched into other areas very quickly. No one could ever track anything back to him, he was so cunning.

Ilya grabbed his coffee and gulped it down hard as Nikolai nudged the muscle man's knee and then skirted away, looking coy and innocent when the man glanced at him. How was it that Nikolai already sat on the chamber of commerce, while Ilya did not?

He knew the real answer: although his father had given most of the power of the factory over to Ilya, his father still attended the chamber meetings. It was still, as far as his father was concerned, his factory, and therefore his position to maintain. Ilya did not wish his father dead. But he hated watching Nikolai pass him on his motorbike, heading for the meetings, giving Ilya a quick wave as he went.

Nikolai giggled and squeezed the muscle man's bicep. The man himself seemed bemused but tolerant of the attention. Ilya had to stop himself from snarling. Nikolai could smile and disarm anyone with it, with his hips rocking with a seductive grace as he walked and those deceptively shy eyes. Shouldn't a man like the one he was fawning over be repulsed? Shouldn't he hit Nikolai? Hadn't Nikolai learned he was vulnerable after Ilya's punishment in the gymnasium? Ilya despised his knowing grin, the sly look that said Nikolai had a secret that he was not going to tell anyone, but he just might if you knew how much to pay. His blood raged to think that he'd fucked another man and the man still had not learned. Ilya still thought on that night and his cock would become half-hard. There was order that must be maintained in the world. Order. And Nikolai brought chaos.

Ilya had been ignoring his anger. It would not do to repeat the events of that night in the gymnasium. Then Nikolai had begun to breathe words into the ears of the workers at the furniture factory. Tempting offers of greater pay, with side benefits that Ilya could only dream of giving them. When five men and two women left the factory, murmurs that became rumblings passed from house to house, eventually reaching Ilya's ears. From his house on the hill, he glared down at the docks, wishing his own hands could bring down lightning to strike at Nikolai's office.

Nikolai glanced over at Ilya and gave him a cheeky wink. *Almost flaunting how he undermines me, the bastard!* Ilya thought.

Ilya finished his coffee, and called the waiter over. He asked for a pen and pad of paper. He wrote a furious note on it, marched over to Nikolai and thrust it in his face without a word. Nikolai took it and began to read.

Ilya waited with his arms crossed for a response. Nikolai read the note, and folded it. He leered up at Ilya.

"Tomorrow," he said.

Ilya nodded, and left Nikolai to his muscle man.

Chapter 3
Thunder

Nikolai

Nikolai rode his motorbike along the coast road, smirking beneath his helmet. He'd bought the bike to celebrate his first year of success in business. He loved it. Furthermore, it enabled him to ride out of town to the larger cities and find deliciously built men who would fuck him hard and rough.

No one had matched Ilya's brutality. Nikolai had ached for days after the fight in the gymnasium, sore and tender, flinching from everyone. When he'd emerged into the world again he'd vowed to make Ilya's life hell.

In the years since then, he found other deals to thread through the town, to keep his business afloat and keep life interesting. Mostly he was amused by Ilya's puffing and posturing, by his sense of assurance he was doing so much right in this town. Though sometimes he would seethe when Ilya treated Nikolai like he wasn't worthy of address, like something beneath his shoe. He would not acknowledge Nikolai on the street, though Nikolai always offered him a cocky wave, a sway of his hips, if only to see Ilya barrel his chest and storm away—people scattering out of his stride—back to his wife to prove that he was unaffected by Nikolai's presence.

Nikolai knew the best way to keep people happy was by generosity and kindness. He hadn't really meant to steal workers from Ilya. Of course, when a man named Goran had come to him with a broken

137

arm and a tale of woe about Ilya's treatment of him, Nikolai's heart had been quietly moved. To him when a poorer man borrows money and is late on repayment there were other ways to deal with it than breaking his arm. A job in Nikolai's business seemed most fitting.

So now, pleased with his busy docks and his eager new workers, Nikolai would look up from the boardwalk on his morning stroll to that towering house on the hill and smile smugly.

Thus he was not wholly surprised when Ilya had handed him the written note in the cafe with a request that Nikolai meet Ilya in in a hotel room in a town some miles south, where they would not be recognised, and where they could talk.

Ilya was already there when Nikolai arrived. Nikolai wore tight fitting clothes, the kind he knew that Ilya would stare at and curse him for. Ilya, in his open shirt and rolled up sleeves, shook his head as his gaze passed over Nikolai. Nikolai suppressed his smirk, raked his eyes over Ilya, but said nothing. There was a small bottle of oil in his pocket. Unnecessary perhaps, but Nikolai suspected not. Outside there was a roll of distant thunder.

Ilya offered Nikolai a bottle of beer; Nikolai knew well that it was a pretence of civility.

Nikolai hesitated before taking it.

"I wonder that it is not poisoned."

Ilya snorted, and leaned back on the wall as Nikolai sat in the armchair. Nikolai put the beer bottle to his mouth and sucked, eyes suggestive, mouth laving the top and neck. Ilya shifted to cross his legs; Nikolai wondered what stirred between them.

There was no need for ceremony or preamble. Ilya said, "I know why my workers have left. I have heard what you promised them. I've lost a good group of people because of your pernicious words."

Nikolai blinked, deliberately coquettish. "Pernicious? I'd hardly call a better offer pernicious."

Ilya's face creased. Frustration, Nikolai had no doubt. Nikolai always had the advantage with words—small as he was, he had had to learn—while Ilya's reliance on strength meant that speaking left him tongue-tied.

Delighting in Ilya's discomfort, Nikolai lay back in his chair, opened his arms behind him, and parted his legs. His cock was growing in his trousers, pressing against the material. Ilya saw it, his eyes unmistakeable on Nikolai's groin. He folded his arms, his expression disgusted, but Nikolai suspected that his balls were hanging heavier, filling with seed.

Nikolai grinned. "It is not my fault you cannot do better."

Ilya's arms tightened, his teeth clenched. He threw his bottle at Nikolai. Nikolai ducked. The bottle struck the wall behind his head, not shattering but spilling beer everywhere. Lightning flashed outside.

Nikolai glowered back at Ilya.

"Always with violence. That is your way, isn't it, Ilya? You know Goran? The man who borrowed money from his ever so benevolent boss? What about his broken arm? Perhaps it is your own ways you need to check, not mine."

Grabbing Nikolai by his shirt collar, Ilya hauled him to his feet. "You stop what you are doing."

Nikolai was so close he could have spat at Ilya. Instead, he leaned forward, and began to caress Ilya's mouth with his lips and tongue. He pressed his body against Ilya, who stood frozen, his mouth hardly moving under Nikolai's attention. Then Nikolai pulled back and whispered,

"Make me."

The thunder rolled again. Nikolai's chest heaved. Ilya's blue eyes became electric, and he began to pull off Nikolai's clothes. Nikolai felt liberated from their confines, enthralled as he did the same to Ilya, revealing his powerful body. Their clothes fell to the floor—there was a clunk as the little bottle of oil hit the carpet—and Ilya's mouth was all over Nikolai's neck.

Ilya shoved Nikolai onto the bed and leapt on top of him. He ground their hips together. His large cock rubbed against Nikolai's slender one, a hot friction that made Nikolai's body tense, for he would not lose himself under Ilya, would not give in, but the sensation was incredible.

"Make me," Nikolai repeated, craning up, rolling his hips as he did so.

Ilya pushed him down again. Nikolai laughed, more turned on by Ilya's forcefulness than he'd realised as Ilya glared at him. Ilya stood and turned away. Nikolai frowned, wondering what Ilya was up to, until he saw Ilya bend to the floor and rise again holding both the beer bottle and the bottle of oil.

Then Ilya emptied the beer bottle, and Nikolai knew his intention.

Nikolai began to dart away. But Ilya only had to press his chest down and trap his thighs with his own to stop him. Ilya placed the bottle next to them and spread Nikolai's legs. He lifted Nikolai's rear up, propping it on his knees, making Nikolai lock his legs around Ilya's waist.

Ilya opened the bottle of oil, poured it onto his fingers. He smeared the oil onto Nikolai's hole for only a few seconds, before inserting two long, fat fingers.

There was less pain than the last time, but only just.

Nikolai flung his head back, moaning. Ilya savagely crooked his fingers around. He quickly found a tender place and rubbed it without mercy.

Nikolai whimpered; he saw Ilya's huge cock growing. He wanted to beg, oh he wanted to, but he wouldn't. He'd wait for all of Ilya's punishment. He could hear, under his the nonsensical murmurings, the desire to beg for more, to want to be punished for his actions. And he knew Ilya would punish him with everything he had.

Nikolai tried to take hold of his own cock, but Ilya smacked his hands away at every attempt. Nikolai swore and tried to fight so he could just give himself some relief, but Ilya made it impossible. And when he wouldn't stop fighting, Ilya withdrew his fingers, picked up the bottle, and slid the neck all the way into Nikolai before Nikolai could even protest.

"You bastard," Nikolai said, teeth clenched, but Ilya cranked the bottle upwards so the rim hit that perfect spot. Nikolai gasped. Thunder struck again, closer than before, and another flash of lightning filled the room with brief, stark brilliance.

The bottle was cool, the glass unyielding. It took all of Nikolai's strength not to try and slide along its length, to feel more of it; he would not show Ilya he found it at all arousing.

Ilya worked his hand like a lever, as if he were pumping water. Each press made Nikolai pant, and he wanted more, his body twitching with each probe.

Above him, Ilya smiled. "You will stop stealing my workers?"

Nikolai wouldn't say yes. Not yet. He gave Ilya a hazy look, and only growled quietly.

Ilya jammed the bottle in as deep as he could. Nikolai winced, and Ilya said in a vicious whisper, "Have it your way."

He yanked the bottle out and threw it to the ground. Ilya grabbed Nikolai's body and hauled him onto his knees. Nikolai almost bounced on the mattress. He tried to drag himself away, but Ilya encircled his waist with one powerful arm.

As much as the bottle had stretched him, Nikolai had forgotten how huge Ilya was. Ilya, chuckling darkly, dripped more oil against Nikolai, then took his time as he urged the head of his cock against Nikolai's hole. And slowly, aching movement by aching movement, Ilya pushed his cock all the way into Nikolai.

Nikolai mewled, feeling full, spread apart by Ilya's cock. Ilya wrapped his body around Nikolai, trapping him. He took Nikolai's cock and balls entirely in his hand, not pumping, just squeezing, holding. Ensnared in Ilya's grasp, completely in his power, Nikolai succumbed to washes of pleasure. With Ilya hunched over him, hips thrusting his cock into Nikolai, it was as if his whole body was swollen, throbbing, like a giant cock himself, meant for nothing but fucking and harsh strokes, or fierce bites and slaps.

Nikolai felt Ilya's grip change. His arms left Nikolai's stomach and instead he grabbed his shoulders. Rather than thrusting himself, he began to pull Nikolai against him. Nikolai felt like a rag doll, flopping back and forth on Ilya, letting himself be impaled over and over again.

Ilya's clutch grew hard, almost bruising. Nikolai hissed, and went to swat the hands away, loosen the grip... when he saw a pair of talons digging into each shoulder. Clawing into his skin like a hawk. Nikolai would have shuddered if his body was not being pummelled. He tried to pull away, but the talons tore like nails, pinning him to the spot. This new pain was excruciating, and as Ilya thrust deeper and harder, the claws began to cut. Nikolai screamed as his skin broke; he saw his blood drip down onto the bed.

Did Ilya not *see*? Maybe not, for Ilya grunted and came. He withdrew sharply and let his seed splatter against Nikolai's hole and buttocks. Beneath Ilya, Nikolai whimpered. How could Ilya not see this? Ilya was violent but never so cruel... what the hell *was* he? And all the while, as Nikolai desperately tried to ignore the pain, he bit back his desire to beg for release. He didn't need to come, he told himself.

Until Ilya reached around, and took the stiff cock and balls in his hand again. It was a hand, not talons, but Nikolai still jerked to the touch.

"You will stop stealing my workers?" Ilya asked.

Nikolai gritted his teeth.

But with one squeeze from Ilya, and a clutch from the talons, Nikolai screamed, "Yes!"

Ilya, only taking a couple of hard pumps, made Nikolai spurt all he had into Ilya's hand. Nikolai's tortured body rocked with the orgasm, his vision swam, and he tumbled to the bed when Ilya dropped him without care. He shivered as the talons left his shoulders.

Ilya smeared the mixture of their spunk over Nikolai's stomach, chest and face. Nikolai tensed, but saw to his amazement that there was no blood on Ilya's hands, though his shoulders still stung from the tearing. Ilya dressed quickly and left, closing the door with a slam. At the same time, a loud clap of thunder shook the windows.

Nikolai tentatively brushed his shoulders. To his shock and relief there were no open wounds, though it felt as if his skin had been ripped. No blood on the sheets, either.

Nikolai lay on the bed, pulling the sheets around him. As the thunder outside swept into the distance, he felt small, quite alone as the rain began a gentle patter. He tried not to think about those terrible talons and what they had meant. For he had felt them in his skin as sure as he had felt Ilya's cock inside him.

Ilya

Ilya stroked his beard as he drove back to town, back to his house on the hill. He was satisfied with the outcome of their meeting, but would it be the last time he would have to punish Nikolai? It gave him pause, as he locked the door of his Mustang in the garage; a tiny thrill ran through him to consider the possibility. The way Nikolai's body had drawn out his orgasm... it was unlike anything else he experienced. Even with Dobrana he had never felt such a surge. The power that ran through him, almost all-consuming... he was sure there were moments that he was not himself. Like he became some kind of ravaging beast. Ilya knew well his own temper, the red rushes of rage that sometimes flooded his being. Yet he'd never forgotten himself, lost himself in the moment. With Nikolai... he shuddered, and left the garage.

Inside, Dobrana was on the floor with the youngest child playing with building blocks, while the other two were on the couch, reading like good children. Unnoticed at first, Ilya smiled on the scene. His perfect brood, and another to join them later that year. Dobrana had said she would give him many children. Ilya was glad for that, and glad to for the many proofs of his virility. They were a well-matched couple.

Dobrana looked up from the floor and beamed at him. Ilya nodded, but he did not go to her for a kiss. Instead, he went to the bathroom to wash away the scent of Nikolai.

As he showered, he thought how he made love to Dobrana, the gentleness of it, how easy it was. Not the sharp fucking he'd given Nikolai. Not the digging of his fingers into Nikolai's shoulders...

Ilya's hands froze on his body. He drew them out to look at them, to see his fingers and nails. In the midst of it, he'd felt something else. The power of rearing up over Nikolai, of having him in his control: yes, that was present, but something more too.

An image flashed through his mind. His hands as talons? No. He must have only dreamed that, imagined it. What kind of imagining was it, though?

He looked again. There was no blood under his nails. Only the lingering sense that Nikolai had been under his command.

Ilya shook himself and turned off the water. This was ridiculous to even consider. He was a man of reason and the modern world: superstition was for the weak-minded and backward looking. Beast and giant talons. How preposterous.

Centuries ago...

Veles continued his frantic flight, ducking and weaving through streets and towns. Every so often he would pause at a hiding place, but Perun's eyes were sharp and always found him. Perun flung down his stone arrows. Lightning blazed where those arrows struck.

"Gromovnik!" the people cried, for though his form was not visible to them, they knew his anger and his power.

"The great dragon..." others whispered, knowing that where each bolt fell, Veles had been.

There was a moment's relief for Veles as he hid behind a hedge. He heard Perun's chariot above him, but Perun had not yet seen Veles. Veles leered, content for a time.

Until he overheard a young man speak.

"He chases Veles... have we displeased them both?" the young man asked, his voice frightened.

Veles peered his head above the hedge, enough to see the young man with his arm around a old woman's hunched back, guiding her, trying to run to be out of the storm. But they could not move fast for her back and her hobbled legs. Rain drenched their clothes and matted their hair to their faces.

"The gods are always fickle," the old woman said, her face hardened by the harsh lashes of living. "And we are at their mercy."

On hearing this, Veles curled behind his hedge, stung and moved by their words. This merry chase was bringing destruction, and it was leaving the people desperate.

Veles wondered how much longer he could run.

He eyed Perun in the sky, who had not yet spotted him. Veles made his choice and reared up. He shot back into the air, turning to face Perun.

"Come get me."

And he flew before the next bolt could strike him.

Chapter 4
Cloud

Croatia - one month ago

Ilya

As he drank a glass of cool cherry nectar, Ilya was content. There was a gentle shower of rain falling, just enough to cool the town's sweltering heat. He stood on his large covered balcony, casting his eyes across the town.

He was wearing shorts. He had been on a long run, the kind he only took when Dobrana and the children—all seven of them—were away. They were with his wife's sister and his only duty was to his work and to himself. He had not quite escaped the heavy drops of water before getting indoors. He wore no shirt, and the light rain had mingled with his sweat and begun making droplets in his beard. His body was filled with the satisfying ache of exertion, both tired and energised.

Ilya took another sip of the nectar. This was *his* town: after all he had done for it, he had earned the right to call it that. Since his father had died seven years ago—and after he had grieved—he had at last become president of the chamber of commerce. The factory was entirely his. He also inherited his father's nickname, so he was now the true Thunderer. Not the one only in waiting, creating his small storms, but able to cast his power where it was needed. From where he stood he felt as if he could scoop the whole town up in his arms and embrace it.

The rain began to fall harder. Steady at first, then faster and faster.

It was a beating rhythm, a quickening pace, and it created a stirring in Ilya's belly. His loins began to tense and tingle. Without any prompting from his hand — or from images floating from his own mind, as the rain beat heavier and faster — Ilya's cock hardened.

Ilya dropped his glass. It shattered as Ilya gripped the railing in front of him, as he breathed deeply, trying to will his cock soft again. Why this, why now? But the rain did not cease and his arousal intensified.

Ilya grabbed the underside of his balls. They were like two stones, his cock like the trunk of a tree. He squeezed the whole lot, wanting it covered and free all at once, but the friction of the material and his hand gave no pleasure. Even when he slipped his hand under his shorts, skin to skin, his cock felt numb. Ilya could have roared in frustration. He wanted to stroke himself to climax now. Not later in the bath, nor in bed, but now. Even Dobrana had she been there would not have been able to satisfy this feeling. His body insisted on it, demanded it, wanted it as much as the hot summer earth must have begged for the pouring rain.

His body knew — even as his mind fought it and he cursed himself — exactly how to fix it.

Ilya pulled on sweat pants and a t-shirt and charged out to his Mustang. The wheels spun hard, water splashing the side of the car as Ilya sped into town, into the docks, and strode into Nikolai's office building. He was forced to push employees aside, one man doubling over, before he kicked open the door to Nikolai's office.

Soaking, he stood before Nikolai, who looked up from his work as if Ilya's entrance was expected. A pulse beat through Ilya's cock. He clamped his jaw, hoping to quell it. Nikolai's eyes cast down to his groin and a lascivious smile crossed his face. *Oh, how typical!* Ilya thought, yet without that smile he may have turned and left. He could not ignore that he wanted this from Nikolai, and Nikolai wanted it from him.

God, is this really what I am? Ilya remembered the thrill of Nikolai bent to his will, Nikolai on his knees, Nikolai's cock hard under his clutching hand. Another flush through his groin. *Yes*, he thought, his stomach sinking. *This is what I am.*

Nikolai stood. He sauntered out from behind his desk, twirling the gold chain at his neck around his fingers.

"You have not come to lecture me on my business practices, I see."

Nikolai moved too slowly; Ilya charged at him, grabbed Nikolai's shoulders, and forced him onto his knees. He tugged down his sweat pants just enough, and pressed his cock to Nikolai's face.

"Take it," he said.

Nikolai peered up at Ilya, and said in the sweetest, stickiest voice, "Make me."

Blood rushed down Ilya's cock. The head leaked with a drop of pre-come, and Ilya grabbed a fist-full of Nikolai's hair and shoved him again.

"Suck!"

Nikolai laughed, but he complied, taking Ilya's cock with an obliging yet cheeky wink.

Nikolai's hot, wet mouth was a blessed relief. Ilya groaned, his fingers almost tenderly brushing Nikolai's cheek as Nikolai sucked and sucked. Nikolai's head bobbed up and down on Ilya's cock. Ilya groaned as his cock brushed against the back of Nikolai's throat. Ilya wanted to shove it all the way down his neck, deep into Nikolai, wanted him to take everything he had, swallow him fully. He rolled his hips, urging his cock down more and more.

Nikolai drew back, spittle lingering like string on his lips and the head of Ilya's cock. Ilya clutched Nikolai's hair, jerking his head back so he had to look up at Ilya.

Ilya gritted his teeth. "I didn't say stop."

A dark smile played on Nikolai's lips. He puckered them, kissing the head of Ilya's cock once. Ilya sighed at the gentleness he knew wouldn't last. Outside thunder clapped, accompanied with a lightning flash. Suddenly, the lights in the office went out. The workers cried out in surprise, the sound ringing through the walls. Ilya gasped, eyes out scanning the window as Nikolai licked his still rock-hard dick. Another flash of lightning, another lick. Ilya's eyes cast down and he froze.

Nikolai's tongue was now forked and slender. It flickered along Ilya's shaft, underneath to his balls. His teeth too, before Ilya's eyes, began to grow, until a pair of fangs rested on either side of his cock.

Panic grew in Ilya's chest. Another thunder clap sounded. It shook the building. More gasps from the workers, and this time from Ilya too. The creature that Nikolai was becoming... Ilya should have run, should have thrown Nikolai away, or even killed him. But the moving tongue and the gliding of the fangs rooted Ilya to the spot.

Nikolai drew back from Ilya's cock and laughed. Ilya felt like a hunted animal succumbing to its predator. As if reading his fears, Nikolai grasped Ilya's hips and pushed him on his back. Ilya stared into Nikolai's now glowing golden eyes, paralysed as Nikolai reared up over him, cobra-like, tongue flicking out, almost hissing.

Then Nikolai threw himself over Ilya's body and attacked him with his hands and mouth.

Ilya could do nothing but lie in frozen horror as Nikolai ravaged him, tearing his t-shirt and sweat pants. Nikolai licked his muscles, bit Ilya's nipples hard. He suckled his balls, and roamed all over with his fangs and nails. Ilya wanted to scream as Nikolai found each part of him that reacted either with pleasure or pain, but the sounds were trapped in his throat like an eagle caught in jesses. Nikolai pinned Ilya down — as if terror was not enough to bind Ilya — winding around his arms and legs. It was the undulating coils and squeezes of a snake; fang-like bites appeared on his body. He quavered in and out of the lightning — sometimes it was him, sometimes it was green scales and long, throttling grasps. The snake that Nikolai had become laughed, and that terrible head shot down to Ilya's cock, taking all of it in that hideous mouth. Ilya's felt his stomach turn, even as his cock was sucked with a brutal wetness.

Ilya came, his orgasm dragged from him as if he was tied to a speeding car. Nikolai swallowed most of it, but pulled back at the last, some of it splashing on his chin. He met Ilya's eyes. Again, he chuckled. Ilya stared back, horrified and still aroused all at once.

A flash of lightning, another thunder clap and Ilya found his strength. He pushed away from Nikolai and slammed the door behind him. The end of the storm beat down on him as he sped home, but was a light drizzle when he stumbled into his house.

He locked himself in the bathroom. His body felt as if it had been torn to pieces. But when he looked in the mirror, he only saw his body. No marks. No blood.

Ilya shuddered, brushing his fingers on the perceived wounds.

He thought of the fangs, the forked tongue, Nikolai's glowing eyes. What had Nikolai, in that moment, become? Had Ilya simply imagined it? As he'd imagined...

His eyes dropped to his nails. He thought about the hotel room ten years ago, about Nikolai screaming under his hands, his... talons. And now he had been under a striking mouth and a long body that had threatened to suffocate him. Nikolai would not have hesitated to do so.

Ilya's knees gave in, and he slid down the tiled wall to the bathroom floor. What kind of... thing... was he? And if Ilya was that, then what in all of heaven was Nikolai?

Nikolai

In his office, Nikolai guided his hand on his cock, smiling and licking his lips.

Oh that surge of power! He could still taste it; it hung on his tongue like the taste of Ilya's cock. It had tasted like rain and fresh cut grass. It had filled his mouth entirely. Nikolai must have made a perfect 'O' with his lips it was so large. Ilya's cock was like the perfect hunk of meat: tasty, succulent, it created a craving akin to a deep hunger in Nikolai's stomach. The thought of swallowing Ilya whole, consuming him entirely starting with his delicious big cock, had made Nikolai suck with a ferocious wildness. He would have all of Ilya, every last inch of him. He'd grazed his teeth a little along the length, earning a gasp from Ilya. Oh yes, Nikolai had had him perfectly. He'd taken Ilya's balls in hand and ground them together like boulders.

The moment he'd sensed his tongue was something else, he'd almost panicked, gulping hard. But the terrified brightness of Ilya's eyes had said it all: Ilya was more frightened than he. That had tasted better than any cock in his mouth.

Stroking himself, Nikolai thought on how he'd ridden the power, turned and twisted with its rolling force. The sensation of his teeth growing, his features smoothing back. Controlled it, though, for to give in to it would not do; he had to watch Ilya's fear beneath him, had to wound him. Such vengeance it was, the years since Ilya had—almost—torn him to shreds.

Now cupping his balls, Nikolai recalled what he'd done to Ilya's body, how he'd enjoyed hearing his expression of agony entwined with pleasure. Nikolai stroked and squeezed, picturing the man beneath him like a terrified goat. *Yes*, he'd thought, *you can suffer as I have under you.* A thought as delicious as Ilya's hot come that he'd milked with glee.

His own orgasm was not far off. Hearing the sounds of the warehouse, workers talking, the whir of forklifts and moving trucks, Nikolai stalled, sinking his teeth into his lower lip, noting that they were his own once more. His own, as if before he was becoming someone—or something—else. A frightening prospect, but Ilya he knew, so conventional in his thinking, would be more frightened than him.

Whoever, whatever he and Ilya were did not matter. Nikolai increased his rhythm, driving himself to the brink. What mattered was that on most days Ilya could use his size, his pomposity, his brute force to win. But not today. Today, Nikolai knew with lightning clarity as he came, the victory had been his.

Centuries ago...

Perun threw another bolt. He almost shouted with victory, but the lightning only singed the tail of the dragon. Veles kept the same straight track through the sky, but each time Perun came closer to him, Veles would be just out of reach.

Perun snarled. The buck goat pulling his chariot looked back at him, as if to say he could work no harder than he already was. Perun saw that his chariot was cumbersome. He would not catch Veles in it, no matter how keen or how much he drove the goat.

His eagle nipped his ear. Perun turned to it. The eagle ruffled its feathers up and rose on one foot, an itching eagerness, only held back by Perun's will.

"Yes," he said, stroking the eagle. "Of course."

Perun removed his axe and held his gloved hand aloft. The eagle took flight, wings spreading wide and mighty. Then Perun leapt off his chariot, up towards the eagle, before he began to fall. The air flapped on his cloak as he plunged to the earth. The eagle dove, like aiming for prey, and with a shriek pierced Perun's chest. Perun screamed. The eagle burrowed into his body, merging with it, becoming him... and Perun ceased falling. Now he could grasp the air, move with it, be part of it. His arms were now wings, and he beat them wildly, and once again began his pursuit of Veles.

Veles turned once, smiling. But Perun saw the sinewy reptilian lips quiver, and Veles's eyes grow wider, attempting to suggest combat but really serving as a mark of growing fear. Perun saw a smile that was hesitant, trying to mask fear. And Perun gained his distance on him. They kept flying and diving, weaving around mountaintops, through clouds, until they were over a lake. Perun was right on Veles' tail. Veles cried out and ducked away, but Perun curved his wings to match him. They were flying in tandem now.

It was time. Perun reached for Veles, talons almost breaking with the strain. He was almost within his grasp. Only a little further...

Croatia - three days ago

One would think, Ilya seethed, *that a half open shirt was not appropriate for a meeting of the chamber of commerce.* Nikolai clearly disagreed, practically inviting gazes as he brushed his fingers down his chest that was boyishly slim and girlishly enticing.

Could no one else see what a reptile he was? Could they not see the fangs in his mouth, that beneath that smooth chest were green, slippery scales? No. No one saw anything but Nikolai the cunning businessman with some eccentricities and a taste for stocky men. The fools!

But Ilya had no strength to point this out. Since their last — encounter — Ilya had wandered through work and home and town with a listless step, unfocussed, as if a fog drenched in sleeping draughts had fallen over him. Dobrana had demanded to know what was wrong, threatening to take the children away if he failed to give them and her the attention they deserved. Worse though, a quiet rumour had spread that he and Nikolai had fought, that their rivalry had come to physical blows and Nikolai had won.

Ilya was only grateful that the true nature of their battle had remained secret. All the rest being true, however, made him feel lower than he'd ever been.

Normally he'd chair these meetings, but today he'd waved everything to the secretary, a fastidious middle-aged man with the kind of attention to detail Ilya did not possess. It was a good working relationship in that regard.

The secretary cleared his throat. "We have before us applications for new businesses in town. As usual the town council has allowed us to vet the applications, and we shall consider each of them in turn. This meeting shall be used to discuss them, and we will vote at the next one."

They went through the applications. Ilya flipped the pages over. The other members offered their opinions, then eyed him for guidance, but he found himself murmuring things like, "Your view is quite correct," or, "That sounds reasonable." He had little energy to do otherwise. He paid no heed to the uncertain glances the men exchanged — and especially not to Nikolai's smirking. They could surely make decisions without his views from time to time.

When they came to the last one, he started to nod, when the secretary said,

"Um… Ilya, have you read this one carefully?"

Ilya looked at his secretary askance for questioning his capacity to read. The secretary though seemed genuinely concerned.

Ilya sighed. "Which one?"

"The one from Mishka Samovic? For his club?"

Ilya held the paper up, peering at it, the words not registering. "What is the nature of the club?"

The secretary coughed. "It is, ah… a sex club, Ilya."

Chapter 5

Storm

The black ink suddenly burned on the page, bright as suns. Clarity came to Ilya like a flash of lightning. No. No, this would not do in his town at all. And this Mishka wanted it on the promenade? Right where everyone could see it! Ilya would not let this happen.

A low chuckle came from Ilya's left. He swerved his eyes to Nikolai, who leaned back in his chair, flicking his pen around his fingers.

"And what is your opinion of this club, Nikolai?"

"Oh, I'm all in favour of it."

Ilya stared at Nikolai. "It would compete with your own nightclub."

"I welcome a battle. It makes one stronger." Nikolai licked his lower lip, and Ilya suspected had they been alone he would have winked too.

Ilya straightened his back, the vigour returning after its month-long absence. "Well, I'm sure that no one else agrees with you." He turned to the rest of the chamber. "Am I right?"

The secretary and two others nodded emphatically. Four more, on the other hand, shifted in their seats or began to play with their papers. Ilya glared at the one closest to him.

"Am I right?" he repeated.

The man shrugged. "Well, Ilya... I can see the merits in such a club. We do get all kinds of visitors here, and our tourism industry is growing rapidly."

"Yes," one said. "I agree. It... fills a gap, so to speak."

"Is it not filled by Nikolai's club?" Ilya said through his teeth.

The third piped up. "I believe this one will cater to more specific

153

interests…" His voice trailed off as Ilya glared, not wishing to hear anything about those 'specific interests.'

"I agree that we need to concentrate on the tourist industry," Ilya said. "But are we looking to attract perverts!"

All eyes shifted to Nikolai, who only grinned as if pervert was a compliment.

"There is money to be made from sex," Nikolai said. "There always has been."

If Ilya could have, he'd have launched himself across the table and slapped Nikolai across the face.

They argued for sometime. Or rather, Ilya and his supporters made their emphatic case, while the others slipped and slid, bleating about money and attracting more people. *Have they lost the point about principles!* Ilya thought. With a vote of five to four, the application would be accepted. He expected this from Nikolai, but not the others.

Ilya smacked his fist on the table. "This is getting us nowhere. We are not voting today, so this will give all of us," he cast his eyes across those who supported the application, "time to reconsider our positions."

The members of the chamber glanced at each other, but there was, as far as Ilya could see, no shift in them at all.

The meeting continued, and when it was done the members packed up and started to leave. Nikolai paused at the door to chat with one of his fellow supporters. He occasionally glanced back at Ilya with an expression of assured victory.

Ilya beckoned the secretary down so to speak to him in a low whisper. "Find out what's going on. Those men would not defy me but for very good reason."

The secretary nodded. "Of course."

Ilya met Nikolai's eyes again. Nikolai ran his tongue over his teeth and slinked away. Ilya suppressed a flinch, but for the first time in a month, his anger had begun to boil again.

Croatia - present day...

Nikolai

When Nikolai had hired Risto, it was as much for his body, taut with muscle, as it was for his ability to protect Nikolai. That he wasn't averse to fucking Nikolai on occasion was a rather tasty bonus.

But the sex was never like it had been with Ilya. Because unlike the others to whom he'd happily given himself over to be dominated, he wanted to beat Ilya at this game. He had once, and he was determined that he would again.

Ilya had broken into Nikolai's house in his threatening way, flung his accusations at Nikolai about the bribes. Of course they had been true and Nikolai did not feel the slightest guilt. Besides, he had mostly accepted them in order to see how Ilya would react. And Ilya had reacted beautifully, looking hilarious standing on his moral high ground, trying to coax Nikolai every way he knew. Nikolai had goaded, teased, flirted, watching Ilya's fury grow. The last straw had come when Ilya demanded that Nikolai obey him. How dare he?

Nikolai leapt to his feet. "Make me."

Ilya's face darkened. Nikolai saw in it his rage and desire, so different and yet one and the same.

Then Ilya breathed, "I will."

Their bodies smashed together like the claps of thunder outside.

Ilya clasped Nikolai's buttocks, digging his fingers in deeply. Nikolai moaned, and tugged down on Ilya's beard until he screamed.

Ilya pulled back just an inch from Nikolai.

"Stop taking the money from Mishka," he whispered against Nikolai's mouth.

Nikolai rolled his hips, his cock rubbing against Ilya's thighs. He sniggered, and whispered back,

"No."

Ilya pushed Nikolai to the floor. Nikolai winced as lightning flashed through the room.

Ilya towered above him. "Why do you keep disobeying me?"

"I am not yours to control."

"You will hurt the town if you continue with your ways."

Nikolai narrowed his eyes, glaring up at Ilya. "This is not to protect the town. This is for your pride!"

Ilya roared, and thunder shook the house. He grabbed Nikolai's collar, hauled him off his feet, bringing them nose-to-nose.

"Nikolai, you will make me do this?"

Nikolai spat in Ilya's face. The gob hit Ilya's cheek, sat like a wet blob.

"Do your worst."

Lightning filled the room. Ilya reached between Nikolai's legs, and twisted...

...While above the lake, Perun made his final stretch, and at last, he snagged Veles' scales.

Nikolai cried out, beat back at Ilya, the pain pure and intense... *and Veles screamed as Perun's talons tore as his scales.*

Ilya latched his mouth onto Nikolai's throat. Nikolai trembled, the searing hot mouth demanding. His engorged erection grew in Ilya's hand.

Ilya muttered against his neck, "You've always been a slut."

Perun twisted Veles to face him. "You will not escape me."

With Ilya's hand clawing at him, Nikolai remembered being helpless beneath Ilya's talons. A pulse of fear transmuted to ferocious rage, and he recalled his reptilian self. This time, when the power ran through him, he welcomed it and let it do as it will.

Nikolai hissed, and the change began.

Ilya... and Nikolai

Ilya gasped. Nikolai's pupils elongated, eyes glowed gold. Ilya stared into those eyes, remembering their sinister seductive gaze in the office. Now, seeing their enraged heat, all the justification of his hatred for Nikolai scorched through his body.

"Snake," Ilya said.

"Dragon," Perun said.

"Yes." Nikolai's voice was not his own.

Nikolai's body began to mould against his like molten clay. Ilya tried to keep his hold, but because of Nikolai's shifting form, his hands could not hold the scales that were sliding away from him...

Veles reeled his body, turning this way and that, but Perun dug his claws in deeper. Then Veles, seeing Perun's sleek feathers, shot upwards, and began...

...to coil around him.

Nikolai saw the horror in Ilya's face, knowing he was being crushed in Nikolai's grip. Nikolai arched around to lick Ilya's cheek, mockingly. The bastard would not win this time. Not this time!

Ilya stood paralysed, fearing for a moment that his life would be crushed out of him. Something though boiled in his chest, and he knew. There had always been a monster waiting beneath his skin. He had long denied it, even fought it. Now, as Nikolai threatened to squeeze him to death, incandescent rage overtook him. An ancient rage he could not ignore, and he knew to defeat Nikolai he must embrace it.

Ilya's beard receded. Coppery feathers ruffled down his chest. His mouth and nose merged and extend, and a giant beak formed as eagle eyes blinked into existence.

And Perun beat his wings as Veles the dragon tried to ensnare him in a hold. He dug his claws in harder...

...and Ilya's hands became talons. They turned on Nikolai, hooking into his scales. Nikolai threw his head back with a loud hissing cry. He curled his neck back and struck Ilya's feathery chest, sinking his fangs in. But as he did so he loosened his grip and Ilya's newly formed wings beat, forcing Nikolai to unfurl from him.

Thunder rocked the whole house, and with the next burst of lightning, the roof opened up. Rain poured into the green room, covering both of them as they both struck at each other, the assault beginning anew.

With his enormous claws, Ilya grabbed for Nikolai. They caught the snake, and Ilya lifted his wings, carrying them both into the air. Nikolai hissed and thrashed against Ilya, fangs glinting in the lightning. Ilya now began to peck, and Nikolai twisted and rolled, each strike sending a sharp pain through his whole body. There was no pleasure now: only the battle, only the fight.

Nikolai retaliated...

Veles sunk his fangs into Perun's flesh...

...and Ilya shrieked. The snake was latched onto him, using his body as leverage to once again try and coil around him. Ilya beat his wings and avoided Nikolai.

They drew higher in the air, closer to the roaring thunder and the lightning infected clouds. As did Perun and Veles. Beneath them, the town, the land, all that lay in their domain and power bore the brunt of the beating rain and rocking thunder, the lightning strikes and the howling winds. In the turbulent air they fought and turned and rolled. Ilya and Nikolai, Perun and Veles.

At last Perun and Ilya delivered a final mighty blow to the dragon and the snake's head. Nikolai and Veles screamed, and they fell, coiling and twirling through the thunderous sky. Veles hit the water with a mighty splash, and with a heavy thump Nikolai landed onto his carpet.

The roof closed in again. Ilya, now himself once more, stood over Nikolai's body. Their shirts were torn. Both of them were soaked with rain, as was the whole jungle of a room. Nikolai's eyes were open, but he wasn't moving, except for a small rise and fall of his chest.

"Perun…" he breathed.

Ilya swallowed. "Veles."

The words, their true names, hung heavy in the wet air.

Nikolai spoke again with a low croak but steady certainty. "This is what we always have been."

Ilya trembled, but only for a moment. He shook it off and said, "Yes. Always."

Nikolai grinned. "You accept it at last."

Nikolai tried to lift himself up, but collapsed back down. No, he'd wait a little longer. He'd had dragon's wings once and he would find them again. He remembered the fields and the sea below him, riding the air as the windsurfers did the waves. And he remembered the dark place, his home in the underworld in the roots of a great tree.

"How fitting," he said, and smiled.

Ilya frowned. "You always knew?"

"Not everything… but there was always more to us than you ever wanted to know, Perun."

Ilya crouched, flexing his fingers that were no longer talons, recalling how they felt reaching and straining for the dragon-snake, the sensation of lightning in his hands, the thunder — actual thunder —

boiling in the sky behind him. This was him, this ancient god. A rare sensation of humility settled over him. He'd always known he had a duty to fill in this world, and there was none heavier than this.

But he was no longer riding a chariot in the clouds. Nikolai lying before him was a man, not a dragon.

He bent down to Nikolai's ear. "Cease your mischief, and refuse Mishka's money."

Ilya stood and started to leave, when Nikolai said,

"You have not won, Perun... Ilya..."

Or whatever we should call ourselves now.

Ilya turned back, meeting Nikolai's eyes. "But I have, Nikolai... Veles... as I always will."

Nikolai laughed, then winced, for laughter hurt his chest. "So you say, Gromovnik. So you say."

Ilya left Nikolai on the floor. He walked slowly back to his Mustang, holding himself like royal china: fragile but filled with dignity. Outside, the thunderstorm had rocked the harbour. There was no one around, but now — with only the lightest of rains — the town was quiet, peaceful even.

Nikolai eventually stood with a shaky step. He went to check on Risto and to find Mishka's phone number.

Meanwhile, Veles burrowed into the earth beneath the lake. He slunk through the soil, past the dirt and the worms, until once again he was back at his the oak tree. The roots shifted a little, and Veles knew that Perun was perching on the branches above.

Perun puffed up his feathers, proud that at last his task was accomplished, and bellowed in a grand voice, "You go to the earth and you stay there!"

Veles sniggered. He coiled around himself, around the roots of the great tree. His wounds gaped with each breath. It would take some time for the bites and the cuts to heal, for his spent essence to grow inside him once more. How long before he emerged again he did not know, but surely he would.

And the fight would begin anew.

As it always had. As it always would.

If you enjoyed this story, you can sign up for a free membership at
ForbiddenFiction.com and discuss it with other readers
and the author at the *Gods Among Men* story page
at http://forbiddenfiction.com/story/JB1-1.000192.

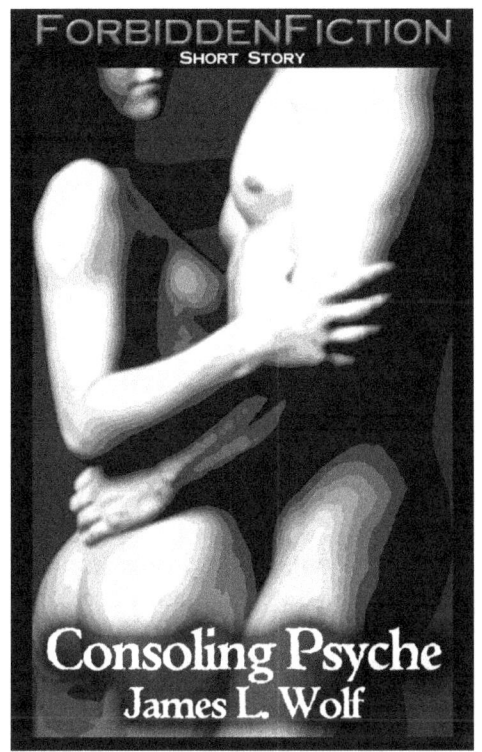

Consoling Psyche

James L. Wolf

James L. Wolf has visited Harbin Hot Springs many times, both before and after transition. Thus, James might be one of the few guys to truly understand that bizarre, funky smell inside the women's changing room at Harbin. He is both an author and story editor at Forbidden Fiction.

Consoling Psyche

Carrie removed her top and began undoing her bra. "Huh. I'll bet you anything he has Narcissistic Personality Disorder."

Leah hunkered down, feeling self conscious. The wooden bench was damp beneath her bare buttocks. The women's changing room at Harbin Hot Springs had a particular sharp odor, as if the sulfur springs, fig trees and natural personal care products of a hundred New Age women had melded into permanent perfume. Leah realized her face hurt. It figured; she'd been crying so much.

"Yeah," she replied softly.

"Come on, Leah." Carrie didn't tell her to snap out of it, but her expression said it all. After all, they were on vacation. Year one of their psychology graduate program was finished — at last! — and they were here to relax and laugh it off. She was supposed to get with the program.

Not that Erik had cared about vacation when he broke up with her last night in the most passive-aggressive manner possible: he'd dumped her by text message. It was such an adolescent thing to do, but Erik was in his thirties, a fourth year student in the program. He was brilliant. Which made her what? Brilliant's disposable snot rag.

Leah forced a smile to her face. It felt ghastly. "Okay, let's go soak."

They stepped outdoors. Even through the shroud of her depressed emotional state, Leah breathed in the sunlight, her shoulders relaxing. It felt weird to be walking around naked with other women and men, also naked. Yet it felt liberating. As they made their way to the soaking pool, the fig trees overhead rustled overhead. Leah had loved this pool the instant she'd seen it, earlier today. She loved the wrought-iron dragons that were the railings of the pool, the faded blue mural on the plaster wall at one end, the feeling of peace as wind chimes tinkled. She settled into water up to her chin and closed her eyes.

There was movement at her side. A man and woman were trying very hard to remain still as they held one another, but Leah could tell by their movements that they were having intercourse. Completely against Harbin rules, of course. The man had a narrow, cerebral face and the angle of his shoulders reminded her of Erik....

Leah turned swiftly for the stairs, creating ripples all around her. Carrie, making friends with a group of women, glanced her way as she climbed out. Carrie probably thought she was going to visit the hottest pool, or even the cold dip. But Leah couldn't. She could hardly breathe right now.

Yet... where could she go? This was ridiculous. She was a calm, rational human being who was going to be a psychologist, damn it. She needed to think things through. Maybe she should get away from people. Right. Leah gathered her resolve, then retrieved her sarong from the changing room and strapped on her sandals. She would hike to that Tea House she'd seen on the Harbin map. The exercise would do her good.

Half an hour later—dusty, panting, scratching mosquito bites—Leah decided she'd been a fool. Now that she was alone, all she could think about was Erik. Hiking up dusty switchbacks didn't help, either. The thorny California weeds poking into the path were probably filled with ticks. Everything was horrible. She was weak; the pain was so bad that she wanted to die. Leah trembled as she crested another switchback. She was going slower and slower. Maybe she should turn right around and go back down the trail, accept herself as the failure she was.

There was a burst of noise from between the madrone trees and a man slammed onto the path, as if from nowhere. He wore colorful, Indonesian-print pants and massive harry boots that looked like sheepskin, though his sweaty torso was naked. After a second Leah realized that his fly was undone and his penis—prodigious and erect—was sticking straight out like a fishing pole. She shrank at the sight, shocked. He was singing loudly and off key to whatever was playing through bright orange, 1980s style headphones perched over his wild hair. He didn't even acknowledge her before harrying off into the forest, penis waggling freely, singing at the top of his lungs.

"Weird," Leah murmured to herself. She stared at his retreating back until the trees swallowed him again.

The path was easier to climb after that. At least the man had given her something to think about besides her own personal doomsday. As her shock wore off, Leah found herself laughing. He'd been so goofy looking. A real individual, California style. She wondered what her mother would say, then grinned. Her mother would undoubtedly worry that he was a pervert and a rapist. Well, he hadn't done anything to her and now he was gone.

The Tea House was disappointing. A destination that wasn't worth the hike, just a tiny round hut baking in the sun. Nothing inside but a few Tibetan prayer flags hanging from the walls. Maybe it would be a nice place to meditate if it weren't so hot. At least there was a view. Leah realized she'd been hoping for solace up here, some new vantage point, perhaps even enlightenment, pretentious as that was. Something. Something to erase Erik from her heart, where he smoldered like red-hot coals, destroying her from within.

Leah sank abruptly onto a nearby rock. Her head settled into her arms and she breathed hard. One tear ran down her face, then another. She didn't even have any Kleenex in her sarong. Leah sniffed and eyed the cliff's edge. By the sound of things, there was a river below. She might throw herself off the cliff. There were probably river rocks below that would break her body as they broke her fall...

A cacophony burst behind her and Leah startled. "Christ!" she said, looking over her shoulder.

It was the same man. He was trotting up the path toward the Tea House with an ancient but apparently functional boom box perched on his shoulder. It blasted music into the calm afternoon. She didn't recognize the tune but it sounded like ethnic world music. Greek, maybe? He paused at the sight of her, then turned down the stereo.

"Sorry," he offered with a half-cocked grin.

"Um. It's okay." It wasn't, but she smiled politely. His penis, she noted, was back in his pants. Thank god. She hadn't wanted to prove her mother right and be victimized, atop everything else.

He eyed her curiously. Leah realized he could see her tears. She

wiped her face with the edge of her sarong and looked away. She
wished he would just leave her to her misery. As if in perverse response to her thoughts, he tossed down the boom box and sat with a
poof of dirt beside the Tea House.

"Want to talk about it?" he offered after a minute.

Leah stared at him, taken back. "Talk about what?"

He raised a bushy eyebrow. "Sometimes it helps," he said with a
shrug. He had nice shoulders, she noticed. Not like Erik's.

"Um. Maybe I should go back now." She liked to keep an open
mind but this was just creepy. She was vulnerable and alone, and this
was a guy who ran around with his willy hanging out of his pants.

The man tilted his head and rested it gently on his outstretched
hand, for all the world like a psychologist himself. "Let me guess. He
was sleeping with your best friend? No, that's not it. He was definitely
having an affair with someone, but you feel it's all your fault, for some
reason. He must be a real piece of work, that guy." He rubbed his face
and snorted derisively. "What a shithead."

Leah stared. She couldn't help it. "Who are you, Sherlock Hol-
mes?" Maybe he was stalking her... except she'd never seen him in
her life.

His expression was sober. "He's not worth it, you know. You have
a lot to live for."

This was going too far. "Who are you?"

He grinned up at her as if she'd asked exactly the right question.
"Peter Adelphos Nebble, at your service. Esquire."

"You're a lawyer?"

"We can't all be psychologists," he noted, almost gently.

"Okay, that's it. Whatever you're doing, whoever you are, you
need to knock it off. It's just creepy." Despite her tone, some part of
her brain registered his smile. It was a great smile.

The man—Peter Adelphos Nebble—rose to his feet and stretched.
It was a long and supple stretch, lengthening his muscular chest.
"Well, if you feel like talking later tonight, I'll be around." Then he
turned and strode down the path, silent boom box in hand.

Leah waited five minutes until she was sure he was gone, then
hiked back down. She felt as if the world had slipped off its axis and
she had landed in another reality. It was too much. Rather than at-

tempt the pools again, Leah headed back to the campsite. The tent was now in the shade, fortunately. She washed dust off her legs in the nearest spigot—finding no ticks in the process—then crawled inside. Her sleeping bag was so soft. She was asleep before she knew it.

She awoke in the middle of the night. Carrie was snoring softly beside her. Leah hadn't even heard her come in. Well, she was wide awake now.

Without thinking, Leah unzipped the tent and stepped out. The stars and Milky Way swirls were bright, without light pollution. Even the moon was absent from the sky. Leah stared upward with awe until her body ached from lack of movement. The pools would be open, she realized. They never closed. Leah retrieved her flashlight and made her way down the silent path. Walking through the dark woods was frightening and electrifying, as if she had stepped back in time. Hell, she hadn't checked her messages or cell phone in hours. Of course, she didn't want to know if he'd sent another text....

Leah gasped. Her flashlight wavered as an enormous shape moved in the path before her. It was a doe. The doe stepped onward, graceful and not at all panicked by her presence. Even as she watched another doe slipped across the path, then another. They ignored the light, making their way toward what sounded like a river.

There was a rustle of brush and a buck—a nine point buck, for god's sake—stepped onto the path. He moaned and grunted, the deep noises resonating from within his barrel-like body. Leah froze. Would he attack her? His tongue flickered in and out of his mouth, though she didn't see anything to lick. Didn't deer like salt? He followed one of the does closely as Leah watched, training the light on them. She caught her breath as he mounted her. She could see his red penis, the movements he made as he maneuvered. The doe's ears were laid back and after a moment she stepped away from him, breaking contact. The buck followed, tongue flicking in and out of his mouth. Then they were gone.

Leah shut her mouth, her heart fluttering in her chest. Insects around her continued to chirp, the river below burbled. It was as if nothing extraordinary had happened. "That," she murmured, "was cool."

The warm pool was silent. Leah flicked off the flashlight and set it where it wouldn't get splashed, then settled in, relaxing. Though she'd thought the pool was deserted, there was a person-shaped shadow in a darkened corner. Yet the pool was absolutely still. Maybe the person was asleep. The stars winked overhead between the fig branches. Leah ran a hand through her hair and realized she was crying again. She was crying without even knowing it.

Damn Erik anyway. Fuck him. She'd thought she'd been helping with the suggestion that he should explore his attraction to Maya Bainfield. She'd meant in therapy, damn it. She and Erik had processed every word and emotion ad nauseam. It was their style. So why did he have to break up with her by text? He'd been sleeping with Maya for over a month, he'd said. Over a month. Since before finals. Such a repulsive way to treat another human being.

The other person moved, making the water ripple. Leah looked away, wishing she could control her emotions and not cry so much. It was embarrassing. Then she blinked. Even in the starlight the wild, curly profile was familiar... it was the man from this afternoon. He reached for something on the side of the pool, then approached her slowly, ripples proceeding him. He handed it to her. It was a handkerchief.

"Kind of dusty, but better than nothing," he murmured, his voice rising above the chirping insects around them.

"Um. Thanks." She accepted the cloth and blotted herself. She remembered his penis waggling comically that afternoon. Then her mind flashed upon the lengthy, reddened penis of the buck. She caught her breath.

The man paused, eyeing her. "Really?" he asked. He was breathing in time with her, she realized.

She frowned. "What?"

He lowered his head. Why did she suddenly have the absurd thought that he had horns? "Mmmm," he rumbled deep in his chest. Like the buck.

Leah fled, water splashing and cascading around her. She did it without thinking. She fled up the steps to the cold pool, where the path dead ended. She knew from exploring earlier today—yesterday?— that the whole pool was set on a platform above the wild forest floor. She could hear her own breath in her ears. After a moment, Leah realized she was aroused. Deeply, totally, completely aroused, so much so her pelvis ached. How bizarre. She began analyzing her own reaction, then froze.

He was behind her. She knew it. Her breath was coming fast, yet she wasn't trapped. She had a choice. A choice, damn it. The doe in the forest had laid her ears back but she hadn't protested—much. Leah should protest. She should say something.

"Do you have a condom?" she said, then covered both hands over her mouth. Oh. Oh.

He stepped around her and settled onto the wooden bench near the cold pool. His penis stuck out in the starlight, absurd no longer. Her eyes were riveted to it. He reached for something in the shadows beyond the bench—a backpack, she realized. She stared, absurdly shocked as he fished out something small and foil wrapped. She'd been joking, damn it! He was calling her bluff. What would she do if he came after her? Leah was panting, her mouth hanging open to take in enough air. Oxygen seemed in short supply just now.

To her astonishment, he lay on the bench face up, flat save for his cock. He put his arms behind his head and waited. He was waiting, she realized, for her. "Do as you like," he whispered in the dark. The foil-wrapped condom was a dim shape beside him, she realized. An invitation.

Leah didn't know how to respond to that. Her brain was on overdrive yet she couldn't think. She licked her lips, then licked them again. Like the buck. Who was the buck here, and who was the doe? Some part of her chided her for lowering herself to Erik's standards and she grimaced. This wasn't about tawdry rebound sex, damn it. Why did the thought of him have to invade every part of her life? Every moment, every breath?

The man chuckled in the dark, then reached down and started to stroke his penis. "Of course, it's okay not to do anything at all." He hummed under his breath—still off key—and began stroking himself faster.

"Wait," Leah pleaded. "Wait. Don't—write me off."

He paused in the dark. Respecting her plea, she realized. Leah advanced upon him cautiously, feeling tiny pebbles beneath her feet with each step. Then she was beside him. What now?

Her body knew for her. She knelt and stroked his cock with a hesitant finger. Leah realized anew how soft a penis could be. Soft with a springy hard core. She played with his cock. Touched the wet head of it, spread her fingers under his ball sack, stroked the length with her knuckles. He moaned and writhed under her hands. Leah grinned. This was fun. She realized that she'd never had the chance to do this, to explore a man without pressure. Without expectations.

The insight lit her on fire. She rocked forward and put her lips against his cock, gazing at up his shadowed face. He made a little noise and she realized the anticipation was torturing him. Leah grinned and swallowed him whole. He gasped, arching his back. She let him go, then took him in again. She was a lioness, playing with her pray. A cobra, coiled around him. She was in charge. The wet cock was soft in her mouth and she suckled it as he wriggled in place.

Leah let him loose. "Put on the condom," she demanded softly. She needed him inside her. Now.

He fumbled the foil pack. She helped, rolling it down over his wet shaft. Then she mounted him roughly and maneuvered him inside until he filled her. She snarled, taking him. He was the one panting now. Leah slapped his chest where his nipples rose in the dark. She grabbed his wild hair, pulling him upward to meet her. His hands were wavering in the dark by his side, as if he were helpless. She grinned, her teeth bared. She could ride him all night.

He arched beneath her and went still.

Leah extracted herself. She watched without emotion, curious what he'd do next. He lay like a slain animal, spread eagle on the bench. After a minute he roused himself. "Want to soak in the warm pool?" he murmured.

She raised an eyebrow in the dark. "Do you have more condoms?"

The warm water enveloped them as they sank within. They were still alone. He fumbled with a fresh condom while she watched him, narrow eyed. Earlier he'd consoled her. Then he'd freaked her out. He'd invited her to play and now he was hers.

He paused in the dark, eyeing her. "I think you should know that I'm not going to be around in the morning," he murmured in an apologetic tone of voice.

"I see."

A smile touched her lips. Nothing could throw her off her game now. In fact, he'd just relieved the rational part of her mind. The part that wondered if he expected something more from her, if he would be nasty and manipulative later on. Leah was tired of being fucked over. If he was leaving then she could remain an anonymous woman in the night. The freedom was breathtaking. Some part of her wanted to protest that she wasn't like this, that she'd never done something like this before.... Leah snarled under her breath. Screw it. She might never get another chance. Why not? She'd already had him. She might as well enjoy him until she was full.

She mounted him recklessly; he held up well under her. The warm pool had a softening effect, but that was okay. Leah quickly discovered that water was not a lubricant. She continued anyway. It heartened her to break the rules, to fuck him in the communal pool. He anchored her and gently held her to him, though she knew he was still taking cue from her. It was intimate, this endless rocking, but after a time she grew tired of intercourse.

"Hold on to the sides," she instructed, her hands reaching under his thighs. She pulled his body into a horizontal position in the water, floating him on his back. Her hands straddled under his hairy buttocks, his legs spread to accommodate her.

Leah had him. She could do anything she wanted to him. And what she wanted was for him to come in her mouth. Leah tore the condom off and tossed it to shore. He groaned loudly as she took him in her mouth again, panting and jerking in the water. She caressed his buttocks and he grew harder, his penis long as the buck's. Her fingers found his anus. With courage she never imagined she had, Leah poked a finger inside. Penetrating him.

His legs kicked the water around her, splashing. Helpless against her will. Salty, funky liquid burst into her and she swallowed it, squinting at the spicy flavor. She was dirty. A dirty, dirty girl.

They cuddled. If the warm pool was lousy for intercourse, it was wonderful for cuddling. He caressed her lightly, and she enjoyed the sensation, not inclined to reciprocate. She was still in charge, she realized. Especially now that she was done.

"That... was very helpful. Thank you, Peter Adelphos Nebble."

"At your service," he whispered hoarsely.

They bobbled silently once more. Then Leah straightened up abruptly. "Hey!"

"Hmm?"

"Your name. Peter Adelphos Nebble. It spells Pan. Like the Greek god. Did you know that?"

He stroked her wet hair. "It's come up once or twice before, I believe. Like me."

Leah drew away from him, control slipping from her grasp. The insight made her feel like she was stoned or drunk, except this was more like enlightened clarity. Everything was falling into place—sort of. The magical night. The strange afternoon. The way he'd known what she'd been thinking. Responding to her lust even before she'd been aware of it herself.

He paused. Then, as if in response to her confusion, he lifted himself out of the pool with a splash. He stood above her, a bright shadow in the starlight. "Just so you know, Erik really was a shithead. Next time choose better, little Psyche."

He strode up the stairs toward the cold pool. Probably to retrieve his backpack, but... it was a dead end. The entire area was a platform above the wild forest floor, right? So he'd have to come back here and what would Leah say in reply? Ugh. Why had he spoiled the moment like that? To make it a fucking mind game? Moments slipped by yet there was no movement on the path. Leah couldn't believe it. This was the only way back. Was he waiting for her to go away? The hell with him. She found her flashlight beside the pool and climbed the stairs one at a time.

No one awaited her by the cold pool. She was alone. She flicked on her flashlight—wincing as her night vision was destroyed—and scoured the area thoroughly. His backpack was gone, as was the used condom. She widened her search, focusing the beam of light into the forest. Insects chirped but nothing moved beyond.

Wait. There...

A nine-point buck gazed at her solemnly, his eyes flashing in the light. Then he turned and melted into the forest.

If you enjoyed this story, you can sign up for a free membership at
ForbiddenFiction.com and discuss it with other readers
and the author at the *Consoling Psyche* story page
at http://forbiddenfiction.com/story/JLW-1.000163.

Maman Brigitte

Slave Nano

Slave Nano is an author of erotica drawing on the themes of female supremacy, BDSM, and fetish. His short stories and novellas have been published by Xcite Books, House of Erotica, Coming Together, and Greenwoman Publishing. His novel *Adventures in Fetishland* has been published by Xcite Books. Maman Brigitte is his first story for Forbidden Fiction Publishing. He is a member of Leodis Pagan Group and has also had work published in the Pagan e-magazine *Eternal Haunted Summer*. You can find out more about his writing on his website: www.slavenano.co.uk.

Chapter 1

A Voyage into Darkness

I cursed the day I met Captain Bernard Dugarry. What a fateful decision, made over too many cognacs in a tavern in La Rochelle, though it seemed the right one at the time. I had been discharged from the French Navy for long service after the American War of Independence, and my life was going nowhere. I thought I'd had enough; that I wanted to turn my back on the sea, but it was in my blood. In my depressed and drunken state I could see no reason to turn down Captain Dugarry's offer. He was persuasive and charismatic. He was young for a captain of a vessel, yet supremely confident and ambitious. The money was good, very good, better than anything offered by the French Navy, and I had been offered a cut from the sale of the slaves when we reached the Indies as a bonus.

It seemed a good match. On his own admission, Captain Dugarry was not concerned with the fineries of sailing; he was a leader and disciplinarian, a businessman as well. He saw profit and wanted somebody to steer his cargo safely across hazardous waters to make it. He needed a skilled seaman, and I was that man; decades of service harrying the British navy down the coast of West Africa, across the Atlantic, and in the Indies gave me experience of these waters. One last job, I thought. One last payday to see me into my retirement, and perhaps then I would be able to turn away from the sea.

I did not know then the journey I was about to embark on was not only a voyage across a sea, but also one into the darkness of my soul.

We departed the port of La Rochelle on the second of February, 1785. Captain Dugarry delayed to leave on that particular day. It was Candlemass, the saint's day of St. Bridget and the feast of the Purification of the Virgin, and he insisted this would be an auspicious day to set off. The night before setting sail he went to the seaman's church at La Rochelle to receive confession. God knows, having already seen something of this man's temper and the extremity of his cruelty, he would need the intercession of a priest to stop him going to hell. We sailed around Spain and down the African coast to pick up our cargo from the slave fortress at Gold Coast in West Africa.

In the navy, I encountered some terrible things. I have seen men blown apart by cannon balls in battle, their bodies a mess of bloodied flesh and shattered bones. I have seen the harsh penalties administered by the quartermaster where men's backs have been torn to bloodied flesh by the cat o' nine tails for stealing a mere drop of rum. I have looked on hopelessly as men have been tossed overboard into the raging ocean, floundering desperately before the sea swallows them up. A sailor is hardened to hardship.

But none of what I experienced prepared me for the sight which confronted me on that day on the slave ship *Le Saphir*. Hundreds of near naked bodies in tattered rags crammed like sardines in a barrel, row upon row, chained together by ankle cuffs. The smell was unbearable; an unspeakable stench of soiled bodies and dried piss permeated the whole deck. The bodies were listless and lifeless. Some blank eyes stared up at me, but most of the slaves barely recognised anybody else was there. I was shocked. I had never worked on a slave ship before and, although I heard stories from other sailors, this mass of human misery was overwhelming. In twenty years of being at sea I never threw up, but I had to use all my powers of resilience to stop myself from retching then.

Dugarry laughed at my squeamishness, "Monsieur d'Estaing, you shouldn't give a damn. I've three hundred and sixty of these bastards; I can afford to lose a hundred and fifty and still make a comfortable profit. I don't give a shit as long as I have enough for the slave markets and plantation owners to make a handsome return." I think this was the first sign of my unease about this adventure, if that's what it could be called. What else should I have expected? After all, Dugarry was right, it was just business.

"Yes, Captain, of course," I replied, but deep down I knew something in my conscience had been piqued.

One night, Captain Dugarry invited me to his cabin for 'some fun', as he put it. When I arrived there were two slave girls already there. Their bodies had been stripped of the rags that passed for clothes and washed down with sea water. Their hands were tied with rope behind their backs and they were gagged. They knelt on the floor; their eyes wide with fear and their black-skinned foreheads dripping sweat.

"Come on in, Monsieur Gerard. I've got some entertainment for us tonight. We sailors need some relief, don't we, eh." I looked on as he took up a leather whip and flayed it across one of the slave girl's breasts. There was a muffled squeal of pain from behind the gag. Dugarry laughed at her sadistically. "I've only just started, you black bitch," he muttered. She would not have understood a word of French, but that wasn't necessary to understand the captain's threat. The whip rained down hard on her cutting a red weal across her breast. When she collapsed onto the floor to protect her exposed tits, Dugarry pulled her up roughly by the hair and whipped her harder.

He threw the whip over to me and laughed, "You whip yours now." I felt uneasy. I'm no prude. I've been to brothels in more ports than I can name. I've fucked plenty of prostitutes in my time, but this was cruelly malicious. Still, what could I do? The captain clearly expected me to join in.

I started whipping the second slave girl's tits. At first I was hesitant and held back, but Dugarry shouted encouragement. "Go on, get stuck in man; give her a good beating. You'll enjoy it once you get going." I increased the strength of my strokes. I could hear the muffled screams from behind the gag. Scarily, egged on by the captain's taunts, I became absorbed in the task, driving myself onto harder strokes, moving onto the girl's back, thighs and arse. Despite disgust at what I was doing, and against the better side of my nature, I found it exhilarating, even enjoyable, to whip the girl harder, challenging myself to go further. "Great work Monsieur Gerard," Dugarry called out, "I'll make a sadist of you yet."

The captain pulled down his crisp white breeches and knickerbockers so they hung around his ankles, removed the gags from both girls, and thrust his hard cock into the mouth of one of them, so deeply and forcefully she started to gag. "Keep whipping her whilst she sucks on me," he ordered.

And I did, but was I doing it because it was an order, or because I was enjoying it?

The captain grasped the girl's head and forced her down on him making her suck his cock. It didn't take long before he reached his climax, pulling out of her mouth and shooting a stream of hot white come all over her face.

The captain took the whip from my hand and gestured to me to take my pleasure from the other girl. Once again, I was hesitant at first, but I was so aroused I needed relief, it was not long before I had the girl's head in my hands forcing her to suck on me as Dugarry whipped her arse. My erect member muffled her screams. Like the captain, before I felt my come about to burst forth, I withdrew and emptied myself all over the girl's face and onto her drooping breasts.

The captain had not finished. He grasped his girl's head and forced her onto the tits of the other girl and made her lick my come off. I caught a glimpse of tears of humiliation running down her cheeks.

When I returned to my cabin that night I was quivering. On the one hand I was disgusted with myself. It was against my nature, or so I thought. But I also had to face the fact I enjoyed it. I was only too aware of the hardness in my breeches whilst I was whipping the girl and the carnal pleasure I relished from having her.

Captain Dugarry's treatment of the slaves was savage. I witnessed numerous beatings, usually with a vicious knotted whip. "The slaves need to know who is in charge. Discipline is everything on a slave ship," he would insist. Yet I could see the sadistic pleasure he obtained from administering these random and cruel punishments.

I felt sickened, but at the same time drawn to the sadistic and charismatic Captain Dugarry. What was happening to me? Was exposure to the hardships of slavery eroding my sense of humanity?

The captain's debauchery continued for the whole voyage. The slaves were used for all manner of perverted acts to satisfy our sexual gratification. I will not go into detail about the depraved activities we engaged in, partly out of shame, but also because graphic detail of our perversions would add nothing to my account. Despite revulsion at what I was doing, and against the better side of my nature, I found it exhilarating, even enjoyable. I would return to my cabin disgusted with myself, but also facing the dark reality that Dugarry's sadism had aroused me, and I had enjoyed it.

We were only a few days away from our destination, the French colony of Port-au-Prince on St Domingue, when one morning the lookout called out, pointing to a swirling mist on the horizon. I had sailed these seas many times; this bank of fog was a strange phenomenon for these waters.

We sailed inexorably into the mist until the ship was completely enveloped in an impenetrable fog. The combination of the thick mist and the rhythmic ring of the warning bell created an eerie atmosphere. I could tell the crew was uneasy, and I knew only too well how superstitious sea-faring folk are.

Indeed, although a fog like this in these waters was unusual, I would not normally be bothered by such conditions. But there was something about this mist that was deeply unsettling. I shared the crew's unease. We were now becalmed and could do no more than sit out the situation until conditions changed. They lasted for the best part of a day, until late afternoon when the mist lifted as quickly as it descended.

Later that night I was in the captain's cabin to partake of yet more of his perverse pleasures. This time he had a male and female slave and was about to embark on yet more debauched games with them when there was a knock on the door. Dugarry was furious. He hated it when his entertainment was interrupted. One of the crew asked him to come down to the hold, as the cargo was behaving strangely.

As we entered, the slaves were in a trance, their eyes wide open and unblinking. They emitted low ululating sounds from their mouths in an eerie cacophony of noise. The captain ordered the crew to whip them all but the slaves were oblivious to this punishment and continued their other-worldly calls. The strange guttural noises continued unabated all through the night making the crew grew more and more agitated.

Pierre, one of the crew and old sea dog, turned to Dugarry. "Whipping 'em'll do no good, Cap'n; they are possessed. This noise will drive us all mad, Cap'n. I've seen grown men try to pierce their ear drums because they can't stand this." The captain told him to stop talking rubbish, that he didn't believe in such things and that a more severe whipping will put an end to the racket. "That'll do no good,

Cap'n. I've seen this before in other parts of the Indies. It's possession, I tell you, and there'll be nothing you can do without a witch doctor." Captain Dugarry stormed off in a furious temper.

When the ship landed at the harbour it was not a moment too soon. The crew was being driven mad with the constant ululating sounds made by the slaves. One of the worst jobs was putting them in the cast iron collars and cuffs whilst they were in this state. The captain wouldn't normally empty his cargo so quickly from the hold, but none of the crew would stay on board with them. Captain Dugarry marched the slaves off the ship to the slave fortress and market on the harbour to prepare them for sale.

In the morning I attended the slave market with Captain Dugarry, who met with the auctioneer, Monsieur Richelieu, and some plantation owners. The slaves had now taken to rocking feverishly on the deck, their eyes rolling up into their heads showing only the whites. Monsieur Richelieu was adamant. He would not keep them in the slave market for any longer than a week. The plantation owners were quite clear; they would not buy any slaves in that condition. Basically, Dugarry had been told the whole cargo was worthless unless he could do something to restore calm.

"They are possessed, Capitaine," Monsieur Richelieu told Dugarry."There's no point denying it. You may not believe it, but on St Domingue, we see this many times. But, I must say I've never seen a mass possession like this before. You may laugh at me Capitaine, but you have to get help from one of the *Guede*."

My ears pricked. I was uneasy. I had heard of the power of the *Guede* from other sailors, though whether their tales of witchcraft and madness were true or exaggerated nonsense I could not say.

Monsieur Richelieu explained the nature of the *Guede*: they were intermediaries between the living and the dead. Only one of them would have the power to cross over into the spirit world and release the slaves from their possession. Dugarry scoffed. He still didn't believe these superstitious tales, but really had no choice. As Monsieur Richelieu told him, in this state, his whole cargo was useless. He might as well throw the whole lot of slaves off the harbour and drown them.

Reluctantly, Captain Dugarry had been persuaded. "So, tell me

Monsieur, where do I find one of these *Guede*?"

The slave market auctioneer explained, but first issued a warning. Seeking the aid of the *Guede* was dangerous; they were powerful and capricious and would not offer their assistance lightly. They would expect a handsome reward for their services.

The captain replied, "That's no problem. I'll get plenty of gold sovereigns from the sale of the slaves. The survival rate on this crossing has been good." God, I thought, I hate to think how many dead slaves would be thrown overboard on a bad crossing.

Monsieur Richelieu continued. "There's one powerful *Guede* who can be sought in the mountains inland from Port-au-Prince; that's Maman Brigitte. It's perhaps a day's journey there and back on horseback." The captain asked how she could be found. Monsieur Richelieu looked into his eyes and said, "You do not find her, she will find you, if she wants to parley with you. Go into the mountains and trust to fate."

Dugarry was exasperated. "Fuck, monsieur, you expect me to go up into these god-forsaken mountains on a gamble that some mad witch woman might speak to me?" Richelieu rolled his eyes and shrugged as if to say, you asked my advice. "*Merde*," exclaimed Captain Dugarry. "Monsieur Gerard, let's get some horses. We'll set off tomorrow."

What further journey into the heart of darkness will my travels take me? One last voyage, one last simple expedition was all I asked, and what did I get? A cruel captain who had drawn me into his sadistic games, a shipload of possessed slaves, and now this trip into the mountains for an encounter with a woman who could cross over into the spirit world.

When we returned to the ship, old Pierre definitely had a view. "Capitaine, you are going to see Maman Brigitte. You will parley with the goddess of death. You are a crazy man. She will suck all of the life out of your soul, and leave you an empty shell. You are taking a terrible risk. Monsieur, if I were you, I would rather throw the bastard slaves into the sea and cut my losses than meet with one of the *Guede*."

Dugarry told him to fuck off and stop repeating old wives' tales, and stormed off.

Chapter 2
An Encounter with the Maman Brigitte

The next day, Captain Dugarry and myself, with two other crew members, set off at dawn on horseback to take the path that led into the Montagnes Noir, southeast out of Port-au-Prince. The captain was in a foul mood and we barely exchanged a word all morning as we wound our way up the mountain paths in the direction Monsieur Richelieu had directed us. Dugarry was furious and frustrated; he just wanted to make his sale, get his money, and head back to France with a hold full of sugar.

Over lunch, as we sat in the Caribbean sun eating fruit and drinking masala wine, he loosened up a bit and admitted to me he still couldn't believe he had been persuaded to make this trip.

"We don't have a fucking clue where we are going. All this talk of soul-sucking demons and goddesses is superstitious nonsense," he complained.

We carried on into the afternoon, climbing higher into the lush vegetation of the mountains, the bright sunlight beating down on us. Suddenly, the horses became agitated, and reared for no obvious reason. Then the mist descended.

Captain Dugarry looked across at me. We knew what we were each thinking, reminded of the eerie fog that enveloped *Le Saphir* and the way it was connected with the slaves' possession. The same fear spread over me, this time the sense of dread was even stronger. The two crew members refused to go any further, so the captain sent them back to Port-au-Prince. We calmed the horses and continued on the path. This must have been what Monsieur Richelieu meant about Maman Brigitte finding us. We pressed on into the dense mist.

In the distance we could see a hazy light, and we approached cautiously. The canopy of trees opened into what we first thought was a clearing, but as our eyes adjusted to the glow of candle-lit lanterns hanging from the trees, we realised we had stumbled into a cemetery. Beneath us were roughly dug mounds, topped by crudely cut wooden crosses with skulls perched on them. I trembled with foreboding; Captain Dugarry, despite all his scepticism and bravado, was also affected. We dismounted, tied the horses up, and proceeded on foot.

We silently wove our way between the graves. Perhaps mad old Pierre was right; maybe we were passing through into the spirit world. At the far end of the cemetery we could see a ramshackle mud hut with dim light glowing in its window. Had Maman Brigitte drawn us into her domain? We jumped in fright as a red crested black cockerel swooped down and settled on top of a skull, eyeing us warily.

What was I doing here? Give me a cutlass and a pistol and an open fight with an English redcoat rather than this scary place.

We approached the hut with trepidation. Captain Dugarry entered first, gently pushing the door open with a trembling hand. I took a deep breath, and followed. The first thing that struck me was the smell: sweet and pungent with an intoxicating aroma. The air was thick with powerful incense, making my head spin.

The room was a chaotic hovel; I could make out rows of shelves with ceramic pots and glass vials, a floor scattered randomly with old animal bones and teeth. Finally, my eyes fixed on Maman Brigitte sitting imperiously in an ornate chair, the ends of its arms carved into the shapes of skulls, and its sides etched with elaborate symbols. A black raven sat in her lap.

Maman Brigitte was a wild and unkempt figure, but at the same time exuding power and danger. For some reason I was expecting an old crone, but she was a young and attractive woman. Her long curly red hair, combined with her dark skin, gave a striking presence. Balanced precariously on her head was a top hat decorated extravagantly with exotic feathers. She wore a fine dark crimson ball gown, which now looked worn and dishevelled. It was as if she was dressed for a ball, but the wild way she bore herself suggested she was mocking the finery and vanity of such rich clothes. Finally, in her hand she held a staff topped with a goat's skull. Her eyes were closed tight, as if she were asleep or had drifted into another world. Suddenly, her eyes snapped open, and glared at us menacingly.

She spoke in a strange accent that combined elements of Creole, French, and even Irish. "What business do you have that you would dare disturb the peace of Maman Brigitte? Come, before you state your business, share a drink with me and then you may say what you desire from the spirit world."

In front of her was a table with a phial of liquid and three glasses. It was as if she was expecting us. She poured out a dark red liquid in each of the glasses and drank hers down in one gulp. The captain and I held the glasses pensively to our lips. I took a sip. It was like fire water, a sensation as if my mouth had been set alight. The captain spat his out, which I did not think wise. If he wanted help, he would do well to accept the witch woman's hospitality, such as it was.

Maman Brigitte laughed, "You fucking soft whities." She pointed the goat's skull cane at us like an accusation. "You cannot share a little drink with Maman Brigitte? Come now, you must accept my offerings if you want to parley with me. Don't you trust me? Do you think it's bewitched? It's only rum and chillies — hot chillies."

I took another sip and felt the liquid burning the inside of my mouth. I decided the best approach was just to take it down in one gulp, which I then did. It felt like my insides were on fire as the hot liquid went down my throat and settled in my stomach. I grimaced but kept the fluid down. The captain followed my lead and did the same.

I had never seen the usually confident captain look so hesitant. He slowly explained who he was, his predicament, and how he had been recommended to seek Maman Brigitte's aid to release the slaves from their possession. The *Guede* sat patiently, listening to his tale with an appraising ear, neither interrupting nor commenting on the story.

After Dugarry finished she responded. "Tell me white man, trader in the bodies and souls of men, why should I help you? Do you know anything of my past, of how I came to be, of why the only debt I owe to slave traders is one of bitterness?" We both shook our heads to indicate we did not.

She continued her account, "Very well, I will tell you. My spirit is descended from many centuries ago back to the Irish Pagan Goddess Brigid. My spirit came on English ships over a hundred and fifty years ago when the Irish were sent out here as slaves. My blood is mixed with the natives and the black slaves to make me the spirit that I am today. So, tell me why you think I should grant any favours to a slave trader, when I am a descendent of slaves myself?"

This was not going well. There really was no reason why this spirit-woman should do the captain of a French slave ship any favours. Dugarry replied in the only way he could in the circumstances, and offered the one thing he had, the promise of riches.

"If I sell my cargo then I'll be a rich man. I can offer you gold sovereigns and wealth you can only dream of." She remained inscrutable and just nodded.

She spoke again, "I may deign to help you. But, you realise that for the spirit world to come to your aid there has to be an exchange, some kind of sacrifice, an offering to appease me."

Shit, I thought, where is this going? The captain is not going to like this. He feigned indifference, saying that if she could not help them he would take the possessed slaves back out to sea on *Le Saphir* and dump them in the Caribbean.

She laughed a high pitched cackle and shook her red mane as if she was actually taking pleasure in the fact somebody was daring to haggle with her.

"You could," she said, "but then you would lose your money and you might have to face the spirits of the sea, and your own conscience, such as it is. Tell me; are you afraid to take up my challenge?" I looked at Captain Dugarry. His face was strained with indecision.

He asked Maman Brigitte what form the offering would take, but she refused to tell him or give him any guarantees, saying the risk and choice was all his. He said he would accept her challenge. Maman Brigitte told him to return again tomorrow with two of the possessed slaves as breaking the spell for these would also release all of the slaves. My heart jumped a beat when I heard the captain's decision. What kind of test had he committed us to?

After we left Maman Brigitte's hovel and were riding back down the mountain path, I expressed my fears over the pact he had entered into. By then, some of his old arrogance had returned and he was dismissive.

"Monsieur Gerard, you are an educated and worldly man, do you still believe in these spirits?" I detected some hesitancy in his reply; did he really disbelieve, or was he exhibiting this bravado to hide his own doubts? I would never know for sure.

In the middle of the night I awoke with terrible nightmares. Visions of swirling skulls in my head, combined with an incessant drum beat, and the eerie call of the slaves had disturbed me. It was only one o'clock in the morning, and the visions continued in my waking mind so that I could not get back to sleep. I sat up all night fixated with fear at the unknown ordeal I faced later that day.

We started early and collected two of the luckless slaves from the slave fortress on the harbour. The slaves were in a terrible state and, according to their guards, had been agitated all night. It was as if they knew a wild power had been unleashed and they were awaiting some final reckoning. Dugarry was dressed in his full captain's uniform for the occasion.

Before we set off up the mountain path, we were confronted by old Pierre with more omens of doom. "You have made a pact with the *Guede*. You must be mad. You cannot trust these spirits. They will suck your brains out." I could do without mad Pierre's warnings at that time. Dugarry just told him to shut up and fuck off.

We rode up the mountain side with the two slaves in shackles. The eerie mist descended on us at exactly the same point. We left the horses tied to trees at the edge of the graveyard and proceeded on foot. The atmosphere in the cemetery was shrouded in the opaque mist and lit by lanterns in the trees. Today there were also candles on each of the mounds of earth below the crosses, illuminating the skulls that hung from them with a ghostly light.

Maman Brigitte stood outside her hovel, awaiting our arrival. She stood before us with her skull mounted staff in her hand; her top hat perched precariously on her head, billows of crimson material around her, and locks of bright red hair on her shoulders framing her dark features. She looked even more wild and dishevelled than yesterday. She pointed her staff, and beckoned us forward. The slaves were wide eyed and fearful.

"You have come to make sacrifice to Maman Brigitte, to make a pact with the spirit world." She offered us more of the fiery drink she offered us yesterday. She ordered the captain to release the two slaves from their shackles for the ceremony. "Embrace my spirit and you will endure, resist and you fall."

We all partook of the drink, shooting it down in one gulp. The mixture was stronger than yesterday, and this time I felt sure the elixir had been drugged. The effect on me was instantaneous; my head started spinning. The nightmare visions of swirling skulls and beating drums overpowered me as I felt myself tottering and collapsing onto the dusty earth of the cemetery.

Chapter 3
The Final Reckoning

When I came to, I was staked out naked on the ground, spread-eagled, and tied with jungle vine to wooden stakes amongst the cemetery mounds. I glanced across at Captain Dugarry who was tied naked and dishevelled onto a crude wooden cross. The two slaves were standing outside Maman Brigitte's hut dressed in skins and furs, with collars of animal teeth around their necks. My body was numb and my head reeling. Why had I let myself get drawn into this strange world of voodoo spirits?

Maman Brigitte was wandering around the graveyard with a bowl sprinkling us all with some liquid, anointing us for a ceremony like a deranged priest. After completing this task, she spread her arms wide, pointed her staff to the sky, making some kind of invocation to the spirits of the dead.

"In this ceremony, the spirits will test the cleanliness of your soul," Maman Brigitte proclaimed. I glanced across at Captain Dugarry; his eyes were glazed over; all attempt at resistance gone. I could tell he had already been subjected to some kind of torture. We had been tricked and trapped. The captain had made a one-sided pact with the *Guede* and now we were both consumed in their world, surrendered into the hands of Maman Brigitte.

She approached me, her staff in one hand and a candle in her other. She knelt over me, resting the staff on the ground. She held the candle close to my face. Her face was luminous in the gentle glow of the candlelight, and her emerald eyes fixed on me as if she was looking *into* me. With deft movements, she pulled the candle back and tipped a pool of molten wax onto my nipples. My body jerked in shock and pain and I let out a gasp.

"Your friend has already suffered for me; now it is your turn. Will you let the power of the spirit world into you? Does your soul need cleansing? Tell Maman Brigitte what darkness is there, and let her in." My head was reeling with the heat of the fire water in my stomach, the pain of the hot wax, the sickening aroma of the incense that pervaded the whole cemetery, and Maman Brigitte's dark skin illuminated by the candle light.

I knew I was at a crossroads. I knew enough from sailors' tales and legends of the power of the *Guede*; that they were intermediaries between the real world and the spirit world. I believed that now. Old mad Pierre was right. But what would I choose? To stay in this world, or pass with Maman Brigitte into the spirit world.

I shook my head in denial. I was not ready to pass. Maman Brigitte passed the candle over my naked body dripping droplets of hot wax on my flesh until she held it over my cock and balls, and poured another pool of hot wax over me. The pain was excruciating, like nothing I had ever felt before, needle sharp but sensuous, all at the same time.

I saw her pull out a red fruit from the folds of her dress. She held it in front of me, watching as my eyes widened in trepidation.

"Red chillies," she explained, "the hottest and fiercest I can find, ripened in the hot Caribbean sun." She held one over me and split it, licking her fingers erotically afterwards as she knelt over me. She took one half and rubbed it gently up the shaft of my cock. I felt the burning sensation. She ran it over the tip at its most sensitive point.

I screamed out in pain, "No, please no!" She laughed at me. She took one end and inserted it into the tip of my cock as deeply as she could without forcing it. My body jerked with pain. She took the other half and reached under me to touch my backside. I felt her fingers searching for the right spot and then the chilli was gently pushed into my arse. My head was spinning with the pain.

Maman Brigitte knelt over me, curls of red hair brushing against my face.

"The slaves will come with me. They have decided to join me. They have accepted they must make themselves a sacrifice to me to release themselves and their fellows from their possession. They have come over to me willingly. But then, their choice is easier perhaps.

What is their alternative? A life time under the whip of a cruel plantation owner. Look, they have already received my brand and will soon be released to become my followers, half way between the real world and the spirit world."

I looked across at one of the slaves, who had a raw burn mark on his arm. It had an intricate pattern interweaving a cross with a heart and a triangle, no doubt symbolising the crossroads between the human and spirit worlds.

"Soon your captain will have to decide, and then it will be your choice. How will you choose? Will you seek atonement for the dark deeds of your life's journey?" I felt the pain of the raw chilli permeate my whole body. "I will leave you to suffer for a while longer, while you make your choice."

I watched as she walked over to Captain Dugarry. She reached and held his face between the palms of her hands.

"Are you ready?" she asked. Dugarry nodded. "There are more tests for you before you can pass. You must complete them for me without question if you truly want to serve." She pulled the chilli that had been inserted into his cock and looked the captain in the eye. "Now eat it for me," she ordered. She held it up to his mouth and he took a bite from it and slowly chewed, keeping his eyes fixed on her as he did. Then she took the second half of the chilli from out of his arse and repeated the order. Once again, Dugarry received the hot fruit in his mouth, took a bite and chewed slowly before swallowing.

I could not believe my eyes. What power had Maman Brigitte now got over the captain that he would do such a thing? Part of me was repulsed, but another part of me was strangely drawn.

She pulled a knife from within the folds of her dress and reached to put a gentle slit in the palm of his hand. Droplets of blood trickled onto the earth. Maman Brigitte took some of the blood into her hands and smeared a red cross on his chest. She looked at him, stretched out on the cross. The once proud and callous captain of a slave ship now sucked into a world completely out of his control.

"You must know I never desired gold and riches from you. I collect souls, and the darker the souls, the better." Her laugh echoed hauntingly around the cemetery. "Now you must consummate your pact with me."

I wanted to scream out a warning to Dugarry, *No, don't do it*, but I could not force any words from my lips. Did he have any idea what he was doing? But I could see he was rendered senseless. He was set on a path from which he could never turn back, and had to accept the consequences, whatever they were.

Maman Brigitte cut the vines that held him to the cross and helped Dugarry down. He was unsteady on his feet, but gradually recovered his balance. Maman Brigitte lay down on one of the grave mounds; she hitched up the folds of her crimson dress and showed herself to him. She flaunted her sexuality and taunted him.

"Enter me, and consummate our union."

Did he realise what he was doing? It was the point of no return for the captain; I believed if he entered her he would be embraced into her spirit world never to return.

He approached, his cock erect at the sight of her cunt offered up to him. He knelt before her. In the flickering light of the candlelit graves, with the white skulls gazing on, he entered her. His body was smothered in the billowing crimson gown as if it had been swallowed up by her. The captain warmed to his task now, thrusting himself into her vigorously. She welcomed him in, holding onto his naked body and pulling him into her so he became enveloped in crimson material and curly red hair. His fires of lust and submission were met, and consumed. Maman Brigitte moaned in ecstasy, and took his cock deep into her.

"You belong to me now." She was a taker of souls, and her lust was to take them, play with them, and offer them up to the spirit world. She would suck his seed out of him and leave him an empty shell, fit only for serving Maman Brigitte, until she decided to release him to the spirit world. I watched Captain Dugarry's body writhing as he finally climaxed. The deed had been done, the pact consummated, and I knew in my heart Dugarry had crossed into the twilight world halfway between man and spirit. Their two bodies lay entwined until Maman Brigitte pulled herself away, and let out a blood curdling howl of laughter and triumph.

She stepped back to a fire that was burning on one of the grave mounds and pulled out a branding iron, the same one she must have used on the slaves. She pushed it down onto the flesh on Captain Dugarry's arm. I could hear the hissing of the hot metal on skin and then the agonised scream of the captain as he received Maman Brigitte's mark of servitude on his body.

I laid there silently in fearful anticipation, knowing Maman Brigitte would now turn her attention to me; it was time to make my choice. She walked back over to me, leaving the captain curled into a broken ball on the graveyard sobbing. She stood over me and hitched up her skirt. She was tempting me, showing me what might be offered if I came over. The powerful scent of her body overwhelmed me. I could see Dugarry's come oozing out of Maman Brigitte's cunt.

"Now it is time for you to make your choice, Monsieur. Will you follow your friend into my domain?" My head was spinning with doubts, caught between a desire to surrender myself to Maman Brigitte and her world, and fear at what that might mean.

Maman Brigitte got down onto the earth and knelt over me, the brown flesh of her thigh touching my flesh. I could smell her sex, erotic and intoxicating. She exuded sexuality.

"Don't think my world is all retribution. I offer you the chance of sexual delights beyond your imagining. You see your captain there, that faraway look in his eyes, that's not pain; that's ecstasy. Maman Brigitte has let him come inside her and that will be the most intense orgasm he's ever had. Come now, admit it, you want it. You want your cock in Maman Brigitte's cunt. You crave it, don't you?

And she was right, I wanted it. How I yearned to succumb to her, to have her lower her cunt onto me and consume my lust. She was wild and beautiful. Was I tempted to give myself up to her? Oh yes, I certainly was. She was an elemental force, a goddess of sex. I didn't doubt her boast she could transport me to a realm of sexual delights. But what was the price of that? What of my soul, sucked into a nether world between life and death?

She loosened the laces around the top of her gown and released her breasts. She hung the glorious brown orbs over my face, flaunting her power over me. They dangled agonisingly over my face and, even though I strained to lift myself up to plant my lips on a nipple, it remained tantalisingly out of reach. She laughed at me.

"Give yourself up to me and you can bury your face in my breasts and gorge yourself on my flesh."

She shuffled backwards so she knelt over my groin, the delicious curve of her cleavage still in my line of sight. She ran her fingers gently along my cock. I gasped in ecstasy. My cock was hard; the sting of the chillies had receded or simply got lost in a maelstrom of sensation. The boundary between pain and pleasure had become blurred for me. One more touch and I'm sure I'd come. And I wanted it. I wanted that release so badly. And yet, as she pulled her fingers away, I realised she was never going to offer it without me fulfilling my part of the bargain and giving my soul up to her. I think it was in that fleeting moment I recovered my sense and my awareness of what it would mean if I succumbed. I steeled myself for my final test.

She leant back and pulled the chilli out of my throbbing arse and held it in front of my mouth.

"Take it. The choice is yours. I will not force you; you must take it willingly." I grunted my rejection. It wasn't even disgust at the act, or fear of the fiery taste of the chilli; my reluctance was because I understood the symbolism of the act. I knew that, like Captain Dugarry, if I received the chilli into my mouth it would be an act that signalled I had surrendered control and had given myself up to her. Was my journey going to end here, in the hands of perpetual torment by this demon?

Maman Brigitte questioned me.

"Are you sure you are making the right choice?" she asked. "You are at the crossroad between two worlds and the chance to atone for all the foul acts in your life. I will receive any soul, even the darkest, like your captain's there. I looked across at the blank glazed expressions of the two slaves and Dugarry. Old Pierre had been right; their souls had been sucked out.

I nodded my head in denial.

"So be it, if that is your choice." She reached for her skull mounted staff, shook it at the sky and then pointed it at me, "Then I release you back into your world." These were her final words to me before I must have passed out.

I finally recovered consciousness two days later. When we had not returned that night, a search party was sent out to find us the day after. They found my prostrate body and carried it back to Port-au-Prince. When I first came round I was still in a delirium. I tried to piece something of my story together. But, when they went back to search there was no sign of Captain Bernard Dugarry or the two slaves. There was no cemetery or hovel or Maman Brigitte. No sign of anything that had happened on that fateful day; only a grizzled, middle-aged sailor who had lost his mind.

I have been out of the sanatorium for a couple of years now. I have lost the desire to be at sea, but it gives me comfort to be near it, and from my cottage in this fishing village in Brittany, I can gaze at the Atlantic and exchange banter with the fishermen. I have plenty of tales to tell about my life, but I never passed on the one about Maman Brigitte. Perhaps I thought nobody would believe me, or maybe I just believed it was best locked away in my journal.

The second of February is always a difficult day for me. It brings back memories of the date I set off on that final strange voyage from La Rochelle with Captain Bernard Dugarry. I have learned that, not only is this the day of the Catholic St Bridget, but also that this date was originally celebrated as the special day of the Celtic Pagan Goddess Bridgid.

I still have nightmares, though they have receded a little in time, but this day always brings them back. I understand the source of my madness now. I often wonder if I made the right choice, that actually Captain Dugarry was right to surrender himself to Maman Brigitte. I have come to believe that my nightmares and my madness were because I made the decision not to give myself up to her spirit world. In a strange kind of way I envy Captain Dugarry, as I have come to learn he made the right choice and my madness is a sense of loss, and that I yearn to be with him and Maman Brigitte in her spirit world in the mountains of St Domingue.

If you enjoyed this story, you can sign up for a free membership at ForbiddenFiction.com and discuss it with other readers and the author at the *Maman Brigitte* story page at http://forbiddenfiction.com/story/SN1-1.000230.

Fools Rush In

Elizabeth Schechter

Elizabeth Schechter is a stay-at-home mom who lives in Central Florida with her husband and son. Her first novel, *Princes of Air*, was published in 2011 by Circlet Press, and her second, a steampunk novel entitled *House of the Sable Locks*, was released in June, 2013. Her most recent work, the *Tales from the Arena* duology, was published in November, 2013.

Chapter 1
Rash Promises

"And I'm saying it can't be done!" The current object of my attentions snapped. Not at me, thankfully. I was sitting at a table in a tavern with a pair of bickering women. The one sitting in my lap was the only one who really held my interest. I'd lost her name somewhere at the bottom of the first bottle of plum brandy, but that didn't bother me. What was important to me right at that moment was that she had the most amazing tits. I was a simple man, then. Nice tits, nice ass, pretty smile, red gold in my pocket and good wine. That was all it took to make me happy. And let me tell you, that night, I was really happy. I had plenty of the last two, thanks to a very profitable heist back in Tarsis. But things had gotten a little too warm for me back in my home town, so I decided to come to Arraki for a spell. For my health, you understand. Which was how I found myself in a tavern in the Thieves Quarter that night. With her.

Now that I look back on it, I honestly don't remember just where she came from. It was like she was just... there, cooing over the tales of my recent exploits and paying me just the right kind of attention. She was a short, buxom blonde with gorgeous blue eyes, and she'd giggled when I'd first pulled her into my lap and told her that she was conveniently pocket-sized. After the first night with her, I wondered if all the whores in Arraki were that pretty and that pliable. After the second night, I stopped wondering about anyone else—female or male—entirely.

"What can't be done, Darlin'?" I asked, tightening my arm around her waist and glancing over at the woman across from us at the table. That one was dark, and she had a hard, rangy look that told me that she was in my line of work. She was young, though. No older than seventeen, I guessed. Old enough to know how to survive on the streets, but too young to have made her name.

"Lace is going to try to break into Kai's Temple," my lovely companion told me. "And it cannot be done!"

Now, telling me that someplace can't be broken into was like telling a devotee of the God of Lust that a woman was virtuous. All that does is give us something that needs to be proven wrong. I picked up my glass and took another sip of plum brandy. "And Kai is...?"

"Kai the Formless," the lady in my lap answered. "The Arraki patron God of Thieves. The Temple is sealed to everyone. I've heard that there is supposed to be a cloistered priestess, but no one knows for sure, because no one ever goes in there."

"I've also heard that the mosaics on the interior walls are made with gemstones, and everything in there is dripping with gold," Lace added. "I need to make my name, and that's how I'm going to do it."

Dripping with gold, hm? I've always wanted to be dripping with gold. I leaned back in my chair. "You really want to throw your life away?" I asked nonchalantly. "Don't fuck with the gods, sweet. You'll live longer."

Lace sniffed at me. "And who are you to be handing out platitudes?" she demanded. "Some kind of priest?"

I laughed, "No, sweet. I doubt there's a god out there that would want me as his priest. I'm just someone who has been doing the old snatch-and-grab a lot longer than you. My name is Davi."

Lace's jaw dropped, "Davi? Davi of Tarsis? Davi the harem thief?" Her voice spiraled up on the last few words, and the tavern fell completely silent.

I smirked, reached up to twirl my mustache, realized at the last second that I'd shaved it off before I ran for my life... excuse me. Before I decided to take an extended vacation in Arraki. I settled for stroking my chin. "You've heard of me?"

I could see Lace now had a serious case of hero-worship building, and my lovely lady was smiling at me in a way that sent heat rushing to all the fun parts of my anatomy. Once again I thanked the Trickster that I'd paid extra for a private room. We'd certainly made good use of it.

"Of course we've heard of you!" Lace gushed. "Who hasn't heard of the Master Thief who stole the thousand emeralds from the Sultan of Tarsis' harem?"

I clucked, fishing under my shirt for an emerald the size of my thumb that I wore around my neck. "Thousand and one," I corrected her as I flashed the stone. Of course, this particular emerald hadn't been stolen. It was a gift from the Sultan's intended bride, a truly stunning eighteen-year-old virgin named Naras. Call it... payment for services rendered. I got entry into the harem and access to the emeralds, she got a way out of a marriage contract she had no desire to go through with. Everybody won. Well, except for the Sultan.

The rest of the night in the tavern was a blur. It seemed as if every thief, grifter, pickpocket, cutpurse, pimp and whore in the place just had to buy me a drink. In return, they all wanted me to breathe on their hands. For luck, they all said. So I went from being a little bit drunk to being very drunk, and I swear by the Trickster that I remember nothing about the rest of that night.

I woke up the next morning hung-over, wondering if it would be worth it to turn myself in to the Palace guards so they could chop my head off. No, I decided. If they did chop my head off, it would still hurt. It would just hurt way over there.

"Drink this."

I didn't recognize the voice, but I drank anyway. Maybe I'd be lucky and it would kill me. The room took a sharp turn to the left, wheeled around three times, settled gently on the ground and spit me out like a peach pit. "What is this?" I gasped.

"Trust me, you don't want to know." The bed creaked and settled, and I turned to see my lovely lady with the pretty tits sitting next to me. She was completely, gloriously naked, except for a pair of wide gold bracelets that she seemed to wear all the time. A brief check under the coverlet showed that I was as naked as she, and I wondered what I'd missed. How to find out...

"I am very disappointed in you, Davi," she said, folding her arms over her chest.

Well, I suppose that's one way.

"I'm sorry, Darlin'," I said, sitting up and letting the coverlet slip down. "I shouldn't have drunk those last two dozen whatever-they-were. What was I drinking, anyway?"

"You don't want to know that, either," she answered. She looked down at me and sniffed. "You really don't remember anything, do you?"

For a minute, I wondered if I'd started something with her that I hadn't been able to finish, then shook off that thought. "Not a thing. What did I do? Or not do?"

"You swore by the Trickster that you and you alone would be the one to dare Kai's Temple," was her answer.

"Oh, I didn't!" I gasped.

"You did. Your exact words were that you would be the one to relieve the god of gold that He was never going to use," she told me. I groaned and rubbed my hand over my face. That did sound like me when I let the bottle do my thinking for me.

"And... how many people heard me say that?" I asked.

She sniffed at me, and didn't answer, which told me more than words could have. If I didn't at least make an attempt on the Temple, I might as well leave town. I sighed dramatically and reached out to take her hand. "So, let me get this straight. I got drunk and stupid, swore to do the impossible, and then you brought me back up here so that I could snore at you. Is that right?" She nodded without looking at me. "Sorry, Darlin'. Is there any way I can make it up to you?" She sniffed again, then squeaked in surprise as I pulled her closer.

"What are you doing?"

"Attempting to make it up to you," I answered with a smile. I ran one finger down her cheek. "Sapphires, I think. To set off your eyes."

"Sapphires?" she repeated, those amazing eyes as wide as saucers.

"Once I've done this job, I'll see you draped in sapphires," I whispered, running my finger down her throat and over her collarbone. "Sapphires and silver and nothing else."

She smiled in return and leaned closer, "You're really going to try it? And you would do that for me?"

I drew her into my arms and lowered myself back onto the bed, holding her to my chest as I did. "Oh, yes, I'm going to try it. And, Darlin', you just wait to see what I'll do for you after this job."

She giggled, running her fingernails over my chest, "How about what you'll do for me now?"

That was just what I wanted to hear. I ran my hand up her throat and into the curls at the back of her head, pulling her face down and kissing her, making it hard and possessive, the way I'd learned she liked it. She moaned against my lips and squirmed against me, her hands trapped between our bodies. I loosened my hold on her long enough for her to get all the way onto the bed, then caught her in my arms again and rolled, pinning her underneath me. She giggled, her cheeks flushed, her lips red as rubies. Once she was settled, I pushed up, bracing myself on my arms so I could look down at her.

"What are you waiting for, oh Harem Thief?" she asked. "You're wasting time."

"Since when is it a waste to admire the woman I love?" I asked. She caught her breath and sat up, so fast that she almost caught me in the chin with her forehead.

"What?" she demanded. "What did you say?"

I smiled at her, reaching out and tracing the bow of her upper lip with my thumb. "I said I love you."

"Oh..." she breathed, looking stunned. "Oh, Davi..."

"Now, are you going to let me show you how much?" I asked, pushing her back down onto the bed. She giggled and raised her arms, embracing me as I lowered myself down over her.

"I love you, too, Davi," she whispered in my ear as she held me. I kissed the side of her neck, then started moving down her body, admiring her every curve, worshiping her beauty with lips and tongue until she was breathless and whimpering under me. When I found her jewel with my tongue, she moaned, arching her back and wrapping her legs around my head. Gently, I pushed her legs up and back, rolling her into a ball and leaving her open and spread so that I could drink deep. It amazed me how good she tasted—like honey mead warmed in the sun, mingled with the finest spices in the world. I could pleasure her like this for hours, and it was incredibly tantalizing to watch her as she writhed underneath me, moaning and screaming with the force of her climax and then going completely, bonelessly limp. I stretched out next to her, studying her as she slowly rose from the depths of pleasure and returned to awareness. When she smiled at me, I leaned down and kissed her.

"You taste fantastic," I told her. She blushed and giggled, then ran one finger down my chest.

"Your turn," she said in a husky voice.

Just what I was waiting for. I kissed her again and moved back between her legs; she hummed softly and raised her knees, hooking her legs over my hips and pulling me towards her. She was primed and ready for me, and I let her set the pace as I teased the entrance of her cunt with my cock. She moaned softly, her legs flexing as she tried to pull me deeper.

"Davi, don't tease," she whispered, her voice catching as I thrust into her before she finished speaking. She was still wet, tight from her orgasm, and for a moment, I wished that this would never end. Then she found my nipples with her fingers, and I gasped and started to pump, hard and fast. I could feel her cresting again, growing wetter, growing tighter. She locked her ankles behind my back, digging her nails into my arm as she pleaded with me in a broken voice to not stop, never stop, more, please, please. I could feel my orgasm, feel it in each thrust, in the way she tightened around me, her cunt throbbing and squeezing me. When she started to shriek, I lost it, pounding into her until I burst, riding wave after wave of ecstasy until I collapsed over her, spent.

I stayed there for a moment, keeping my weight on my arms so I wouldn't squash her, then rolled to the side and pulled her into my arms. She cuddled against me, her head resting on my shoulder. When her breathing finally returned to normal, she murmured, "When?"

"When what?"

"When are you going to try the Temple?" she asked.

"Oh," I answered, and considered the question. Then I shook my head, "Soon, I think. Before the gossip hits the wrong ears. Where is this Temple, anyway?"

She raised her head and smiled, "I'll take you."

Chapter 2
Into the Temple

It was just after midday when we stopped outside what she called the Temple Wall. Which was pretty accurate. It was, indeed, a wall. I left her standing there and made my way around it, a longer walk than I'd expected, finally coming back to ask the obvious question, "Where did they hide the gate?"

She laughed, "That's the usual first question. There is no gate. Hasn't been for as long as anyone can remember. We told you last night—the Temple is sealed. No one goes in there."

I remembered someone saying that, but I'd thought it hyperbole. Instead, I was faced with a real challenge. I found myself oddly excited. This might be fun! "No supplies? No food or anything? No deliveries?"

She shook her head, "There's a rotating portal to let supplies in."

"I saw that. Not very big."

"Exactly. It isn't big enough for a man. And I don't even know why it exists, because the Temple is the same. No gate, no door, no anything. The only opening is... well, come with me." She led me down the street to a small park, then pointed back at the Temple. "Look just under the dome."

Now, there's a reason I don't do second-story work, and it has nothing to do the fact that, for some reason, most people usually hide their valuables in either the root-cellar or that crock right up on the top shelf of the kitchen. You know, the one with the crack in it that you can't put mead into anymore? Yeah, that one. No, the reason I don't do second-story work is that it involves climbing, which makes me dizzy and ill. So I do not, under any circumstance, climb anything other than stairs. The idea of scaling the side of a building made me nauseous, and here I was, about to do just that. I'd backed myself into a corner, and if I didn't go through with this, word would spread. I didn't think that my sweetheart would actually tell anyone, but if we weren't stinking rich by dawn tomorrow, then everyone would know I failed. So I really didn't have a choice.

I squinted and nodded, seeing the regular dark spaces in the gray marble, "Windows?"

"For ventilation. That's the only access."

I frowned and looked at her, "How do you know that? If there isn't any way to get inside the gate, how do you know that there isn't a door to the Temple?"

She dimpled, "Because I scaled the wall and took a look around the Temple grounds last year."

I coughed, "You?"

Her smile vanished. "Yes, me. I thought I'd try my luck at that treasure, and I decided that it was too much trouble to take the risk."

She folded her arms over her chest and turned away from me. I gave myself a good mental kick and went to rub my hands up and down her bare arms. She didn't shrug me off, which I took as a good sign.

"Darlin', I didn't realize you and I were in the same line of work," I said. "I apologize."

"Some of us like to keep our doings a bit more discrete than the Harem Thief does," she snapped back, looking over her shoulder at me. "Now, are you going to listen to me?"

I stepped back and bowed, "I yield to the expert. How do we do this?"

She relaxed when she realized I wasn't being sarcastic, taking my hand and leading me to a bench underneath a tree. A nice place to sit and talk, and if any of the people passing by were paying attention to us, we would look like a pair of young lovers making up after a spat. I pulled her close and whispered in her ear, "Didn't take you for a thief. You're very good."

She smiled and rubbed her cheek against mine. "Yes, yes, I am," she whispered as she kissed me. She rested her head on my shoulder and murmured, "Now, there's a place where the outer wall is rough.

There are wonderful handholds, and it takes less than a minute to get up and over. It's an easy drop on the other side."

I buried my face in her golden hair, "What's the watch schedule?"

"Every twenty minutes. Plenty of time." She tipped her head back and gave me a lazy smile, her blue eyes sparkling. "And I'm going with you."

I couldn't react to that statement without calling attention to us, so I forced a smile and said, "No, you're not," through clenched teeth.

She laughed and tapped me on the nose, which would have been adorable if I didn't want to strangle her right then. "You need me. You'll never get into the Temple without me and my equipment," she said in a soft voice, then pulled free from my arms and stood up.

"I'll meet you here an hour past sunset. I'll have everything we need," she purred, then turned and walked away, vanishing into the greenery.

When I returned to the park that night, she wasn't there. I sat down on the bench and waited as full dark fell, wondering if I'd been made a fool of, and I nearly jumped out of my skin when she appeared out of the darkness as if she'd been conjured there. As I tried to slow my heart down, I noticed what she was wearing. Gone were the low-cut bodice and hiked-up skirts; now she was in breeches and boots, with a long-sleeved jacket that came down to her knuckles and a heavy-looking bag slung over her shoulder. Everything she wore was mottled black and gray, and her face was smudged with dirt or soot, the better to hide in the shadows.

"Come on," she said softly. "We don't have a lot of time." She pulled me from the bench and into the shadows, shoving a bundle into my hands. "Put this on. The guards have just passed the Temple. Once they pass the park, we'll have just under twenty minutes to get over the Temple wall and up the side."

I didn't answer, shaking the bundle out to reveal clothing in mottled gray and black, similar to what she was wearing. I stepped back into the bushes and stripped, pulling on the shadowy clothes and wondering just how she had been able to get something that fit me as if it had been made for me. I rolled my own clothes up and left them under the bush. I could retrieve them later, if all went well. And if it didn't go well, I wouldn't need them anymore, and whoever found them was welcome to them. I kept my emerald, though, tucked under the jacket. For luck.

When I rejoined my partner, she was standing in the shadows of the trees and was almost impossible to see. She nodded when she saw me, and fussed over me for a moment, pulling the jacket's hood up over my hair, then rubbing her hands all over my face. Whatever it was that she smeared on my skin itched. I grimaced.

"You can wash it off later," she whispered. "Stay in the shadows. The guard just passed. Let's go." She flowed out of the shelter of the trees, moving like a ghost. I followed her, not quite as gracefully. This morning, the walk from the Temple to the park had taken two, maybe three minutes. Now, it seemed to take half the night, and I was sweating by the time we got to the wall. She gestured to the left, and I followed her lead until we reached a place that didn't look any different than the rest of the wall, until I rested my hand on it and felt the uneven stone. She grinned, her white teeth flashing in the darkness, then swarmed up the wall and over. I heard a distant thump as she landed on the other side.

Well, if she could do it, so could I. I fumbled my way up the wall, certain that at any moment someone was going to grab onto my ankle, pull me down and haul my ass to prison. I almost fell over the top of the wall in my haste to get out of that imaginary guard's reach, and I dropped down on the other side and kept going, sitting down hard and panting.

"There, that wasn't so bad, was it?" she cooed. I glared up at her, but the effect was lost in the darkness.

"How did you say we get in there?" I asked, knowing the answer and not wanting to believe it. What had I gotten myself into? And was there any way to get out of it? She pointed up, and I grimaced. "How about we agree to say we did it, and never speak of this again?" I offered.

"Really? The Harem Thief is giving up?" she said with a snicker. "Afraid of heights?"

"It isn't the height that bothers me. It's the stop at the bottom when I fall," I muttered, staring up at the distant dome of the Temple. "So, are we going to fly?"

"Not so simple," she answered. She started rummaging through her bag and pulled out a hand crossbow and a quarrel with a thin cable attached to it. The rest of the cable dropped to the ground in a coil.

"That is never going to reach the top," I said as she took aim.

"It isn't meant to. I did some scouting after I left you today, and there's a ledge halfway up. We'll go in stages." She fired the crossbow and I watched as the cable unfurled until just a few inches were left on the ground. She tucked the crossbow back into her pack, picked up the end of the cable and tugged on it, then pulled harder. "It's ready. Let's go." She handed the cable to me.

"You go first. I'll keep you steady." Trapped. Nowhere to go but up. I tried to cover the fact that I was completely, absolutely, terrified, giving her a quick grin. I took the cable from her... and the next thing I knew, I was standing on the ledge with her arms around me.

"Idiot!" she scolded. "Why didn't you tell me you have no head for heights?"

I looked at her, a much more pleasing view than the ground all the way down there. "How did we get up here?"

"We climbed. You did fine. When we got to the ledge, you turned around to help me up and froze. You don't remember?" I shook my head slowly, and she sighed and kissed my cheek. "It's fine. That happens, sometimes. So I hear. Now, do you want to go the rest of the way up, or back down?"

"I came this far. Maybe I won't remember the rest," I joked, forcing out a laugh. She grinned and coiled the cable up, repeating the process of setting the line. And again, the minute I took hold of the cable, I blanked out, coming to myself this time standing in one of the windows at the top of the temple. Looking down into heaven.

The entire inside of the temple glittered in the light of torches that ringed the interior of the space. In the flickering light, I could see bright flashes of red and blue and green, like brilliant stars below my feet. And for once, I didn't mind looking down.

"Oh, me," she breathed next to me. "It does look amazing from up here..."

"Incredible," I agreed. "If we come out of here with even a fraction of what is down there, we'll be set for life." I looked down at the vast wealth below me, and then at her. "Darlin', when we get out of here... what would you say to staying with me?"

She looked at me oddly, "I am staying with you."

"I mean..." I hesitated, then decided that if she said no, I could always fling myself down into the gold below. "I mean marry me. Raise up our own little thieves guild. You'd have to teach them the second-story work..."

She stopped me, "You... you're serious?"

I nodded. "Dead serious. Sapphires and silver and a wedding ring."

"Oh..." she looked down, then back up at me, a gamine grin on her face. "Shall we get down there?"

Thankfully, I didn't remember a minute of the trip down, either. I found myself on the ground, the cable still in my hand, wondering just how I'd managed to get all the way down without remembering the stop in the middle. I heard a soft thump, and turned to see her straightening and coming towards me.

"Darlin', I have never seen anything so beautiful," I said as she walked into my arms. She smiled up at me and put her arms around my neck, drawing me down to kiss me.

"Davi, I want you," she murmured against my lips.

I had sudden visions of rolling around with her, naked on a pile of gold the size of a feather bed. I laughed and pulled her tightly to me. "Oh, I like the way you think, Darlin'."

She ran her hands over my chest and pushed me back. "Over there, in the corner. There's a pile of silk."

I turned away to see what she was talking about, and gasped in pleasure and surprise as she came up behind me and wrapped her arms around me, caressing my chest through my jacket, running surprisingly strong hands down my belly and over my hip, her body pressed against my back. For a moment, I thought there was something strange. Her body felt... different. But then one of her hands started working its way down into my breeches, and I gave up on thinking and reached back, running my hand down over her flank.

"Darlin', you'd better give me a chance to get laying down," I said over my shoulder. Her answer was a low chuckle. I turned in the circle of her arms, and found myself looking into blue eyes that were full of amusement... and on the same level as my own. That stopped me long enough that I noticed the beard. I yelped and jumped backwards, pulling out of her—his!—arms and staring. He was my size, wearing mottled gray clothing similar to mine, with shoulder length blond hair, brilliant blue eyes and a rakish grin that looked familiar. A glint of metal caught my eye; I saw the wide gold bracelets on his wrists and my jaw dropped.

"I..." I started, then coughed and cleared my throat. "That's... a nice trick, Darlin'. Someday, you have to show me how you did that."

Chapter 3

Tricks and Tricksters

He laughed again, "Oh, I do like you, Davi. I'm going to enjoy having you around. Welcome to my Temple."

"Your...?" I started to repeat, then shook my head. "Oh, no! No, no, no! You're... you're him, aren't you? What's-his-name...?"

"Kai the Formless. Yes," he answered, grinning at me. "Patron of thieves. You call me Trickster, and I like that. You're one of my most devoted sons, you know."

"Thanks. I... uh..." I had been about to apologize for breaking into his Temple, then remembered that it hadn't really been my idea in the first place. "You tricked me!"

He grinned, "That's what I do."

"I never told anyone I was going to try and rob the temple, did I?"

"No. I told you that, and made you believe it," he shrugged. "Truly, I couldn't think of any other way to get you here. If I'd asked you nicely to come here, would you have?"

"Ah..." I looked down and away. He had a point. "All right. So you tricked me into thinking you were a woman, manipulated me into thinking I had to rob your temple, and I've no doubt that you did some kind of magic to make sure we got past the guards so that I got in here in one piece. Not to be rude, but why?"

He sighed dramatically, just the way I do when I'm about to try and sell someone their own shoes. Before he could start, I held one hand up. He looked surprised, then nodded. "All right. I had to. I couldn't lose you, not when you were finally close enough for me to reach. The form you were so intrigued with was that of Arna, my

208

priestess. She died recently."

I frowned. Arna. Not usually a woman's name, that. And for some reason, the name sounded familiar. I didn't know anyone named Arna, so I wasn't sure why. It would come to me, eventually. "Sorry to hear that," I said while I thought. "What does that have to do with me?"

"Do you remember what you told Lace? That you doubted that there was a god who would want you as a priest. You were wrong." He looked at me, starting down at my boots and working his way slowly up until his eyes met mine again. He smirked at me and said, "I need a new votary."

I was about to repeat myself and ask what that had to do with me, but that was the moment when I remembered where I'd heard the name Arna before. And the Arna I knew hadn't been a woman. He'd been a thief, a legendary one, one who'd made his name before the age of twenty and had never stopped making his mark on the upper echelon of Tarsii society. No one was safe from his reach, right up until he vanished. Which had happened over five hundred years ago.

"Wait... you're telling me that your priestess was Arna the Rogue, the most famous thief in five generations," I said slowly. "And he ended up... here. As a woman?"

"Sometimes. Sometimes he was a man," Kai answered and shrugged. "It depended on our moods, really. I think you can agree that he made a most fetching woman, didn't he? Of course," he looked down at himself, "He wasn't bad as a man, either."

I nodded slowly, wondering just how far up the cable I'd be able to get before Kai stopped me. Which raised another question. "You... you did something to me. To get me up the side of the Temple."

"I was running out of time, and you never said a word about being afraid of heights." He rested his hands on his hips. "Davi, let me finish. I need a votary. It doesn't have to be a priestess. It can be a priest. I just need to have someone here in the Temple, someone to serve me, see to my needs. I'm... well, I got into a bit of trouble, a few millennia back. And Mother... grounded me."

"Grounded?" I fought the urge to have a giggle fit—it wasn't often that I heard a god admit to having been sent to his room and told to play nice.

"Well, I couldn't help it! I am what I was made to be, and Fersis' shield was so shiny..."

"Fersis?" I did laugh this time. "You stole the Sun God's shield?"

Kai pouted at me. He actually pouted, and when he spoke again, he sounded like a small child who'd been caught with his hand in the date jar. "Yes. But I gave it back, and said I was sorry. Anyway, Mother got upset. She always did like Fersis better. So I'm confined to my Temple until she decides I've learned my lesson."

I shook my head, confused. "But you came out! You were with me!"

"Loophole. I can walk outside for one mortal week to find a new votary when the old one dies. But I have to find a new one within that week, or I'll be alone. Do you know what happens when a god is alone? We need to have someone to actively worship us, or we fade away into the darkness." He looked at me, and I saw a hint of desperation in his eyes. "You're my choice, out of all the thieves in Arraki. I want you. I like you. You're funny, and you're interesting, and..." He stopped, looked down, then looked back at me. "You can stay with me, be mine. You'll have every luxury, everything you desire, anything that is in my power to grant. I'll keep you alive far longer than you would otherwise live, keep you young and handsome. You'll serve me, be my priest. Or priestess, if you want to try that. I don't mind either way. Please say you'll stay?" Kai leered at me and took a step closer, "I can promise that you will never be bored."

My mouth went dry, and I think I whimpered. "I..."

"You just spent most of a week with me in your bed. You promised to drape me in sapphires and silver. You were ready to take me right here, right now," his voice dropped, became lower, sultry, seductive. "You asked me to marry you. You're already half in love with me."

"More than half..." I croaked.

"Do you object to men, Davi? I can be female for a few hundred years. Tell me what you want, Davi." He closed the gap between us, standing close enough that I could feel the heat radiating from his body. And a small part of my brain was dying to know what he looked like under those clothes. "You aren't the only one who fell in love, Davi. Be mine. Please. And let me be yours."

"Or...?"

He sighed, "Or... I will cloud your memories of me and transport you out of my Temple. I will not force you. I will not try to coerce you. I had to bring you here, so that I could make the offer. But if you do not want to stay, I cannot keep you. There's no point—if I keep you here against your will, you're not a votary. You're a prisoner. You won't worship me, you'll hate me. And I don't want your hate. There are no tricks now, Davi. No magic, no manipulation. Just me, asking you to stay." He paused, then turned away, but not before I saw disappointment plain on his face. "If you want to go..."

"I didn't say that," I whispered.

He looked at me over his shoulder, wide-eyed as a startled deer. "You'll stay with me?" he asked, looking into my eyes.

I nodded slowly, wondering what I was getting myself in to. He smiled at me, and the joy in those eyes made me not care.

"Take this, my priest," he murmured, taking from his wrist one of the wide bracelets. "Take this and be marked as my own." He took my left hand in his and slipped the bracelet onto my arm, and I watched in wonder as the metal warmed and shifted, forming itself to the shape of my wrist. I admired it for a moment, then smiled and slipped the emerald off, dropping the cord over his head and settling the stone onto his breast.

"Now you're marked as mine," I said, smoothing the stone down and touching the skin underneath.

He covered my hand with his. "You promised sapphires," he reminded me.

I grinned up at him, "I'm a little short on sapphires right now." I had a thought, and the question fell from my mouth before I could stop myself, "Kai, you're using Arna's face now, right?"

He nodded, turning slightly, "Both of them. I thought... my powers are limited, outside these walls. But from what I could see in your mind, I thought she would appeal to you."

"Oh, she did." I smiled slowly. "So... what do you really look like?"

The minute the question was out of my mouth, he changed. Sharp-faced, high cheekbones and eyes like storm-clouds under unruly black curls, he was a little taller and a lot thinner, wearing a wrapped shirt and loose breeches instead of the shadowy clothes that he'd worn as Arna. He looked down at himself and shrugged. "This is the form Mother gave me when she made me." He said, his voice a wonderful baritone rumble. He peered shyly at me through ridiculously long lashes, and I felt my heart stutter as I recognized the look as one of hers. That made me look harder at him, and I studied him for a long time, long enough that he started to fidget. "Should I change back?" he asked quietly.

"No," I answered. "I like this face." I cocked my head to the side and smiled at him. "Emeralds suit this face better. And you're right."

"Right about what?" he asked.

"I really was more than half in love with her. With you, I mean. It was her face, but it was you behind the eyes." I crossed the space between us and reached up, cupping his cheek with my hand, feeling his skin grow warmer under my touch. I had no idea that gods blushed so beautifully. "I like this face," I repeated. "Because this is your face." I slid my hand to the back of his head, running my fingers through curls like warm silk, and pulled his head down to mine. His arms wrapped tightly around me, and the kiss was as warm and welcoming as any that he'd given me whilst wearing his female disguise. I slid my arm around his waist, laughing against his lips as he started tugging at my jacket.

"Impatient?" I whispered as I pulled away from his kiss and slid my hand out of his hair and down to his shoulder.

"You have no idea," he answered, then scowled slightly. For a moment, I was afraid he was annoyed at me, then I felt a cold draft against my skin, and warm skin against mine where our bodies touched. When I looked down, every stitch of clothing that we both had been wearing was gone. The only things that remained were our bracelets and the emerald, flashing green in the torchlight. I looked up at him to see amusement and desire in his eyes. "Clothing only gets in the way," he growled.

"It does," I agreed, shifting my hips against him and feeling his cock pressing hard against my stomach. I ran my fingers over his side and down over his hip. "You said something about a pile of silk in the corner?"

He laughed, taking my face between his hands and ducking his head to kiss me again. I'd never before been kissed by someone taller than I was—even when I'd been with men, I was usually the taller one. It was interesting, if a little hard on the neck. I ran my hands up his back, tightening my fingers over his shoulders as he ran one hand firmly over my ass. Then he grinned and took my hand, tugging me after him. I followed, surprised when Kai pushed aside a tapestry and revealed a large door. He looked at me over his shoulder, then led me into what I knew had to be the main sanctuary, a room decorated with more gold than I'd ever seen in my life. At the center of the space was the altar, glittering with inlaid gold. As I watched, Kai raised his hand—there was a flash of light, and the top of the altar was piled with fur and shimmering silks.

"Better than a pile of rags in the corner?" he asked, pulling me towards the altar without waiting for an answer. Laughing, we clambered up onto the makeshift bed and he pulled me into his arms again, his eyes meeting mine as he stroked my sides and back.

"I wasn't expecting to fall in love with you, you know," he said. "I wasn't expecting you to propose marriage. Or to take my bracelet so easily. I'm amazed." He pressed his lips to mine, then started moving down my jaw and over my neck. I preened under his attention, until curiosity got the better of me. I pushed him back gently and asked, "What was that about the bracelet?"

He smiled lazily and stretched like a cat, then held up his left arm. "This is what ties me to the Temple. So long as I wear it, I can't leave, except for that loophole I told you about. Now that you're wearing one, you're bound here, too." He must have seen something in my face, because he sobered and propped himself up over me. "I'm sorry. Should I have told you that before?"

"Yes..." I said slowly. He blushed again, looking chagrined.

"Does that... would that have made you change your mind?" he asked in a small voice.

I considered the question, then realized that it would have made no difference. I had always wanted to be rich. Now I was, beyond my wildest dreams. I'd always wanted to be a legend, like Arna. I'd made that name for myself by becoming the Harem Thief. I'd wanted her, the girl I'd somehow fallen madly in love with, the girl that turned out to be the god who was watching me, waiting for my answer.

"No. It wouldn't have made me change my mind," I told him, and watched the worry fade from his eyes like mist in the morning sun. I leaned forward and kissed him, then pushed him onto his back.

"What are you doing, Davi?" he asked.

I leered down at him as I straddled his legs. "I want to see if you taste the same," I answered, leaning down and kissing his throat. I worked my way down his chest, stopping to pay lavish attention to his nipples, making him moan and squirm so much that I had no choice but to pin him down, my hands on his upper arms as I nibbled and licked him into a frenzy.

"Davi!" he groaned, a delicious sound. "Davi, don't tease!"

I laughed with my lips pressed against his skin and continued my exploration of his body, pausing for a moment to ponder his navel—why would a god have a navel?—then traveling further, until I reached my goal. He gasped and thrust his hips up as my mouth closed over his cock, his hand tangling in my hair and pressing gently. His skin was salty-sweet, and surprisingly different from how he'd tasted before. I swallowed him entire, then rose up and started to play, swirling my tongue over the head of his cock, sucking the first droplets of nectar from him before moving on to lick the shaft from base to head and back. He had a magnificent cock, and I couldn't wait to feel him. But it had been a long time since I'd been with another man...

I raised my head and asked, "Where do you keep the oil?"

He groaned and looked at me, his eyes glazed, "You stopped!"

"Kai, where do you keep the oil?" I repeated. I had to ask the question once more before he understood enough to ask, "Why do you want oil?"

"For this," I answered by running my finger down his length. "You're a monster, and I can't take this without something to ease the way."

He grinned, "Oh, you want me to fuck you. We don't need oil, Davi." He shifted and sat up. "Lay down. On your back. I want to watch you."

"Kai..."

"You've never been with a god before," he said, cutting off my protests. "Trust me. We don't need oil."

He had a point. I never had been with a god before. How could I

214

know what I needed? I nodded and lay down, rolling onto my back and looking up at him. "Now what?" I asked.

"Now?" he asked, smiling down at me. "Now you let me play. It's been a long time since I last had a man like this. Arna didn't care for it." He ran his hands up my legs, then slid his fingers under my knees and lifted them, pushing them towards my chest and positioning himself against me. I felt the head of his cock probing against me, and fought the urge to push him away. I couldn't get past the fear that this was going to hurt....

Then he entered me, and it was as smooth as if he had used oil. There was no pain, nothing but the pure pleasure of being filled. I gasped as he moved, looking up to see him smiling down at me. Then he started to pump, and I closed my eyes and moaned as he pressed down on my legs, pinning me in place and holding me there with his power. I struggled for a moment, straining against him, and heard myself whimper.

"Like that, do you?" he murmured, his voice husky, his hands sliding down my legs and over my chest in a soft caress. "I'll have to remember that. There are chains around here somewhere. Would you let me bind you, Davi?"

Just the idea was enough to make me moan with need. I nodded, unable to find words, then cried out as he thrust harder into me, his cock hitting just the right spot. Without warning, my right hand was freed.

"Touch yourself, Davi," he ordered, bending over me and bracing himself with his hands on my shoulders. "I want to see you come."

I did not need to be told twice. I reached down and wrapped my hand around my cock, fumbling for a moment until I got the rhythm and could pump in time with his thrusts. He moaned his approval and started moving faster. His movements were becoming more erratic, his moans more strident, and his fingers on my shoulders tightened. I yelped in surprise when it suddenly felt as if his cock was growing inside of me, expanding, filling me completely. It was that sensation that drove me over the edge, and I screamed my climax to the distant roof as my seed splattered all over my chest. A moment later, Kai followed me, cresting with a wild cry before slumping over me. He released me from his power, and I sighed happily and curled into his side. "I think I'm going to enjoy this," I mumbled.

He chuckled, running his hand down my spine. "It shouldn't be too much longer before Mother remembers me and releases us."

I nodded, then raised my head, "Kai, who is your mother?"

He blinked and looked surprised. "You don't know?"

"There aren't any goddesses worshiped in Tarsis, and I don't know the local gods. I didn't know about you until... well, you told me about yourself in the tavern."

"Ah," he said as he nodded. "I'm surprised you don't know, though. Mother was... everywhere. Sirina, the Mother-Goddess? I thought she was worshiped in Tarsis, too."

All at once I went cold. "You have been here a long time, haven't you?"

He frowned, "I don't know how many mortal years. I've had... four votaries. I think it's four. Why?"

I let out a long breath, "And Arna lived over five hundred years ago, according to the stories I've heard about him. Four votaries... two thousand years. That explains why I didn't know you, and why you didn't know...."

"Didn't know what?" Kai asked. I grimaced. There was no easy way to say this.

"All of the temples of the Mother-Goddess were destroyed almost two hundred years ago," I answered slowly. "The followers of Fersis rose up against her. Her priesthood was wiped out, all of her followers put to death. Her worship is still outlawed. My grandfather told me that there used to be a Mother-Goddess worshiped once, but I didn't know her name until you told me." I swallowed and rested my hand on his stomach. "Kai, how long before one of you... how long before a god fades, like you said?"

He shuddered, closing his eyes. "I'd wondered..." he murmured. "I'd wondered why she never came for me."

"I'm sorry," I said.

He nodded, then looked at me and smiled. "I have you, though. You'll be here with me now, and I will love you for the rest of your life."

And that's how I came to be Kai's High Priest. I've been here a long time now. Long enough that I'm not even sure anymore just how long it's been. They haven't been bad years. Far from it. The food is the best I've ever eaten, Kai's company is wonderful, and the sex is amazing. The first time he turned me into a woman was a little strange, I will admit, but I got used to it after a few years.

The only problem is that I'm getting older. I can't help it; there's only so much aging that he can stop. I just can't keep up with him like I used to, and I know my time is almost up. In a few years, I'll be gone and he'll be going hunting again. That's where you come in, whoever you are, and that's why I wrote this journal. To tell you about what you'll be facing, and to ask something of you.

Be gentle with Kai. I know that sounds strange, given that he's probably tricked you into his arms. He's easy to love, once you get to know him. So give him a chance, at least. He's lonely, and he's trapped here. He needs you.

Welcome to the priesthood. Take care of him for me.

Hunting Artemis

Annabeth Leong

Annabeth Leong has written erotica of many flavors. She loves shoes, stockings, cooking, and excellent bass lines. Forbidden Fiction publishes many of her dark erotica titles. Find her at annabetherotica.com or on Twitter @AnnabethLeong.

Chapter 1

Forbidden Glimpses of the Goddess

The day I came to Delos, as a girl of ten, to dedicate myself to Artemis, my mentor took me out beside the stable before the ceremony. Most of her advice washed past me. I had eyes only for the barren earth around the temple, the gleam of forest beyond, and the girls in white who whispered and giggled and peered at the newcomer.

I do remember one thing she said: "We run so hard and shoot so sure, Nikia, not only for love of the goddess and the hunt, but also because we must take revenge for all we sacrifice."

A dry, brown woman, she had skin the gray-brown color of a nut husk. I glanced up and found unexpected heat in her eyes. She cackled and thumped me on the shoulder, making me buckle under the strength of her arm.

"When the fire between your legs awakens, you'll call my words wise," she said.

Ten years passed before I did—when Theron came. On the first day of autumn, I went with the temple's delegation to greet him. Theron sat foremost in a fleet of smaller boats dropped into the water from the decks of his black ship. The sun glinted off the hard curves of his muscles as he steered toward shore with great sweeps of the oars. I couldn't make out his features from where I stood, but my body thrilled at his perfect, manly geometry. Even in the noonday heat, his brown hair gleamed with a touch of moonlight. I wondered if the goddess' fingers had recently touched his brow and brushed back his thick curls.

He disembarked with his hound at his heels, and as the high priestess spoke a welcome, I went to him and knelt in the sand, holding the ritual cup before me. He smelled of leaves and rain, as if fresh from the hunt. I tried to fix my eyes on one of his sleek calves, but they wandered up and mapped the lines of his thighs. I wondered what lay between his legs. Theron took the cup from my hands without a glance at me, without the slightest brush of flesh to flesh. He drank to the goddess' honor, his tall, lean body upright and quivering faintly with devotion. His bright brown eyes and pointed nose gave his pretty, noble face a hungry look. I breathed him in, imagining my body falling against him and my hands winding around the places my eyes had been.

Theron stepped past me and spoke the next words in the ritual.

I asked Eurydice about him at dinner, but my friend had little to say. "He is some great follower of Artemis from Thessaly. He brought a dozen steeds with him as a gift to the temple." She shrugged, whipped her black hair off her thin shoulders and looked at me suspiciously.

I tried to keep my voice light. "How long will he stay?"

"How long do any of these travelers stay? They come by the sun and leave by the moon. Who knows?"

Theron entered, and I snapped my mouth shut, swallowing what I planned to say. A hush fell over the room, reminding me I wasn't the only woman in awe of him. I smiled at Eurydice, and spent the rest of the meal focusing on the arch leading up to the white ceiling, and the carvings on the pillars around the hall. I could do without her curiosity.

My charade aside, I noticed every movement of his hands, and every change in the tilt of his head. I wished I sat beside him. I lingered after dinner rather than retire to the room I shared with Eurydice. When the moon rose above the forest trees, he crept to the stable. I wandered in after him with my bow slung over my back.

Theron's black-eared hound raced in circles at his feet. His fine black horse edged sideways as he saddled it. I watched him reassure it with strong, sure fingers and wished he caressed me instead. Theron narrowed his eyes and looked at me.

"Do you go alone on a midnight hunt?" I said, fingering my

bow.

He turned away and mounted without a word, but I stopped him with a hand on the horse's neck. I knew better than to touch Theron. "Let me ride beside you," I said. "My duties multiply, and I do not often hunt."

"The ritual hunts are not the same as the real thing." He nodded. "I won't wait long."

I grinned, chose my horse, and saddled her in a rush before he had time to change his mind. When I returned, Theron gave another short nod and headed for the forest. Though I tried to hunt, I cared nothing for the flash of deer between the trees. I raced after the rich, male scent of him, strong and big enough to fill the forest. I could have followed him with my eyes closed, and yet I did not want to. I felt grateful for every moment he rode ahead of me, leaving me free to stare at his elbow, the tip of his ear, or the start of his spine above his shirt. In my heart, I feared Artemis would judge me for paying more attention to a man than to the chase.

Finally, the familiar rhythms of the hunt took over, and I found myself sighting and stalking deer. Theron, however, blundered on despite the silvery animal bodies, never touched his weapons, and made no particular effort to ride quietly. After the third time he startled my quarry, I turned on him, surprised at the anger in my voice. "What is it you're seeking here?"

His guilty eyes met mine. His brash confidence had fallen away, and beneath the veneer, he seemed haunted and harried. With an urge to lay my hand over his, I pressed my horse forward, but he pulled his mount into shadows illuminated only by the barest dusting of moonlight.

I went on the attack. "You're not really on a hunt, and it's clear you're not in this to be alone with me."

Theron swallowed. "It's the goddess," he said, his deep voice full of shame. "I dreamed of her the night before we landed at Delos. I must ride every night seeking Artemis."

"You know as well as I that Artemis will suffer the touch of no man." I didn't really mind his heresy, but I wanted to shame him as punishment for ignoring me.

His head snapped up, then dropped a moment later. "Then there's only one thing left to do."

He cleared his throat, dug his heels into his steed, and bolted off into the forest, so suddenly my horse shied. I collected her and tore after him, keeping my body low to avoid being flung from the saddle by a low-hanging branch.

Caught up in the chase, I felt his speed, as the lingering howl of his heart's desire joined with mine in longing. The leaves whipping about my face became his hair, the wind tearing at my clothes became his hands, and the horse between my legs, his body. I closed my eyes. His distinct scent seemed to spread through the forest. I breathed him in, bucking against the saddle and riding ever wilder. Surpassing him in speed, only the moon watched me.

When the mare and I tired, I fell against her neck, crazy for the touch of a lover. Theron, not yet spent, charged past me, crested the hill beyond, and hurtled down the other side like lightning. His horse's hooves ripped over the ground like thunder. His hound, staying abreast of his wild ride, yipped an otherworldly challenge to the night.

We tell a story among the girls of the temple about a man named Actaeon, a Theban prince and hunter. One day, he followed his quarry into a vale on Mount Cithaeron. As soon as Actaeon entered the vale, his animals went strange. His horse balked at some unseen thing and threw him, and his hounds lost the scent of the quarry, circling Actaeon in confusion before wandering away into the undergrowth.

Actaeon scarcely knew why he had come to that place. The air intoxicated him, and he walked on as though dreaming.

After an hour, he heard water nearby, and followed the sound to a hidden pool. Before stepping out into the clearing around the water, he froze at the sight of a woman bathing there. Tall and powerful, she stood in the center of the pool, snatching handfuls of water and sluicing her bare skin. Her short hair curled tightly about her head, and dark eyes burned from her face. Actaeon became entranced by the glow of her skin and the patch of dark curls between her strong thighs. He could not tear his eyes from her large nipples, covering half the surface of the small breasts perched atop her muscled chest.

And though we imagine the goddess Artemis does not wish to be described thus, we do it all the same, lingering on every beauty Actaeon saw. In hushed tones we talk about how Artemis stepped out of the pool and sunned herself on the rocks at the edge, running her hands over her face and neck. Before Actaeon's astonished eyes, the goddess teased her nipples, pulling and pinching them until her sharp breathing filled the clearing. Her pink tongue licked the edges of her mouth as she gasped and trailed her right hand down her belly and between her legs. Slowly, she spread her cunt and slid one long finger into the opening. The goddess writhed upon the rock as she stuffed her sex with more fingers, reveling in her private ecstasy.

Her muscles rippled gloriously, bunching in her sides as her body strained toward satisfaction. She exhausted herself before achieving bliss, however, and uncurled her body and rested on the rock, one hand still cupping her sex. Breathing hard, she turned her head to the side and saw Actaeon in his hiding place. The prince's hand pumped his straining cock. In truth, it took all his control not to charge into the clearing and take her into his arms. Artemis snatched her hands away from her cunt and leapt to her feet, turning a furious gaze upon him.

Ignoring his stammered apology with a wave of her hand, she turned Actaeon into a stag, and as the creature wobbled away on its new feet, she set his own hounds upon him.

Seeing no sign of Theron again, I dismounted and walked my mare back to the stable. I prayed, begging the goddess to forgive him for what he wanted from her, and to forgive me for what I wanted from him. I tried to placate her with hymns, and even accused Aphrodite of plotting against us.

Nearing the stable, I spoke the truth of my heart into the night. "Lady of the hunt, I don't know if I am fit to be in your service. If there is something you would have from me, take it and release me."

At breakfast in the morning, Theron sat with eyes blackened and shadowed by the night's ride. I would come to know the look well, for every night he went riding after the goddess, and every night I followed him until my horse could no longer run. And though he rarely looked at me, our kinship grew.

Autumn faded and winter threatened every evening. The leaves fell and crunched sharply underfoot. The wind traded claws for teeth, biting ever deeper during the midnight rides I took in pursuit of Theron. The naked trees struck obscene poses against the sky, digging into the earth with fisted roots and spreading their branches apart like pairs of legs.

Theron hadn't eaten in days. The endless hunt had wasted him, wearing thin the beauty of his face. The hard man beneath attracted me even more than before.

A hand closed over my shoulder as I crept behind him one night. "Nikia," Eurydice said. "What are you doing?"

"I go riding at night."

"So I hear. They say it's him you ride." She jerked her chin toward the stable, where I knew Theron would be saddling his horse.

Would he notice my absence? Or had I been creating a bond that only mattered to me?

Eurydice misunderstood the blush in my face. "It's true, then," she said.

I flashed a smile. "Eurydice, any fool can see he cares only about the goddess."

"And what about you?"

"I see nothing but him."

Her hand clutched mine. "Walk with me."

We walked behind the stables, in the direction opposite Theron's nightly ride. The trees thinned until the shore appeared and the pale beach beyond it. Barely in sight, the mast of Theron's black ship poked up into the darkness. We stepped onto the beach. She darted ahead on bare feet, but my shoes gathered sand until I stopped to remove them.

"They say they built the temple here in Delos because this is the place where Leto birthed Artemis, and where Artemis in turn played midwife for her twin brother Apollo," Eurydice said in a tiresome, pious voice.

"I know the story," I said.

She silenced me with a sharp slash of her white hand through the night. "On her birthday nights, when the moon is dark, they say Artemis comes to bathe here in honor of her mother." To my surprise, Eurydice cast her robes aside and stepped toward the chilly water. She gasped as the first of the waves reached her feet, but pressed onward until they slapped her knees, her thighs, then between her legs. Her body glowed, framed by the ocean, and her nipples stood dark and hard against her breasts when she beckoned to me. I shed my clothes and obeyed, allowing her to take me in her arms.

"We are like the goddess," Eurydice said. "Strong and brave. Forget that man." She bathed me as she spoke, scooping up water and smoothing it over my skin, holding me up against the force of the crashing tide. Her touch, though innocent, ignited a fire between my legs. I shivered as my flesh awakened beneath her chaste, teasing fingers. She ran her hands through my hair and over my face, her fingers fluttering against my eyelids, lips, and nostrils. She drew light circles over my back, but did not touch me any of the places where I most wanted to be touched. I clung to her and pressed my breasts against her breasts, sliding so her thigh slipped between my legs. Nearly sobbing from the tension, I pressed against her thigh and she allowed it. Soon I crashed against it, even as the waves crashed against me, until the breath shuddered out of me in a long spasm.

Eurydice kissed me on the forehead as the pulsing between my legs continued. "Forget him," she said again and patted me on the shoulder blade.

Confused, I moved to kiss her on the lips, but she stepped back as the water churned and filled the space between us. Without her body against mine, I trembled.

She waded back to shore and retrieved her clothing, wrapping it around her body as if nothing had happened. I longed to lie down at the edge of the waves and press my fist between my thighs, but I climbed up after her and collected my own clothes. From the look on her face, she thought she had saved me from my lust for Theron. She didn't know that the relief bursting forth like a long-held breath transformed back to desire the moment I breathed in again. He would have understood. Nothing could replace him for me, just as nothing could replace the goddess for him.

Chapter 2
Sacrifices Made for Artemis

Eurydice caught me going after Theron every night for a week. Each time, she took me to the ocean. Finally, my shaming need and her indifference became unbearable. The next night I didn't go out, but lay in my bed and pretended to sleep.

When the moon reached its height, I could stand no more. I went to the stable and took a fresh horse, hoping to catch the second part of Theron's nightly ride.

Flashes of silver peeked out between the trees, but tonight I would not stop to watch the deer. I rode on carelessly, sparing no glance to anything but the trail before my eyes. My guts tangled and twisted as I pictured Theron's face. In my dreams, he smiled when I approached and pulled me into his arms. Awake, I imagined him sneering, sending me back to my bed alone.

I passed beyond the area that I had traveled well with him, and the path before me grew rockier. I slowed for fear of harming the horse. A stone's throw ahead, between two slender trunks, silver flashed again, then stayed and glowed. It was no deer.

Catching my breath, I followed Artemis' beckoning finger, cursing myself for allowing thoughts of Theron to blind me. I knew not why she called to me, her unworthy servant, but I followed, wondering if she planned to punish me or banish me from her temple. I saw only the curving finger, the strong hand, and the well-muscled forearm used to handling a bow. She led me into the forest's darkest heart where the smell of animals crowded thick and close upon my senses. The moon failed to reach this place, and I had to trust the finger to lead me on a path my horse could manage.

The smell of sex, sharp and wild as the sea, spiraled up my nose, making my body throb. My horse shied and threw me into the bushes. I walked on, following the silver glow without reservation. A hound—the tilt of its black ears familiar to me—burst from the undergrowth, whining at my heels and running ahead to guide me. I followed, not understanding the dog's urgency.

A long time later, I heard water nearby, followed the sound, and crept up to a hidden pool. Before stepping out into the clearing there, I froze. The fog lifted from my brain, and I saw Theron, a deep wound in his gut leaking into the pool, staining the water with a thick red swirl. I rushed to his side while his hound whimpered and licked its master's forehead. I dared not look into Theron's face, for fear I'd collapse into useless sobs.

I gathered him in my arms, pressed my hand against his neck, and prayed life still flowed in him. A breath, weak but warm, fluttered the hair beside my face, and I cried aloud. I wrapped a rough bandage around his wound, tearing my attention from the feel of his soft skin. His distinct scent had been polluted by the acrid stench of blood and pain. I needed a horse. I could barely lift him, much less carry him back to the temple.

His horse, the fine steed from Thessaly, stepped into the clearing then, and I did not pause to question why. It came easily at my call. I coaxed it to kneel so I could roll the man into the saddle. After a struggle, I let the horse rise again and climbed up behind Theron.

I held him on the long ride back to the temple, my desire for him pushed to the back of my mind. I didn't cry. Instead, my eyes felt drier than seven deserts. If he died in my arms, I might be free at last, and so would he. I spent the next hours regretting the thought.

Daylight loomed on the horizon by the time we returned, and the sun's rays scattered gloriously over the land. I saw only how pale Theron looked in that exuberant light. Though he breathed and some times mumbled, his mind lay somewhere far away. At the last bare stretch from the tree line to the temple, the horse and I wanted to break into a run, but I held us back since it seemed Theron could not withstand it.

From a distance, the priestesses ran, bringing aid. I gave Theron over to their care and stumbled numbly to the room I shared with

Eurydice. They could ask their questions later. For now, I would let them tend to him.

The sun streamed through the windows of the room, striking me in the face with light as pitiless as the heel of a palm. I'd never been in my room this time of day before.

Eurydice sat beside me. She took my hand and began to relay a strange story. "A bird came into the high priestess's window late at night. The creature made such a nuisance and racket of itself that, still half-asleep, the high priestess took her hunting knife and killed it. But the bird's death cry rang with the voice of prophecy, and the priestess got up at once, carried its body out into the courtyard, and sliced it open to see what message the gods had written within.

"At the sight of its entrails, the high priestess entered a trance. She saw Artemis bathing alone, with none of her maidens present to attend to her. Ares, god of war, stalked the goddess of the hunt, hoping to slake his lust. The priestess saw a warrior sacrificing himself for the goddess, and a maiden sacrificing herself for the warrior."

I stirred and shook off Eurydice's hand. "I've never heard this story."

"It's the story they're telling about you."

"What's this talk of sacrifice? Is Theron—"

"Alive, and they sing your praises for saving him."

Her expression resigned, Eurydice's fine features hardened. She knew those nights in the ocean hadn't abated my longing for Theron at all. I smiled, an offering of peace, and to my relief, she returned it. "Do they plan to ask me why I was out there?"

"You were led by the goddess," Eurydice said and winked at me. "It won't stop the young girls from talking, but nothing does."

"I have to see him."

"Artemis appeared to the priestesses in a vision," Eurydice said with a smirk. "You, and you alone, are to tend to him. And when he is well, you are to leave Delos forever."

"Banished?"

She nodded and watched my face for a reaction. It should have destroyed me to think of leaving the island that had been my home for half my life. Instead, I felt exhilarated. I'd loved hunting night after night, but the thought of the wide world before me, free of vows, made my heart soar more than any midnight ride could. I kissed Eurydice on the cheek to say goodbye, and her answering sigh made me wonder if I had read her wrong on our nights together. It didn't matter now. I went to him.

Pale and weak, Theron tossed in anxious sleep. Though rest healed me, it left him untouched. The healers assured me he would live, but most of winter would be over before he recovered.

They left me alone with him, no questions asked. I soon got over the shock and began to come to terms with the realities of his body, which needed to be fed, washed, lifted, and turned. I saw his every ugliness and scar. I saw his face by evening light, by morning light, by noon light, and in the darkness. Sleeping in the corner of his room, I never spoke except to murmur to him or pray to Artemis.

What spell had controlled me through autumn? At the time, I'd thought I loved Theron, but now my feverish longing faded as I attended to his care day after day. When the healthy Theron spoke, walked, and hunted, I dreamed about his body. Now, with his body in my charge, I dreamed of the man. I wanted to see expression in his face. I wanted to see his lips curve into a smile or a frown. I still marveled at his body, but what obsessed me now were the memories of his wild laughing as he charged through the woods. I would stare for hours at his features, trying to tease out the history of his life. Childhood play, I imagined, left as its mark the old scar on his elbow. A badly-made sandal shaped his crooked second toe, I decided. Love, to me, meant knowing every inch of him, and at the same time knowing him to be a mystery.

Desire no longer drove me. I waited for him patiently, trusting he would one day return.

Theron's eyes opened one day in late winter as I dressed the wound on his familiar body. He caught my wrist.

"Nikia," he said.

I answered with a smile.

"How long have you been here?"

"Most of a season."

"And the goddess?"

"She led me to you."

Theron shook his head. "Ares tore me in half. His body blazed so I couldn't see him. I couldn't do anything to protect Artemis."

"What you did must have been enough."

I tried to calm myself by turning my attention back to the routines I had built around his inert form. I couldn't. Meeting his eyes and hearing his voice restored my desire, and my anger at his obsession with Artemis. I blushed as I ran my hands over the wound, averting my eyes from the bare skin of his stomach and the trail of fur leading down below. He caught my hand again. "She wanted me there, watching her," Theron said. "I would never have dared to be there without her knowledge."

White-hot jealousy crowded out my vision, and rage as deep as the ancient anger of the Titans pounded through me. I went on with my work, trying and failing to lock him out of my heart.

Theron grew stronger every day, and I knew I would soon leave Delos. Tendrils of spring peered around doorways like timid little girls. The sun, which had sneered down on us like a cold and distant monarch through winter, turned to gentler pursuits, taking an interest in tracking soft shadows over sloping meadows and wind-blown beaches.

I took Theron outside. Obeying the order of the goddess, everyone hid from us. "What is her plan for us?" he said into the eerie silence. I shrugged, avoiding the thought of losing him.

"Will you stay on Delos?" I said. My face gave more meaning than my words.

"Yes," he said. "I'm sorry, Nikia."

I shrugged again. It would never satisfy me for him to submit to my caress as Eurydice had done. I'd had months to resign myself to this.

The priestess came one evening. "The temple will prepare a boat for you in the morning," she said.

I did not speak of this to Theron. I cooked his evening meal, waving off his attempts to help. At the end of the meal he took my hand and pressed it to his cheek. I stared at him, heart pounding in my chest.

Emptiness woke me in the middle of the night. I couldn't smell him. Remembering autumn, I pressed the sleep from my eyes with my fist and got up to follow him to the stable. He waited there with two of his fine black horses saddled. He tossed me the reins of the mare. "You'll need to be able to keep up with me tonight," Theron said.

I nodded, feeling self-conscious. We mounted, and our horses rushed from the stable as if from the starting gates of the games at Olympus. We raced faster than the first horses rushing up to shore from sea foam under the whip of Poseidon. The magnificent horses of Achaean heroes, which pulled bright and deadly chariots behind them as they thundered toward Trojan enemies, could not have caught us. The moon witnessed our ride, our horses as sure on the night trails as at the height of noonday, and the forest sounds fading to a whisper as we gave ourselves over to the thrill of speed.

We came once again to Artemis's secret place in the heart of the forest. Intoxicated by the heady scent of the goddess's body, we dismounted just outside the clearing. Theron took my hand before we passed through the undergrowth and onto the wet brown earth beside the pool.

She appeared then, her body deadly and glorious. She wore nothing but bow and hunting knife. Her eyes flashed at our intertwined hands. I pulled away from Theron, but she stopped me with a gesture. "I won't be jealous," Artemis said, her voice large as battle but soft as a flower. Theron fell to his knees, pulling me with him.

"Rise and come here," she said to me. When I obeyed, she took me in her arms. The pleasure of her touch pounded through me, too strong for my body. "I will know the touch of no man," Artemis purred. "But my Theron deserves some reward. Give him this for me." She bent her head and kissed me full on the mouth, her sweet tongue pressing my lips open and slipping into me. I would have fallen, except the goddess held me up and pushed me into Theron's waiting arms.

Trembling, I wound both arms around his neck, letting him support my weight. He shook, too. Even in the full presence and terror of Artemis, I smelled Theron's body and longed for him. I gave him her kiss, and a little of mine, too.

His eyes on the goddess, he caught his breath, still holding me, and said, "If the goddess will accept it, I would have you repay her this in turn from me." Theron loosened my robe and let it drop from my shoulders and into the mud. He picked me up and wrapped my legs around his waist, then lifted my breasts to his lips, kissing and sucking on the nipples. I groaned and ground against him, my blood thudding in my ears. *At last.* I didn't mind being a vessel for her, as long as he touched me that way. When he set me on the ground again, I turned back to Artemis in a daze. Her eyes flashed, but she nodded her permission, and I took her nipples in my mouth one after the other, nibbling them gently as Theron had nibbled mine, trying to transmit to the goddess every nuance of the lips and teeth I had dreamed of for so many nights.

I ferried caresses between them for what felt like hours. I trailed kisses down his chest for her, ending by dragging teasing fingers up both his thighs. For him, I pressed my lips to the insides of her elbows, the flesh behind each knee, and the place where her neck met her shoulder. I vibrated with the touch of mortal and immortal alike, until my mind thrummed with pleasure and power. My fingers explored Artemis's sex, as Theron had explored mine. When I didn't think I could walk another step, Artemis made me lie down in the earth beside the pool and beckoned Theron closer.

"Look at me but do not touch," she said, this time to him. The goddess looked down at me then. "Do you give yourself to me and him?" she asked. I swallowed hard and nodded. Artemis settled her sex over my face, her scent going straight to my head. I gripped her thighs with both my hands and opened my mouth wide to her, letting my nose press into her opening as I suckled the hard nub between her legs. She gasped and laid her hands over mine, squeezing. Theron probed the wetness between my legs, then replaced his fingers with his long, hard cock. The sensation as the two consummated their love through me filled me more than to the brim. I forgot myself as man and goddess gasped above me.

I think the orgasm started in Artemis, but it passed from her into my mouth and down my body, until I shuddered and rolled my hips up to meet Theron's thrusts. Then it caught hold of him, too, and he clawed at my hips at his own release. Almost before Theron finished pouring out his seed, Artemis disappeared, leaving us alone in each other's arms, and yet not lonely.

We fell asleep at once, exhausted by the force of her immortal presence. I had no dreams, only the sensation of his warm arms around me, holding me up even in the land of sleep.

The light of the next morning's sun brushed against us like feathers. I opened my eyes to Theron. I feared he would be disgusted by me, since I no longer served as channel for the goddess. But he stroked my hair as he woke and smiled into my gaze, meeting my lips with a kiss meant only for me. "We are much the same, the two of us," he said.

If you enjoyed this story, you can sign up for a free membership at ForbiddenFiction.com and discuss it with other readers and the author at the *Hunting Artemis* story page at http://forbiddenfiction.com/story/AL1-1.000228.

About the Publisher

 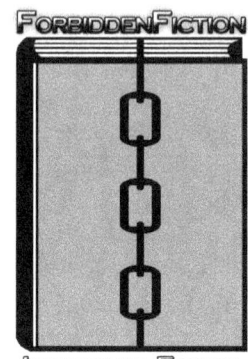

ForbiddenFiction.com is a publisher devoted to writing that breaks the boundaries of original erotic fiction. Our stories combine intense sexuality with quality writing. Stories at ForbiddenFiction.com not only arouse readers through sensations, but also engage them emotionally and mentally through storytelling as well-crafted as the sex is hot.

ForbiddenFiction.com is also designed to be a social reading environment. You'll have fun even if just reading the latest post each day, yet you will have the chance for so much more. Readers and authors can be part of ongoing discussions of specific works and individual authors as well as more general topics.

Sign up for a FREE Membership today at ForbiddenFiction.com

www.ingramcontent.com/pod-product-compliance
Lightning Source LLC
Chambersburg PA
CBHW070058260626
47160CB00004B/1246